PRIMARY DUTY

(THE FORGING OF LUKE STONE—BOOK 6)

JACK MARS

Jack Mars

Jack Mars is the USA Today bestselling author of the LUKE STONE thriller series, which includes seven books. He is also the author of the new FORGING OF LUKE STONE prequel series, comprising six books; of the AGENT ZERO spy thriller series, comprising twelve books; and of the TROY STARK thriller series, comprising three books (and counting).

Jack loves to hear from you, so please feel free to visit www.Jackmarsauthor.com to join the email list, receive a free book, receive free giveaways, connect on Facebook and Twitter, and stay in touch!

BOOKS BY JACK MARS

LUKE STONE THRILLER SERIES
ANY MEANS NECESSARY (Book #1)
OATH OF OFFICE (Book #2)
SITUATION ROOM (Book #3)
OPPOSE ANY FOE (Book #4)
PRESIDENT ELECT (Book #5)
OUR SACRED HONOR (Book #6)
HOUSE DIVIDED (Book #7)

FORGING OF LUKE STONE PREQUEL SERIES
PRIMARY TARGET (Book #1)
PRIMARY COMMAND (Book #2)
PRIMARY THREAT (Book #3)
PRIMARY GLORY (Book #4)
PRIMARY VALOR (Book #5)
PRIMARY DUTY (Book #6)

AN AGENT ZERO SPY THRILLER SERIES
AGENT ZERO (Book #1)
TARGET ZERO (Book #2)
HUNTING ZERO (Book #3)
TRAPPING ZERO (Book #4)
FILE ZERO (Book #5)
RECALL ZERO (Book #6)
ASSASSIN ZERO (Book #7)
DECOY ZERO (Book #8)
CHASING ZERO (Book #9)
VENGEANCE ZERO (Book #10)
ZERO ZERO (Book #11)
ABSOLUTE ZERO (Book #12)

CHAPTER ONE

September 21, 2006
8:15 am Central European Summer Time (2:15 am Eastern
Daylight Time)
La Canada Real
Coslada, Madrid
Spain

"Where is he now?" Jaafar Idrissi said.

The two men made their way together along the bleak alleys, between the tumbledown wood and cement dwellings of the largest shantytown in Europe. The morning was cold and overcast, and a chill ran up Jaafar's back, despite his windbreaker jacket and the sweater he wore underneath.

It had rained last night, and fetid puddles of brown water remained in the pitted earth of the walking path. These people had neither electricity nor running water in their homes. The two men walked through this hellish compound not because they lived here, but because it was a good place to talk and not be overheard. The residents here were too hopeless to concern themselves with the talk of others. And the police rarely bothered to make their way through this maze of despair.

Up ahead, a group of children were playing on three makeshift slides. The slides were made of what appeared to be large PVC plastic pipes, cut in half lengthwise. The pipes were pitched up against a mound of dirt and junk. At the top was a pile of discarded car and truck tires that the children climbed up to enter the mouth of each tube. At the bottom was a mound of sand trucked in from somewhere. The sand had become a thick yellow muck from the rain.

It was a disgrace of a playground. Things of this nature, a mere 20 kilometers from the center of Madrid, the wealthiest city in the country, that global hub of media, fashion, education, entertainment, sport, and government, tended to raise the anger within Jaafar.

Was it so hard? Would it be such a terrible challenge to give the children of the poor and despised something worth having? This

1

shantytown, this so-called "illegal" settlement, was home to thousands of Romani Gypsies and new Moroccan immigrants - the wretched of Spain. And it showed.

"He is in Barcelona," the young man walking with Jaafar said. "He is staying at the Hotel Arts."

Jaafar shrugged. "And what makes this of interest to me?"

Jaafar was 41 years old. Beginning three years before, he had been the originator, and primary planner, of an idea so outrageous that even he didn't believe in it at first. The idea was to plant rucksack bombs on commuter trains headed to the Atocha Station, the central train station of Madrid. It was a success beyond all expectation. The attacks, in March of 2004, killed 194 people and injured more than 2,000. It spread terror throughout the country, and all of Europe.

Four participants in the attack killed themselves as the police closed in on them. Two of those were the only men who knew of Jaafar's involvement. Twenty-one other men went to prison, likely for the rest of their lives.

Jaafar dreamed of the event. Jaafar planned the event. And when the time came to drink of the poison cup resulting from the event, Allah himself took the cup away from Jaafar's lips...

And left him free to do it again.

Jaafar shook his head, almost in disbelief. He was among the Blessed, and even now remained hidden from the eyes of the enemy. He seemed to be an aging ex-convict, a man who had spent 13 years in foul Spanish prisons for the trafficking of hashish from Morocco.

He seemed to be a cast-off, a man who lived in a two-bedroom flat on the 18th floor of a high-rise, one in an endless parade of identical high-rises. He seemed to share that tiny flat with his mother, his young wife, their infant son, and his nine-year-old niece, the child of his drug-addicted prostitute of a sister.

In fact, all of these things were true. His existence seemed anonymous, pointless, just another throwaway impoverished immigrant who had done prison time and had come out older but no wiser - the energy of his youth dissipated, his prospects for the future grim.

This was him, and it also wasn't. He had masterminded the largest terror attack in Europe in decades and hadn't been caught or suspected. He hadn't even been questioned. Hundreds of men had been brought in for interrogation. But not Jaafar. He was too old. He was broken by prison. He couldn't have been involved.

A miracle had occurred. A message from Allah had been sent and had been received. *You have been chosen.*

2

He stopped walking for a moment and looked at the younger man. In a sense, this man was a messenger as well. He was bringing a different kind of message, but it might also come from Allah. Jaafar was highly attuned to this possibility.

Hotels, guest houses, restaurants, and taverns were staffed by Moroccans, up and down the country. They were eyes and ears. They saw things, and they heard things, and some of these things found their way back to Jaafar Idrissi.

"The man wants to go up to the mountains, to the Valley of Aran. A small village there is the birthplace of his grandparents."

The man in question was Richard Sebastian-Vilar, a justice of the Supreme Court in the United States. He had been traveling in France and had crossed into Spain. The formal handoff from one security detail to another, French to Spanish, had made the national television news.

Now Vilar was staying at the famous Ritz-Carlton hotel in Barcelona, the Hotel Arts. There were believers working in that hotel, with access to the rooms. It was easy to plant listening devices - only the grand suites reserved for Arab princes, billionaire corporate CEOs, and heads of state were out of reach.

But a judge? There was no grand suite for a judge.

"Yes," Jaafar said. "Very touching. The Pyrenees are lovely this time of year. So I hear."

Jaafar had never been to the Pyrenees. He had spent his entire life living in the most dismal surroundings. When he was young, he thought of his conditions as a punishment. But he had not understood Allah's plan for him. The young are blind, and he was no exception.

"He wants to go there by himself. He does not want his security to overwhelm the villagers, or to color his return to the home of his ancestors."

Jaafar nodded. "Ah."

"Yes."

"How many men are available?" Jaafar said.

"At least ten," said the young man. "Possibly fifteen."

"Fifteen martyrs who will give their lives?"

"If necessary. A few of these men are among the best we have."

Jaafar thought about that for a moment. "The best we have."

Who are we? The groups of believers in Europe struggled for survival and resources, were hounded by individual governments and the international police, and still carried out successful operations. Then the faraway leaders claimed these activities as their own.

3

"And the target remains at the hotel?"

It was a subtle change in wording. To Jaafar, this Vilar had just gone from being an ordinary man to a target.

"Yes. He will leave for the Pyrenees in the afternoon tomorrow. His itinerary says he will spend two days there, return to Barcelona for a night, then fly to Madrid. Two days in Madrid, then a return to the United States."

"He is making a very fast visit," Jaafar said. "There are so many things to see in Spain. What is his rush?"

"He must be back in time to cast his important vote," the young man said.

Jaafar nodded. "Of course."

"The village is isolated," the young man said. "He will be most vulnerable there. It is close to the border with France, and the border in the mountains is porous. The old siege tunnels are still there, but hidden - we know many of them, and have moved men through them before. The target will stay in a small *pension*, with limited security. This is our best opportunity to remove him."

Jaafar raised a finger. "Prepare as though it will happen. If he goes to the mountains with a large contingent, call it off. We cannot afford a public gun battle with security forces. Especially not now, not with what is coming. But if he goes with a small group, or by himself..."

The young man stared at Jaafar. Behind him, an old woman wearing a ratty brown hijab came out of a low-slung cinderblock shed and dumped a pot of water on the muddy ground.

"Take him."

CHAPTER TWO

11:20 am Central European Summer Time (5:20 am Eastern Daylight Time)
Berchtesgaden Alps
40 km from Salzburg
Austria

"How many seconds?" Ed Newsam said.

Luke Stone looked at him. Big Ed wore wraparound sunglasses, a black t-shirt with white lettering seemingly painted onto his massive chest, cargo shorts, and light mesh hiking boots. The lettering across his shirt said Black & Proud. As always, his hair and beard were close-cropped and impeccably cut. Even while hiking in the mountains, it was as though his survival depended on his crisp appearance.

They were sitting on the edge of a cliff, enjoying a break after a long hike. Ed had just inhaled a banana with a packet of spreadable peanut butter smeared on it. Luke was drinking iced coffee from a small thermos he had brought along on the hike. In between sips, he was eating a chewy energy bar.

He felt good - relaxed, at peace, maybe better than he had in a long time. It was nice to be away from work for a little while. It was nice to have nothing on his mind.

The day was bright, with blue skies as far as the eye could see. Their packs were on the ground just behind them. To their left, and above, the wide plateau of a snow-capped summit loomed. Almost directly below their feet, but far away, a tiny village with a white-steepled church was nestled in the valley, among dense stands of trees.

They had left the hotel in Salzburg early this morning, just after six. It had taken about an hour to drive to the village, where they had parked their rental car. After that, it was just over a four-hour hike to this spot. They had passed through lovely green alpine pastures with cattle grazing, and meadows strewn with yellow wildflowers. Then they had gone up a series of steep switchbacks, higher and ever higher. All the while, the bare rugged stone of that icy peak dominated the panorama.

It was beautiful here. Breathtaking.

5

"At a guess?" Luke said.

Ed shrugged. "Sure. But make it a good guess."

"Uh, my scientific guesstimate is you want to pull at two or three seconds, as soon as you know you're clear."

Ed nodded. He took a sip of water from his canteen. "That's what I was going to guess."

"As long as you've cleared the ledge," Luke said, "it's probably better to be too early than too late." A thought occurred to him. "If you haven't cleared it, I guess it doesn't matter what you do."

Ed laughed. "Agreed."

They sat for another long minute, enjoying the spectacle laid out in front of them - green valleys and foothills, steep rocky cliffs, and a snow-covered peak.

Luke glanced at his watch. "So what do you think? You want to head down? We told the girls we'd catch a late lunch. If we boogie now, we can make it."

Luke's wife Becca, and Ed's wife Cassandra, were back in Salzburg with the kids. Gunner was nearly 18 months old now and growing bigger every day - especially his head. Luke sometimes wondered how he held that thing up. Ed's daughter Jade, a little bit of nothing at five months, was already shaping up to be a stunner like her mom.

This little junket had been Don Morris's idea. The governments of the United States and Austria were doing an intelligence cooperation and training, funded by the taxpayers of each country. Some of their people came over to the states and visited intelligence and police agencies there. Some of our people came over here and did the same thing. There wasn't much to it. A lot of shaking hands and smiling, then nodding heads with utmost seriousness, while waiting for the translators to finish interpreting what was just said.

Luke and Ed were ambassadors to the Austrian BVT from the FBI Special Response Team. Luke didn't even try to pronounce the German words that the letters BVT stood for. Ed had tried for a little while but had given up. Cassandra, who had spent part of her childhood in Germany because her father had been a US Marine stationed there, could say it easily, and didn't seem to understand why it was so hard for others.

Either way, being here was their reward for being good boys, and it gave them the opportunity to take the wives and babies on a little getaway. They would be in Salzburg for a couple more days, and then they were scheduled to go to Vienna.

Luke stood. He stuffed his thermos into a pocket on the underside of his pack. He slipped the wrapper from his energy bars into one of the zip pockets of his cargo shorts. He double-checked his pack one last time, then shouldered it.

Ed was doing the same.

Luke looked out at that vast empty space in front of him. He gestured out at it with a nod of his head.

"What do you think?"

Ed shrugged. "I'm a dad now, so it would be reckless and irresponsible to get myself killed for a quick thrill. You know what I mean?"

Luke nodded. "Yeah."

He took a deep breath. He was almost ready to go. There was no sense doing a lot of thinking about this. There were two things to do here.

1. Jump out as far as possible.
2. Pull the chute.

That was the whole game. Focus on both things, but one at a time.

He and Ed stood, facing each other hundreds of feet in the air. Behind Ed, Luke saw the steep jutting mountain. A stiff breeze whistled down from the peak.

"See you on the ground."

Ed smiled. "Right behind you. Don't die on me, sucker."

Now Luke smiled. "You."

He was about 5 meters back from the cliff's edge. He burst into a run, straight at it, like a young boy racing down a dock to jump into a lake. He reached the edge, planted his right foot and pushed off, leaping as far out into the void as he could.

He was away, and instantly he dropped.

The mountain was gone, and the ground rushed upward toward him. The speed was dizzying and increasing every second. Between his feet, there was nothing but open space. He seemed to be spinning.

He was falling very fast. His own reactions seemed slow. The wind whistled in his ears. His hand found the cord and pulled.

A second passed, then another. He felt, rather than saw, his chute flying out above and behind him. The chute opened, pulling his upper body backward, kicking his legs in front of him. Then he was flying. He steered toward the open green space at the edge of the village, now very close below him.

Alpine meadows passed him on the right and the left as he dropped below them. The white church was here, and the tidy houses of the village, people still living in a tiny community high in the mountains. A still image of the movie *The Sound of Music* passed through his mind.

A few locals were standing by a low white fence, chatting. They turned to watch him as he arrived. He touched down lightly, soft impact, nice landing, and then he was running across the grass, his chute drifting down below him.

He stopped, and looked back at his chute, the red, white, and blue of it finally settling on the ground.

"Oh, baby," he said. He could feel his heart racing, just a bit.

He gazed up at the mountain, to see how Ed was doing, or if he had even come. No worries there. He had come. His chute was red, black, and green, an incredible sight, the Pan-African flag flying against the pale blue sky and the backdrop of the snow-capped mountains. He came down, following nearly the identical descent path Luke had taken just seconds ago.

In another moment, Ed was on the ground, landing with ballerina grace for such a large man. He took a few running steps and stopped. He raised his arms in victory, grinning in delight. His chute drifted down behind him.

"Beasts!" he said.

Luke shook his head and laughed. "You hungry, man?"

"Famished."

They had hiked out from this spot over four hours ago. They were back down here in less than two minutes. It was a great way to start the day.

"Let's go meet the girls," Luke said.

CHAPTER THREE

6:45 am Eastern Daylight Time
Hartsfield-Jackson Atlanta International Airport
Fulton and Clayton Counties, Georgia

"Mohamed, are you okay?"

The man who spoke was to Mohamed's right and just behind him. He was a big young guy, strong, a volunteer like all of them. Mohamed felt him looming there. He couldn't remember the guy's name, just that he was a New York City fireman.

Mohamed was surrounded by guys like this. The broad backs of the two guys in front of him told Mohamed all he needed to know about those guys. There was a three-man film team from one of the New York TV channels somewhere ahead of them.

They were moving up the mobile ramp in a group. They had just departed a Delta Airlines flight from LaGuardia airport. Delta had made it clear that they didn't want Georgia state troopers on the ramp. It was a safety hazard for people disembarking the plane. The cops were probably waiting at the departure gate. All of this would become clearer in about one minute from now.

Mohamed nodded. "Yeah. I'm okay."

He was anything but okay. He felt like he was about to pass out. He was breathless as they walked up the ramp. This wasn't for him. His mother told him he was crazy and threw her hands up in despair. His wife cried when he left. He was 32 years old, and he had a two-year-old son.

His father had taken him aside in a hallway of his parents' apartment in Jackson Heights. "You don't owe anyone anything. This isn't why we came here. We came to this country to be left alone."

Looking at his father, Mohamed could see the man he would be one day. His father was small and thin, with the beginnings of a stoop. The bit of hair he had left, perched on top of his ears on either side of his head, was white. His glasses were thick, with a bifocal line in the middle of each lens. His skin was very tan, a sort of dark cream, and his face was richly lined.

"I thought we came for freedom," Mohamed said.

His father nodded. "We did."

Mohamed shrugged. "So that's what I'm fighting for."

Fighting? Mohamed had never been in a fight in his life. His family had left Egypt when he was a child. His small physical stature made it impossible for him to fight with the violent and energetic American kids at school. And they mostly left him alone to pursue his studies. He was beneath their contempt.

He showed an aptitude for computer science. He went to City College on a full scholarship and became a programmer. He made very good money now, had bought a house in the Long Island suburbs not that far from his parents' place, and was building a life for himself and his family. It was all he had ever really wanted.

He made the New York to Los Angeles commute on a regular basis. The company would pay for him to take a direct flight from JFK to LAX, and that's how he normally went. But certain states were instituting travel restrictions on people from North Africa. People like Mohamed. And civil liberties groups had put out solicitations for volunteers to challenge the restrictions... so...

Now here he was, trying to catch his breath as he walked up the ramp toward the departure lounge. His entire body tingled. His face felt numb. The Georgia cops had the passenger manifest, so of course they knew he was coming up the ramp.

They probably knew exactly what he looked like. Even if they didn't, it wouldn't matter. How many skinny, five-foot six-inch-tall Egyptians were getting off that plane? And how many of them were surrounded by six-foot-plus bruisers who were true believers in the promise of America that had brought their parents and grandparents here from Europe?

"Get ready," the fireman said. "Because here we go."

Mohamed glanced at the guy. He was white with buzz cut blonde hair. He wore jeans, sneakers, and a red t-shirt with the white letters NYFD tight across his chest. He had grown up in Breezy Point, Brooklyn. He said his father was a retired cop.

His grandfather had come by boat from Ireland with no shoes on and had spent his life working at various detention centers as a jail guard. It was amazing how Mohamed had near total recall about the guy's story but couldn't remember his name.

The guy looked at Mohamed and smiled. It was a genuine smile. His blue eyes squinted. They resembled the eyes of an eagle, or some other bird of prey.

He's enjoying this.

He clapped Mohamed on the shoulder. The weight, and strength, of the man's hand was terrible in its own way.

"You did the right thing. We're with you, my brother."

Mohamed felt helpless, like he was on a conveyor belt being fed into a shark's mouth. He had a laptop bag over his left shoulder. The computer inside of it was an old one he hadn't used in a couple of years that he still had lying around. If it was damaged or lost, it wouldn't be a big deal. He had reformatted the hard drive last night, almost as an afterthought. There was no data in there for anyone to look at.

He was trailing a rolling suitcase behind him. Even if he could defend himself, he would never be able to defend himself. Not with all this stuff hanging off of him. He felt like he was about to start crying.

"Oh God," he said under his breath.

"Steady," the fireman said. "We're with you. All the way."

Easy for you to say. Easy for you to say. Easy for you...

They were with him, but they weren't Egyptians. They weren't Algerians. They weren't Libyans. They were born here. They were volunteers, they were willing to be arrested and go to jail, but they were hardly any different from the cops who would arrest them. Mohamed could almost picture a rough sort of camaraderie developing between the cops and the men they were arresting. That would never happen for him.

The small group came out of the tunnel and into the departure lounge. To Mohamed it was like entering the arena. He could be in ancient Rome, a Christian being fed to the lions. The lounge was crowded with people. Faces turned to look at him.

Cameras. There were cameras everywhere.

A phalanx of cops was there, in gray shirts and dark pants. Some were wearing hats, like cowboy hats. They were big, all men, brawny, thick-bodied.

A man came from the side and stepped in front of Mohamed. Mohamed absorbed the man in almost surrealistic detail. He was a big-bellied man, tall, middle-aged, overweight and unhealthy, but very strong looking. His nose was fat, swollen, with broken veins. He had a star pinned to his chest, over his breast. He had a large black belt around his waist, with various heavy-looking items hanging from it. One of those items was a gun. A pair of silver handcuffs appeared in the man's thick hands.

"Mohamed Anwar Zaki?"

Mohamed nodded. His mouth was dry.

"Yes," he heard himself say. His voice was far away. It didn't sound like him at all. "What seems to be the trouble?"

"Son, you are under arrest for violating Georgia state order 5632, which prohibits foreign nationals from certain jurisdictions…"

"I'm an American citizen, sir."

The man was reaching for Mohamed's wrist. "Well, you're just going to have to explain that to the…"

BOOOM!

The man's face disappeared. His body followed, both going to Mohamed's left and down to the floor. The fireman suddenly appeared, stepping into Mohamed's field of vision, following through on the savage punch he had just delivered to the cop's head.

The sound of it! The sound of it had been like an egg splattering on the sidewalk after falling from a great height.

Instantly, there was fighting everywhere. People were shouting. Someone screamed. The volunteers and the cops were fighting. Mohamed fell to the ground. A body fell on top of him. It was a Georgia cop. The man was heavy. Mohamed was being crushed under his weight.

Someone else fell on top of them. A few feet across from Mohamed, a bearded, pony-tailed cameraman had fallen. He was still filming, his camera lying sideways on the ground. It was pointed at Mohamed.

Another body fell on top of Mohamed. It was a pile on. They were killing him. He was going to be squashed under here, like an insect.

"I give up!" he screamed. "I give up!"

CHAPTER FOUR

"I don't want to watch that anymore," President Clement Dixon said.

There was a small TV mounted to the kitchen wall. CNN was on, and they were showing an altercation that had taken place at the Atlanta airport maybe an hour ago. Georgia state police and some local sheriff's deputies had gone to the airport to arrest an Egyptian computer programmer who was on a stopover during a trip from New York to California. A melee had broken out at the exit gate.

The image on the screen at the moment was from a camera that was on the ground. It was filming sideways and showed the young Egyptian under a pile of cops and protestors, screaming in what looked like terror and agony.

Thomas Hayes, Vice President of the United States, thought it was one of the more troubling and bizarre bits of footage he had seen in a while. Which was probably why the news channels were running it over and over again.

Dixon clicked it off with the remote control. The image disappeared.

"How are your eggs?" Dixon said. He gestured at Hayes's plate with his chin.

Hayes smiled. Okay. He could let the travel ban go for now. The battle was there to be fought, but he and Dixon didn't need to fight it right this second. Others were already doing that.

"How do you think they are? Delicious. This place is a 5-star restaurant."

They were sitting in the tiny dining area of the Residence Family Kitchen. Hayes was continually surprised by how small rooms and spaces were in the White House. The Residence kitchen was no exception. They were both big men, Hayes bigger than Dixon by quite a bit, and they filled the space almost entirely.

The White House was built for an earlier era, and smaller people. Abraham Lincoln, at six feet five inches tall, was an anomaly for his time, and notoriously too big for his White House bed.

The food though, was superb, as always. Eggs, sausage, toast, and coffee. It seemed simple enough - every greasy spoon diner in America offered it, but here it was a cut above the best eateries in New York, Chicago, Paris, wherever. Hayes had been everywhere in his time, and he would swear on a Bible if need be. The chef here was as good as they came. He went above and beyond, every single time.

Hayes reflected how incredible it was to sit here with the President of the United States, just informally having some breakfast, and chatting about what was happening, strategies, and goals going forward.

Dixon wasn't even dressed for the day yet, but he was Dixon to the core of his being. His hair was shaggy, and he had a thick moustache. His features were often compared to those of Mark Twain. He wore faded and beat up old blue jeans with American flag patches on them, a United Auto Workers t-shirt, and slippers on his feet.

Clement Dixon, US Representative for more than three decades, two-time Speaker of the House, old school liberal firebrand that the *New York Times Magazine* once referred to as "the Conscience of a Nation." And now President of the United States, stumbling into the office simply by being third in the line of succession.

He looked every minute of his 75 years. Maybe more.

Thomas Hayes and Clement Dixon were long-time allies. Hayes worried about the old man sometimes. Dixon seemed to have lost a step since the Air Force One hijacking. There were days when he just didn't seem up to the job.

And there was a lot to do. The insane travel ban on North Africans imposed by 19 conservative states was causing chaos in airports, as well as train and bus stations, all over the country. Jails and detention centers in places like Atlanta and Dallas and Orlando were filling up with hapless people from Morocco and Algeria and Tunisia who were simply traveling - to visit family, for work, to go to goddamn Disney World.

The lawsuit against it, sponsored by the federal government, New York, New Jersey, Connecticut, California, Oregon, and Washington State to name a few, would be taken up by the Supreme Court next week.

Of course the ban was unconstitutional. It was a no-brainer. But Hayes felt the messaging from the White House had been flat, and with the composition of the Court these days... Well, you just never knew

14

what kind of idiocy a group of unaccountable penguins in dark robes was going to churn out.

Hayes felt that the ban would be struck down, but the vote would be close, probably 5-4. And Richard Vilar, as always, was a wild card. He was a man who seemed to have no fixed opinions about anything. He could turn it either way.

Hayes sometimes wondered if Vilar was some kind of amnesiac. Did he have a valet who had to remind him who he was every morning? About the best you could say of him was he was consistently inconsistent.

This was really too important an issue to have someone like Vilar casting the deciding vote. The American way of life - immigrants coming to a new land to reach for better, both for themselves and their descendants - hung in the balance.

Dixon of old would have been out front on this, banging his fist on a podium somewhere, shouting out, "This decision is an obscenity!" Or: "Future generations will cringe when they read of this!" Or even: "Today I'm ashamed to be an American!"

Thomas Hayes needed to shake him awake and bring him back to the fray. This morning was as good a time as any.

"What are we going to do about the Court case?" Hayes said. "I feel like we're hanging back a little bit and leaving this to the states. I think we need to put our thumb on the scale."

"We co-sponsored the bill," Dixon said, using language inappropriate to the situation. There was no bill. There was a lawsuit. And the federal government didn't co-sponsor bills. Thankfully, Dixon caught himself immediately.

"You know what I mean."

Hayes nodded. "I do. But there's a lot more we can be doing. The fact is, we have all sorts of cudgels we can use against these clowns. We have the bully pulpit, and you're one of the best speakers in America. But that's not all. Texas and Florida may be economically powerful, but Georgia, South Carolina, Mississippi, Alabama, West Virginia, Louisiana… you get my point. These are net receivers of federal dollars. Some of these states would be medieval basket cases without the constant infusions of cash they get from us. They want to pull this kind of stunt? Just by delaying a few well-targeted payments, we can make their lives a living…"

Dixon raised a hand.

"Thomas. I want to tell you something. That's why I invited you for breakfast, before the day gets started."

To Hayes, 7:30 wasn't really before *the day got started*. Hayes had been up and moving since 5 am, but never mind that.

"We need to talk."

All of a sudden, Dixon seemed very old indeed. A sense of dread came over Thomas Hayes, and the realization that in his zeal for the job, he might be missing something important. It was a weakness of his, and he knew that. He was a hard charger, and sometimes he charged right past things that were obvious to other people.

Was Dixon dying?

"I'm here, Clement. I'm listening."

Dixon's shrewd, piercing blue eyes looked at him directly.

"Are you? Are you really?"

Hayes nodded and met those eyes. "Yes. I am."

"I don't really know how to say things, except by saying them. It's not my age. I just never was someone to beat around the bush. I'm going to finish out this term as President, which is my duty, but I'm not going to run for a second term. I just don't have it in me anymore."

He glanced down at the food in front of him, then looked up at Hayes again.

"Clement…" Hayes began.

Dixon raised his gnarled hand again, and Hayes knew better than to speak.

"I never expected this. And I never really wanted it. I was always the outsider, and I was comfortable in that role. When this landed in my lap, and you agreed to come on board, that changed things for me. I became optimistic again, like when I was young. I think you and I have started something great here. But the hijacking knocked the stuffing out of me. And more than just metaphorically. I've seen multiple doctors about this. I've been having minor intracranial bleeds from the impacts I took."

Hayes's heart did something funny. He wasn't sure what it was. He would almost call it a belly flop. It seemed to stop beating for as long as it would take for a fat man to hit the water. Then it started again with a SPLASH!

"Oh, Clem…"

"It turns out 75-year-old heads aren't supposed to take beatings. The blood vessels are fragile compared to those of younger men."

He shook his head.

"There haven't been any strokes, and no memory loss, but it's clear I'm not the man I was. My processing speed just isn't there. I find myself drifting off, wool gathering during meetings."

"That's your imagination," Hayes said. "Everybody does that."

"This is different," Dixon said. "I'm tired. And that's okay. I'll serve out this remarkable term, and relish this opportunity the Lord, or maybe circumstance, has brought me. But to run for the office, a year of constant battle and stress? On the road, on TV, the crowds, the hotel rooms, the reporters, the polls... I'm just not going to do it. I can't. I'm out of gas for that sort of thing."

There was another long pause between them.

"I'm going to keep up appearances, maybe dial my schedule back just a little bit. Nothing noticeable. But I want to begin handing the reins over to you."

Hayes raised an eyebrow.

"We're in great shape, Thomas. Our popularity is as high as it's been since we stepped into office. The economy is good. The hijacking, as much as it hurt me physically, has done wonderful things for my reputation. I'm sure you've read the articles and seen the polls. People think of me as a fighter, even now, after nearly a year has passed. You and I, together, have created an aura of stability after a period of turbulence. And when the time comes, if you decide you want the presidency, I will endorse you in the strongest possible terms."

Hayes nodded. "I want it. I can tell you that right now. I would never run against you, obviously, but if you really aren't going to..."

Dixon nodded as well. "I'm really not going to run. And I'm glad to hear you say that. There's no one I'd rather see take it. There is a very good chance you can practically stroll into this office, and for the American people, it will be a seamless transition. They deserve that."

Hayes was a little bit shocked by the suddenness of this. But he recognized that Dixon was right - he could simply walk in the door.

"I'd like you to keep quiet about the details of what was said here today," Dixon said. "My health is no one's business but my own."

"Agreed," Hayes said. "Of course."

"But I do know that you'll need to start moving. Putting out feelers for a running mate, vetting people, bringing staff together. I would just ask that you keep it as quiet as possible for the time being. I'd like to make the announcement in my own time, and in my own way, without the press running out ahead of me."

Hayes nodded. "Understood."

"But there's a lot you can do under the table..."

"Believe me," Hayes said. "I'm going to start today."

Dixon nodded. "And you should." He paused. For a moment, he seemed as if he might become teary. "You're a good man, Thomas.

17

You're going to make a fine President. I wish we had done more together, but what we've done…"

He trailed off.

"It's been incredible, Clem. And it's been an honor to serve under you. I look forward to finishing this job."

Dixon reached a hand across the table and Hayes took it. Now that Dixon had described the health problems he'd been dealing with, Hayes imagined he could feel the weakness in his friend's grip.

This entire time, Hayes had been waiting for Dixon to steer the conversation back to the travel ban. Surely, he wasn't going to leave the issue lying there, was he? But Clem had made his intentions clear by not saying anything more. He wasn't interested, or maybe he was just too tired to go the extra mile. It seemed like he really was willing to just leave it to the courts, and not try to shape public opinion at all.

The man was old, yes, and he had gone through the wringer. Who survives such a thing? A hijacking, a plane crash and fire, a shootout with extremists on the streets of Mogadishu? Clement Dixon had. And it had taken a lot out of him.

"Go to it," Dixon said. "But keep it quiet."

"I will."

* * *

Ten minutes later, Hayes was in the West Wing, walking briskly toward the exit with David Halstram. Halstram had become his body man in recent months, close to him at all times. David was probably eight inches shorter than Hayes, prematurely balding. Hayes noticed this whenever he looked down at him.

Halstram was young, but with his receding hairline and his glasses, he looked old. Yet he had one of the fastest minds Thomas Hayes had ever encountered. And energetic? The kid seemingly never slept and was never tired.

If he wasn't so young, Hayes would have already made him his chief-of-staff. He was headed in that direction like a guided missile. Hayes's current chief-of-staff, Geri Macario, was already feeling the footsteps.

It is what it is.

Politics was a tough arena. Utterly unforgiving. Geri would need to step up her game, or nature would take its course. She could have no illusions about that. She'd been around the block.

Now, David was filling him in on the upcoming schedule.

"David, we need to talk," Hayes said.

Immediately, David shifted gears. He was ready for anything. Thomas could tell him he was fired, and David would probably be ready with seven reasons why it was the wrong move at this time.

"Okay, Thomas. Tell me."

Hayes shook his head. "Not here. Outside."

They moved through the crowds coming and going at the main entrance to the West Wing. Hayes's Secret Service detail had fallen in step with them. A phalanx of big men surrounded them now as they stepped out into the morning light.

The motorcade was in front of them, the vice-presidential limo bookended by two big black armored SUVs.

Hayes stopped.

The whole procession stopped as well, but the Secret Service men gave them some distance. They knew the deal. When Thomas Hayes spoke outside, it was only for the ears of the person he was talking to.

David Halstram looked up at him.

This was a moment. Thomas Hayes knew it.

From his earliest days, he had always been the top performer, everywhere he found himself. High school valedictorian, captain of the rowing team, president of the student body. Summa cum laude at Yale, summa cum laude at Stanford. Fulbright Scholar. President of the Pennsylvania State Senate. Governor of Pennsylvania.

He had always believed that he could find the right solution to any problem. He had always believed in the power of his leadership. What's more, he had always believed in the inherent goodness of people. He still did.

He could handle the long hours. He could handle the various departments and the vast bureaucracy. He could handle the Pentagon. He could live with the Secret Service around him twenty-four hours a day, intruding on every aspect of his life.

He could navigate the world of DC politics. Politics was his life breath. True, they hit harder here in Washington than in Harrisburg, but that was to be expected. This was the big leagues. And don't forget that Pennsylvania politics also included Philadelphia and Pittsburgh, probably two of the hardest hitting cities in the country.

He could handle DC. He could handle the giant, magic sprawl of America, all of it, New York City to Los Angeles, to Hawaii to Alaska. The cities, the small towns, the various factions and infighting. He was in love with the USA.

19

He could handle the world stage. The friends, the enemies, the hungry masses. All those peoples, all those faces. Looking to him for leadership.

He was ready for this.

And right now, he was about to step into the role. It was becoming real, right in front of his eyes. He was going to run for President of the United States, and in all likelihood, he was going to win. Who could stop him?

David Halstram was still looking up at him. Expectantly, like a puppy dog. Hayes could see it. David was going to grow, and mature, and he was going to turn into a pit bull, a war dog that Thomas Hayes could unleash on his adversaries.

Hayes's heart skipped a beat. This was it. It was about to become real.

"I want you to discreetly put together a very short list of possible running mates," Hayes said, his voice barely above a whisper, his lips barely moving. "It's this simple. I want the most popular liberal politicians in America. I want people who have broad appeal on both sides of the issues. But relatively young, people who are unlikely to undermine me, or run against me. And people who are known to keep their mouths shut. I want exactly three of them, no more, no less."

David's eyes lit up like fireworks. "Thomas, what are you saying?"

Hayes raised a hand. "This is not for public consumption. It has to happen in secret. The people on the list can't really know they're being vetted. They can suspect, maybe they can even know it deep inside, but they can't be sure. And they can't say a word about it to anyone. That much is certain."

David watched him.

"Can you do that?" Hayes said.

David smiled. "You bet I can."

Now Hayes smiled. "We're going places, kid."

20

CHAPTER FIVE

4:50 pm Central European Summer Time (10:50 am Eastern Daylight Time)
Hotel Arts
Barcelona, Spain

"As you know, Spain is my ancestral home."

Richard Sebastian-Vilar sat at a table on the roof deck of the hotel in the waning afternoon sunlight. From where he was, he could look directly across the shimmering infinity pool at the towering artwork known as El Peix d'Or, or the Fish of Gold, by the American sculptor and architect Frank Gehry. To his left, the Mediterranean Sea also shimmered, just not as brightly as the pool.

A young man in a blue dress shirt and slacks sat with him, a small SONY digital recording device on the table between them. The device had replaced the tape recorders journalists had carried around with them up until the recent past. Its red light was on. The young man worked for one of the regional newspapers here in Barcelona.

He smiled. He spoke in impeccable English. "From what I saw on TV two days ago, France is your ancestral home."

Vilar smiled in turn. "Well, both. My paternal grandparents came from Sete, near Montpelier. But my maternal grandparents came from the village of Bossost, in the Valley of Aran."

"So you are Aranese?" the young man said. He was being playful, but his questions were pointed.

"Aranese, yes. But Spanish as well, and Catalan, of course."

It was a complicated history that would be nearly baffling to an outsider. Catalonia, with Barcelona as its capital, was an autonomous region within Spain. And Aran was a tiny autonomous region within Catalonia. All of this stemmed from covenants made between the small kingdoms that existed here in the Middle Ages, when the southern half of the peninsula was controlled by the Moors, and before Spain became one political entity. And to make things even more complicated, each region had its own language, though Aranese was closer to a dialect of Catalan than a distinct language of its own.

21

"You sound like a politician, more than a judge. You are a member of every group."

Vilar laughed. "The heritage is complex, and I embrace all of it. Spain is a melting pot of ethnicities, in its way, just like America."

"In Spain, our melting pot status has long been a source of trouble. And it has taken darker tones than ever in recent years. Between the Madrid bombings carried out by Moroccans and Algerians, and the presence of the international mafias in Marbella..."

Vilar nodded. "It has been difficult. I understand."

"Very difficult."

There was a long pause and the young man stared at Vilar earnestly.

"How will you vote?" he said, swinging for a home run. He must know that a judge, no less a Supreme Court judge, would never reveal his vote before the case had even begun. It was impossible.

Vilar shrugged and smiled. "I will hear the arguments as presented, and cast my vote based on precedents set in case law over generations. That is the way I always decide a case. I do not come in with preconceived notions."

The young man wasn't swayed. "But surely this trip is more than a homecoming, and the timing is no... how do you say it, coincidence. You have traveled to France and Spain, two countries that have had terrible troubles with terror attacks by immigrants from North Africa, just a week before hearing a court case in America about a ban on immigrants from North Africa."

Vilar nodded. "You're a very wise young man. Call this more than a homecoming. It is also a fact-finding tour."

The court had a case in front of it, the temporary banning of North Africans from entering the United States. A group of US states and their attorneys general had banned entry by North Africans across the board - Moroccans, Algerians, Tunisians, Libyans, and Egyptians. The states were the usual suspects - places like Georgia, Oklahoma, Missouri, North Carolina, and Louisiana, but also the powerhouses of Texas and Florida. North Africans were banned from landing in, or even traveling through, their territories.

This was causing travel bottlenecks all over the country because Texas, Florida, and Louisiana all had major international airports, and Georgia and North Carolina had major domestic hubs. North Africans could not get on flights landing in or taking off from Dallas/Fort Worth, Houston, Miami, Fort Lauderdale, Orlando, Tampa, New Orleans, Atlanta, and Charlotte.

Thousands of people had been denied travel. There were massive logjams as security attempted to identify people based on their heritage. Some American citizens of North African descent had been detained for days. Meanwhile, JFK, LaGuardia, Minneapolis, Detroit, O'Hare, Newark, Logan, Philadelphia, LAX, San Francisco, SeaTac, Dulles, Reagan National, BWI, and Portland had all refused to honor the ban.

Many North Africans were no longer attempting to fly. But volunteers were getting on planes in cities that did not enforce the policy and were being detained and taken away in airports that did enforce the ban, while news cameras filmed like crazy. News teams had also been detained. They were traveling incognito with the volunteers, then whipping the cameras out and broadcasting live when security moved in.

The situation was a mess.

The travel ban states were trying to force this down everyone's throat and make it public policy. The federal government and the non-complying states were challenging it. And the Supreme Court would hear the case on an emergency basis next week.

The court had morphed into a very political body in recent years. It had become ideological, no longer above the fray as it was intended. Vilar considered himself old school, a throwback to the days when the court was supposed to be non-partisan. He joined the court 12 years ago.

The young man persisted. "But surely, you must have some idea which way you are leaning."

Which way would he vote? That's what everyone always wanted to know. Vilar was the only real centrist left on the court. Once again, he was likely to cast the deciding vote. But as always, he would judge the case on its merits. He insisted, as he always did, on not revealing which way he would vote beforehand. He also insisted on hearing the case first before deciding. Even internally, within his own mind, he hadn't yet considered which way he would vote, such was the force of the principle with him. People seemed to have trouble believing that, but it was true.

Vilar glanced down at his watch.

It was a beautiful, blue-toned Breitling Chronomat, many years old. It was rare, and probably quite expensive. Vilar had no idea how much it cost because it was a gift to him from a friend. More important than the watch itself was the time.

"I'm sorry," Vilar said. "I promised my wife and daughter I would be ready to go to dinner with them by 5:30. My daughter is very young." He added the last part to explain the earliness of the hour. The Spanish were notorious for eating dinner at 10 o'clock or even later. Restaurants were often packed at midnight.

"Of course," the reporter said, instantly respectful and gracious again. He stood and held out his hand. Vilar did the same, and the two men shook.

"Your honor, it has been my great privilege to meet you."

"I feel likewise," Vilar said.

The young man turned off his recorder, gathered his things, and headed for the elevator. As soon as he did, Karl Adams, an operative from the Supreme Court Police, made his way across the roof deck toward Vilar.

The Supreme Court Police coordinated security for justices when they traveled abroad. Karl and two other men from the tiny agency were with him on this trip, and Karl kept corralling large contingents of police and military units to travel with them.

It was annoying. Richard Sebastian-Vilar was a judge, in a sense, a private citizen. He would just as soon travel alone with his family. He was not the president, he was not a member of Congress, he was not a Third World despot. Why did he need so much security?

He watched Karl approach. Karl was the overburdened, anxious, eyes in the back of his head type. Vilar did not enjoy that about him. But he could respect that Karl was a marathoner and a triathlete and kept his body in a high state of physical readiness. Vilar had been a marathoner himself and was proud that he had remained fit and trim well into middle age. The two men had bonded over races they had both run in various parts of the United States.

But right now, marathons were clearly not on Karl's mind. Vilar met him at the white iron railing at the edge of the deck.

Karl leapt right in without preamble. "Your honor, we've got to make some decisions about tomorrow. The Barcelona police are wondering if we're going to request an escort into the mountains, and I have to say…"

"I've decided," Vilar said.

Karl nodded. "Okay. You have? What's the verdict, in that case?"

Supreme Court justices were in charge of how much security traveled with them. They could choose to have none. Vilar had not chosen that. But he was tired of being flanked by operatives everywhere he went. From here, he could see four armed men, just on the deck alone. There were more downstairs, outside the door to his suite, protecting his wife and daughter as they got ready for dinner.

24

"It's a tiny village," Vilar said. "I don't want to go up there like an invading army. That's not how I want to return to the place of my forebears. If you and your two men want to accompany us, that's fine. But let's leave the military and police escort here in the city."

"That's your decision?" Karl said.

Vilar nodded. "Yes, it is."

"Judge, I don't want to impose anything on you, least of all something that makes you uncomfortable. But I would like to remind you that security environments are always in flux. There is no reliable way to predict..."

Vilar raised a hand and smiled. He didn't like to pull rank and, as a general rule, refrained from doing so. But he was a Supreme Court justice, after all, and this man worked for the Supreme Court.

"Karl," he said. "Save it, okay? If anything goes wrong, you can tell everyone you begged me to go up there with tanks and fighter planes, and I said no."

"Judge..."

"But I promise you, nothing will go wrong."

CHAPTER SIX

7:15 pm British Summer Time (2:15 pm Eastern Daylight Time)
St. Pancras Railway Station
London, England

The man finally made it through the security checkpoint.

It was a busy night, the lines a slow-moving crush of humanity. It seemed these evening trains to France were always crowded. The inspection itself was cursory at best. He put his rolling overnight bag on the conveyor belt and watched as it disappeared into the tunnel to be X-ray scanned. Then he stepped through the human scanner.

The guards he faced barely seemed to look at him. His skin was a deep, rich brown, which at times meant extra scrutiny. But he was dressed impeccably, in a well-tailored suit and topcoat. His hands were neatly manicured. His face was clean-shaven, his short dark hair slicked back and showing a touch of gray along each side. He wore a gold wedding band on the ring finger of his left hand.

If he were stopped by security personnel, and taken in for questioning, the name on his passport and driver's license was Yosef Ensour. He was a 45-year-old Jordanian-born barrister, living in London. He rode the Eurostar train to France twice a month because he was a wealthy do-gooder.

The refugee camp at Calais was large and growing all the time. People, the vast majority of them men, displaced by wars and political upheavals in the Middle East, in Egypt and in Libya, and by drought in North Africa and the Sahel, were accumulating in that squalid camp.

They arrived at Calais hoping to sneak into the Channel Tunnel, the very tunnel Ensour was about to ride through aboard the fancy new Eurostar train, the fastest high speed in the world. If these men could enter the tunnel on foot, the theory went, they could simply walk into England and begin new lives.

Someone must have successfully done it, at some point. Otherwise, why would thousands of people pin their hopes on such an outlandish idea? To be sure, no one was getting through these days. The French had encircled the refugees with high fences, razor wire, guard towers and electronic monitoring equipment. The French police and immigration authorities routinely went through the camp, looking for men with criminal records to deport back to their home countries.

Yosef Ensour, bleeding heart that he was, fluent in Arabic and English, with the ability to speak and understand some French, and armed with his legal background, waded into the camp for a couple of days every two weeks, and gave free immigration law counseling to the people he encountered there.

Of course, none of this was true. The Calais Jungle refugee camp was all too real, but the man's name was not Yosef Ensour. He was not a lawyer, and he wasn't from Jordan. He was a decade younger than 45 and colored his hair with a commercial cream that gave him that touch of gray, for men who wanted the distinguished, sophisticated look that came with age and experience. The wedding band on his ring finger was certainly gold, but he was not married. And he had never spent any time in the camp - indeed, if he entered it, he had no idea if he would make it back out again.

Better to steer clear of such entanglements.

Now, he passed into the wide-open atrium of the gleaming train terminal, rolling his overnight suitcase along behind him. He was on the ground floor, and the glass and steel ceiling was three stories above his head. All along the concourse, evening crowds sat in restaurants or in bars, eating, drinking, and chatting, creating a background hum. There was a pleasant air of... if not excitement, then certainly energy. These people were headed to the Continent tonight - Paris, perhaps, or Brussels, or Amsterdam.

His train was above him, on the second level, preparing for departure. He could see it from here. They hadn't called it yet. There was plenty of time.

He stopped into the men's room. The light in here was bright and white, nearly glaring. He moved along the row of stalls to the last one. It was empty. He went inside, closed and locked the door behind him, removed his topcoat and hung it on the hook, then sat on top of the toilet seat, still fully dressed.

Perhaps a bit carelessly, he allowed his rolling suitcase to fall over sideways onto the floor. He stared at it as it lay there. It was almost new, dark gray in color, non-descript in every way. It could easily be mistaken for the hundreds of other nearly identical suitcases rolling along the corridors out there.

As he watched, two hands appeared from under the barrier between his stall and the one next to him. The hands seized his suitcase and pulled it under the barrier. In an instant, Ensour's suitcase was simply gone.

He carefully controlled his breathing. It was always like this. Even though he knew it was coming, he was never quite ready.

An instant later, the hands reappeared, pushing another suitcase under the barrier and into Ensour's stall. It would be easy to believe that the new suitcase was the same as the one that just disappeared seconds ago. In fact, they were the same color, and the same model, churned out in their millions by the same manufacturer. The two suitcases were even approximately the same age, with the same amount of wear and tear.

Then the hands were gone. The suitcase was lying there, fallen over sideways. Outside, in the public men's room, the door to the stall next to his opened, and someone walked away, trailing a suitcase behind him. Ensour could hear the wheels rolling on the cement floor. He knew what items could be found in the suitcase that had just left - he was intimately familiar with them because he had packed them himself. Clothes for a couple of days away. Pajamas. Toiletry items. Very mundane things.

Ensour, which was not the man's name, pulled the new suitcase closer to him. Immediately, he noticed it was quite a bit heavier than the earlier suitcase. Curious, he zipped it open, just a bit, and pulled back the flap.

There were blocks of C4 plastic explosive in this case, more than enough to blow out the side of a train while it was in motion. Perhaps enough to blow out the tunnel itself. There were blasting caps and long, looped fuses in here. There were two semiautomatic pistols with pre-loaded magazines lying alongside them.

Ensour did not know if these things were real or not. Maybe they were just very convincing replicas. He wasn't going to inspect them any further in the hope of finding out. All that mattered was he had done it again. He had carried out his task exactly as assigned. Whoever the man in the other stall had been, he had done the same.

Ensour had successfully passed though security, a professional man, a long-time Londoner, above reproach or suspicion. And then these weapons, which had no doubt taken a different route into the station, had joined him here. Assuming the explosives were real, in 20 minutes he would get on the train equipped to cause a disaster that could kill everyone, or nearly everyone on board.

It was the third time he had done this in the past month. Whoever had devised this method, had come up with a way to defeat the security

28

at St. Pancras train station, thus making the train itself, as well as the tunnel, vulnerable to attack. Indeed, the train was slowly becoming a high-speed rolling bomb.

"Praise Allah," Ensour murmured, very quietly, under his breath.

He zipped up the suitcase and got ready to leave the stall.

CHAPTER SEVEN

September 22
2:05 am Central European Summer Time (8:05 pm Eastern
Daylight Time, September 21)
Vielha Tunnel
Beneath the Pyrenees Mountains

"In the name of the Prophet!"

The man's name was Hamzah. In Arabic, the name meant strong and steadfast, and he lived by these ideals. When he spoke, it was to himself, and under his breath. The sound was just barely audible in the cab of the large tractor-trailer, where he was alone anyway.

He was driving the truck under the mountains from Alta Ribagorca comarca to the town of Vielha, on the other side. He had left a warehouse on the outskirts of Barcelona earlier this evening, with a precious cargo.

Just up ahead, another truck driver was unaccustomed to the poor lighting and visibility in this tunnel, and the head-on traffic coming from the other direction in what was a very narrow space. The man kept riding his brakes and slowing his truck from a reasonable speed, down to a crawl. Then, as his courage returned, he would speed up again, only to hit his brakes again a moment later.

Hamzah had nearly rear-ended him three times now. He resolved to simply slow down and let the other truck get far ahead of him.

At one time, this was the longest road tunnel in the world. Completed in 1948, it was old, outdated, and had recently been announced as the most dangerous tunnel in Europe. More people died in here than inside any other tunnel on the continent. It was also notorious for its lack of security - there were no checkpoints on either side. You simply drove a curving road set up as a wind break, came upon its dark, gaping maw, and entered the death trap at your own discretion.

Ahead, the red brakes lights of the other truck came on again. An instant later, another tractor-trailer, invisible until the last second, whooshed by going in the other direction. That one didn't slow down at all, and Hamzah's truck lurched from the wind blast of its passing.

It was really quite dangerous under here.

They were building a new tunnel, parallel to this one, in the hopes of replacing it, but the project had been hampered by delays, cost overruns, and accusations of corruption.

In Spain? You don't say.

Hamzah smiled to himself. He had left Morocco more than a decade ago. He had lived in Spain nearly all of that time, and he knew nothing got done in the entire country unless the right beaks were allowed to dip into the right fountains first. It was just the way the place worked.

The truck ahead was traveling 30 kilometers per hour now. Hamzah was right on his tailgate again. The red brake lights never wavered. The man should find a new line of work - driving trucks through the mountains was clearly not for him. Hamzah sighed and pressed his horn.

"Come on! Come on then!"

This tunnel was the only thing connecting the small enclaves of Spain on the north slopes of the mountains with the rest of the country to the south. Many people thought of these mountains as the border between Spain and France, but it wasn't entirely true. Places like the Valley of Aran were Spanish, just on the wrong side of this geological barrier.

Things like that interested Hamzah. He liked to study maps. It interested him in this case especially because the border here was wide open. A man could easily walk from Spain into France, and no one would challenge him. Recreational hikers who traversed these mountains crossed the border regularly along their path, lodging in a French village one night, and a Spanish village the next.

These facts were important. The precious cargo Hamzah was carrying were men. The men were bringing weapons, and they were prepared to go to war. They were well-provided for, with food, water, and bedding. The truck had enough gaps in its structure to provide them with ample, free-flowing air from the outside. The mountain evening was cool, even cold

When he arrived in Vielha, 15 minutes from now, Hamzah would park the truck at a rest area outside the town where many truck drivers parked overnight. Then he would sleep. Tomorrow, in the late afternoon, he would drive the truck up to the village of Bossost. The

31

village was very close to the border, and closer still to the old siege tunnel complex left from the second world war.

If Allah willed it, tomorrow evening, the men inside this truck would acquire their own precious cargo, move it into France, and then along towards its final destination.

CHAPTER EIGHT

6:05 pm Central European Summer Time (12:05 pm Eastern Daylight Time)
Bossost Village
Valley of Aran, Pyrenees Mountains
Spain

It was a shock when the shooting began.

"What do you think, honey?" Richard Sebastian-Vilar said, just moments before.

He was walking the steep, winding cobblestone streets of the village with his wife and daughter, and the mayor of the town, a man named Paulo Robles.

Karl Adams and the other two agents in Vilar's three-man security team flanked the group at a polite distance. All three wore dark suits and sunglasses, despite the fact that the sun was already fading to the west.

Mayor Robles was the same age as Vilar, just in a different way. Besides being mayor, he also owned the town bakery, and he looked like a baker - short, portly, bald at the top of his head with dark hair growing along his ears, and a thick salt and pepper mustache. But Robles navigated the high-altitude hills with no apparent effort, while slim, fit Vilar was breathless. The man was acclimated to his surroundings.

And Robles was an eccentric. He was dressed in a white suit, with a white vest, white shoes, and a walking stick painted white.

"It's beautiful," Sydney Vilar said. "Completely beautiful."

Vilar glanced at his wife. She was as beautiful as the surroundings, long blonde hair, much younger than he was. Her face in the near distance, with the whitewashed houses in the village, and the mountains looming behind her created a stunning image, one that should be in a travel magazine.

Between them, holding each of their hands was Grace, their eight-year-old daughter. Sometimes, back home, they would run with Grace in the park, holding hands with her in just this way, and when they got enough momentum, they would pull her high into the air as they ran. Grace loved that game. But it wasn't possible here, not in these hills.

It had been a great day. They'd arrived in the afternoon and eaten a late lunch in a tiny café with Mayor Robles, who spoke basic English, was charming and gracious, and knew absolutely every person in the town by their first name, knew that person's family, and knew the family history as it interlocked with the history of the town and the region, and all the other families who lived here, or once had. The man was a compendium of lore concerning the village of Bossost and the surrounding countryside.

Many people visited with them at their table, eager to say hello to the long-lost village son returned from America. And a Supreme Court judge? It just went to show you how people from the village were. They chose to remain here, because it was the best, but in the wider world, they could become anything.

Tomorrow, in the morning, there would be a formal breakfast at the community center. Mayor Robles would be there, of course, as the master of ceremonies. But many people from this town, and from others nearby in the mountains, were also coming. There were second cousins of Vilar's still here, and they would be there as well.

It was a wonderful homecoming, not what Vilar might have imagined (he had somehow pictured himself walking these cobbled streets alone and unidentified), but wonderful, nonetheless.

Vilar was here, in part, because he had sent himself on a fact-finding mission. And what facts was he finding? Had he discovered anything useful? Perhaps what he was learning was something he had already known.

Most people were inherently good, friendly, and welcoming. People were people, everywhere you went. The United States was a melting pot of peoples and cultures, a nation of nations, and the people…

He smiled and shook his head. He was getting ahead of himself. He was doing research, and that was fine. But his job was to hear the facts of the case brought before him. He would wait until then to decide anything.

Now, Robles was taking his leave from them. They were at the top of a long narrow alleyway of a street, between two rows of tidy homes with flowerpots under the windows. There were no cars - this alley was built for donkey carts from centuries ago. A modern car probably wouldn't fit between the sidewalks. The small guest house where Vilar, his family, and Karl Adams were staying was here. The other *pension*, the one where the other two members of the security team were staying, was diagonally across the street.

The mayor's home, so he said, was further up the hill, a little bit outside the town. As they shook hands, Robles glanced up the hill. The sun had set, and night was coming in. About 50 meters away, a large tractor-trailer truck had pulled up at the top of the alleyway, blocking it. It seemed prepared to park there.

Vilar glanced at it. There were no markings on it.

Robles shook his head and smiled.

"It is no good. Cannot leave it there. I will talk to him."

He made a motion like a hand on a steering wheel.

"The driver."

Vilar nodded. "Of course. Don't let us keep you. Thank you for everything."

"We are so proud," Robles said.

There was a loud clatter as the rear door of the truck opened. Little Grace jumped at the sound. "Oooh!" she said. Sydney stood on the stone front steps of the pension with Grace, holding her hand. They were at the threshold of the doorway.

Suddenly, there was a spurt of blood from the mayor's head.

Vilar stared at it. There had been no sound. Robles tumbled to the cobblestones. He seemed to move in slow motion. The silence went on and on.

Then Vilar was on the ground himself, Karl Adams on top of him. Vilar's head bounced off the hard stones. Adams was shouting something at his men, but Vilar had trouble making out the words.

"Get… them… inside!"

Sydney and Grace were screaming soundlessly, their faces masks of anguish. One of the guards pushed them inside the building.

TAT-TAT-TAT-TAT-TAT.

A burst of gunfire shattered the quiet of the tiny alleyway. Vilar wasn't sure if he'd ever heard gunfire before. Ten feet away, across the cobblestones, a bloody Paulo Robles, the mayor of this village, lay in a pool of even more blood, a river of it, more coming all the time. The dark red of the blood stood out in sharp relief against the white of Robles's suit. His eyes were open, unblinking. They stared at Vilar.

Why did you come here?

Adams was dead weight on top of Vilar.

"Karl! My wife! My daughter! Protect them. Don't worry about me."

Men were moving quickly down the alleyway now. Coming this way. They were dressed in dark clothes, with black masks across their faces. They carried rifles.

Vilar tried to make sense of it. Were there attacks here in the mountains? For what? This was far from anywhere.

TAT-TAT-TAT-TAT-TAT.

"Karl! Get off me!"

The man was smothering him. This wasn't the way to do the job. They had to get inside the guest house. Vilar squirmed around, trying to shrug Adams's body off of him, like a dog trying to shrug off fleas. His head was not clear. It had bounced off the pavement when Adams tackled him. But they had to *move*!

"Karl!"

He crawled out from beneath his security man. He glanced back at him. Karl's lifeless body was sprawled across the stones, much like the body of Robles. Karl's eyes were heavily lidded, half-closed, staring, not blinking. His mouth hung open.

To Vilar's left, an iron gate to the guest house came down with a clang. Behind it, a heavy wooden door slammed. They were locked inside, Grace and Sydney, someone had locked them in. Who? Who had done it?

Are they safe?

There was another body on the street here. A man, another member of Vilar's security detail. Dead, he looked dead. There was blood all around him, and his arms and legs were thrown out at strange, unnatural angles, like he was a broken toy.

Vilar looked up in the direction of the truck. The masked men in dark clothes were here. It was impossible to say anything about them, except they seemed to be wearing vests and they were heavily armed.

It was full night now. There was no one else in the street. Somewhere, bells were clanging, like church bells, but clanging furiously, an alarm clarion.

The closest man in black stepped up to Vilar. Vilar expected to be shot. The man would simply shoot him in the head. This was a terror attack, and there was nothing to stop it. Vilar felt no fear. Mostly, he felt the pain where his head had hit the pavement. Also, Robles's face, and dead eyes, wide open, were etched into Vilar's mind.

Shock. I'm in shock.

The masked, armed man swung his heavy boot and kicked Vilar in the head.

36

CHAPTER NINE

"I don't know if I'm ready for this," Thomas Hayes said.

He looked across his desk at Geri Macario, his chief-of-staff. Geri was 50, and she looked every minute of 60. Three times divorced, Geri Macario, who had been in Washington since dinosaurs roamed the planet, and who had a reputation as the work hard, play hard type. Eighteen-hour days in the trenches and late nights in the bars and restaurants were written on her face.

Geri smiled. Her teeth were white. Whiter than bleached bone lying on in the sun. Whiter than the whitest paper to be spewed from an office copier. Her eyes were blue.

"I think the kid has a case of puppy love," she said.

Her hair was blonde, the kind that came out of a bottle. Her nails were long. Her skin was lined. She had no illusions about anything. She was a serious person, as serious as a heart attack. Confidence came off her in waves. She could beat people down in a full-frontal assault, if the situation called for it. If that wouldn't work, she could creep up behind them and slip the knife into their kidneys.

Hayes glanced down at the surface of his desk and ran a finger along the smooth wood. It was a nice old desk. Apparently, it had occupied this office for nearly a hundred years. The big old bookcase against the far wall was the same way. There was something reassuring about longevity, and continuity. There was something reassuring about a system that cared for and maintained old, valuable things. The people came and went, they stabbed each others' backs, they cut the knees out from one another, but the system went on and on. America wasn't going anywhere.

When Hayes had arrived in DC, an outsider, the former governor of Pennsylvania, the party had given him Geri. It was the right move at the right time. She was a consummate pro. A bit cynical. Maybe she didn't have quite the energy anymore that her legend described. But her hand on the tiller was steady. She had been invaluable steering Hayes's ship through some rocky waters.

Hayes nodded. "Puppy love? Maybe so."

He didn't like to think it, but it was certainly shaping up that way. David Halstram was young. His head could still be turned by a shiny object. Maybe he wasn't quite ready to fill the shoes of a Geri Macario after all.

David had a hero worship thing happening. And he had a teenage crush thing happening. It was a little bit startling. It had opened Hayes's eyes. He had assigned David to identify, vet, and bring in three popular liberal politicians, people who would make a nice complement to President Thomas Hayes, people who could work the campaign trail hard, people who would run interference, people who could ride herd in the Congress, people who knew what they were doing.

So far, David had brought him two names. The first was Michael Parowski. That one was the hero worship.

The guy was a six-term Congressman from northeast Ohio. He was handsome in a rugged sort of way. He was also a bit of a brute, a former ironworker and Golden Gloves fighter. He liked to make a spectacle of himself, wading into massive crowds at union rallies and ethinc celebrations. Shaking hands, slapping backs, hugging old ladies, laughing, and shouting, mugging for the cameras.

He was popular, for sure. A champion of the unions, and for the little guy. A man's man, a macho man, who would do whatever he could to hog the spotlight. On top of everything, there were whispers that he was still friends with Mafia figures he had known while growing up in Cleveland.

That sounded like a great person to have at meetings in the Oval Office, wandering around in the West Wing, and privy to national security secrets.

"There is no hint, not even the merest suggestion, that Michael Parowski is dirty or corrupt in any way," David had said, when Hayes raised this issue. "The man has a thousand friends."

"Where there's smoke, there's fire," Thomas said.

David had shrugged. "There's no smoke."

Hero worship. Lots of young political workers were star struck by a larger-than-life type like Michael Parowski. Hayes had assumed David was past that phase, but it seemed he had assumed incorrectly. In any event, Parowski was a non-starter.

Now came puppy love.

38

Hayes and Geri were in Hayes's upstairs study at the Vice-Presidential Residence, the beautiful, turreted and gabled Queen Anne style 1850s mansion on the grounds of the Naval Observatory not far from the White House. This house was white as well, and if anything, it was a lot more pleasant than the White House itself.

This room, in particular, was probably the best room in the house. It had floor-to-ceiling windows that faced west and south, granting panoramic views of the green rolling lawns of the Naval Observatory campus.

The light in here always seemed perfect. At midday, like now, with the sun hitting the roof, the light was understated, almost blue, very pretty. In the late afternoons, with sun moving to the west, the light seemed to explode into a thousand spectacular shades of orange, yellow, red, white.

Each day was different, and every time a cloud crossed the sun, it was different yet again. On a breezy day, with clouds skittering across the sky, it was like a light show in here, the play of it through the windows like a symphony for the eyes.

They were sitting here, waiting for David Halstram to bring today's guest upstairs. That guest was Susan Hopkins, the junior Senator from California. It was clear that young David Halstram, not yet 30, was smitten with her. And why not? He had probably spent his teenage years drooling over photographs of her in magazines.

What to say about Susan Hopkins? She was popular, all right, one of the most popular politicians in America. She was a former fashion model, maybe even a "supermodel," who had begun her career draped in designer lingerie, and 15 years ago had graced the covers of *Vogue*, *Cosmopolitan*, *People*, and especially the *Sports Illustrated* swimsuit issue.

She was that rare liberal politician who was popular with conservative men, for obvious reasons. They didn't care what she believed in.

But modeling was a short window for most women. As her career petered out, she had slowly faded from the public eye. Until a couple of years later, when she turned up again, marrying Pierre Michaud, scion of the French ruling class, and sudden internet billionaire. Susan Hopkins had jumped lily pads from famous top model, to one of the wealthiest women alive. And even that wasn't enough for her.

She gave birth to twin daughters, then dipped her toe into politics. Running in liberal California on her looks and charm, and well-funded by her husband and his friends, she had easily won the Senate seat vacated when her predecessor retired.

Hayes got the sense that Susan Hopkins was some sort of voracious Pac Man creature, eating everything put in front of her. Model? Not enough. Rich beyond measure? Not enough. Kids, family? Not enough. Senator?

Not enough. The job didn't even seem to interest her.

She was already in her second term in the Senate, and in all that time, eight years so far, she hadn't moved a single measure forward. She was ineffectual within the chamber, to put it mildly. So she had taken a different tack, and seemed to have completely given up on making and passing laws. Instead, she appeared in magazines a lot, but they were not the magazines from her youth.

Parenting. Ladies Home Journal. Self.

And the reasons she was in the magazines were different as well. She talked about busy moms staying physically fit in just minutes a day. She talked about bullying in the schools, and ways to put a stop to it - by recognizing, not if your child was being bullied, but if your child was the bully. She shared the healthy recipes of her private world-class chef. She reminded women to get mammograms and annual wellness exams.

Senator Susan Hopkins, in terms of the knock-down, drag-out world of Washington politics, was a glass-jawed lightweight. She was lighter than air. Unable to accomplish anything in DC, she used the megaphone of her office to talk about uncontroversial off-topic matters and keep herself in the public eye.

And now here we were. David Halstram wanted to make her Vice President.

"This is probably a lark," Geri said now. "It's an excuse for David to meet her."

"He can do that on his own time," Hayes said.

Geri smiled. "No he can't."

"Anyway, I guess we shouldn't dismiss her out of hand."

Geri shook her head. "I never dismiss any woman. She could surprise us. I'm open to that. When she first announced in California, most people thought it was a joke."

Across the room, the door opened. David Halstram poked his bespectacled head in, almost sheepishly. "Thomas? Geri?"

"Is she here?" Hayes said.

"She's with me now."

Hayes smiled and stood. If anything, Thomas Hayes could be gracious. As a young boy, he was taught his manners well. "Bring her in. We're eager to meet her."

The door opened fully now. David stepped back and allowed Hopkins to enter ahead of him. The first thing Hayes noticed was she was shorter than he might have expected, even in heels. The second thing he noticed was that she seemed to glow.

She and David stepped into the room bare seconds apart. But David, who was taller than her by a few inches, also seemed to disappear behind her. More, David suddenly seemed to be rendered in black and white, like a newsreel from the 1940s, and Hopkins seemed to be in full Technicolor.

She was wearing a blue suit that hung perfectly on her body. The color of the suit was not muted - you would almost call it electric blue. Her hair was cut in a short blond bob, conservative even for the Washington crowd. She wore a strand of simple pearls around her neck. Her face was…

Ethereal.

There wasn't really any other way to put it. Of course. The reason these people became world famous as models, or as movie actors, was because they inhabited a different reality from ours. They did not look like us.

Thomas Hayes had been married for 31 years. He loved his wife utterly. Yes, in the deep dark past, he may have had his dalliances. He may have done things he now regretted and didn't like to think about. But he was completely committed to his wife, and he thought of her as beautiful.

But that wasn't like this. He had never been in the close presence of someone, male or female, who looked like Susan Hopkins. The magazine photos and the TV images didn't do it justice. It was hard to believe she was even real.

And it was because of this, he realized now, that she had simply been handed just about everything in life.

"Susan," he said, stepping around the desk, "I'm Thomas Hayes. It's a pleasure to meet you." They shook hands. He towered over her. He was probably a foot taller than she was.

"This is my chief-of-staff, Geri Macario."

"Geri. The legend. Great to meet you."

Geri and Hopkins shook hands as well. Everyone in the room was in black and white now, everyone except Susan Hopkins. She was like a glowing orb in their midst. Hayes gestured at the high-backed chairs that formed a sort of sitting area in the study.

"Won't you have a seat?"

"I have to tell you, Thomas," Hopkins said. "I love this room. This whole house. It must be incredible to live here."

Hayes smiled. She also had her non-physical charms.

"It is. It's an amazing place. I can't get enough of it. The White House is the Addams Family house in comparison."

They sat down, Geri, Susan Hopkins, and Thomas Hayes. David Halstram hovered at the edges. Hayes glanced at him. He looked like a cat that had just swallowed his owner's pet tweety bird. He looked like he might break out laughing at any moment.

Unreal. Just unreal.

But also a lesson, maybe. David Halstram wasn't as hard bitten as many in Washington, not yet, but he wasn't a babe in the woods, either. Hayes kept him close because having David nearby was like wearing a bulletproof cloak. He saw what was happening before it became clear to others. He was on the phone with people before Hayes even realized the call needed to be made.

David's mind was zooming along, out in front of everyone. And the kid barely touched caffeine. He was like this naturally. Hayes pictured him waking up in the morning, his eyes simply popping open at the appointed time, ready to go.

"To what do I owe this honor?" Susan Hopkins said.

Hayes focused on her now. Maybe... *maybe...* there was something to this. Or maybe, after she left, the spell would be broken.

"Susan, I've wanted to meet with you for some time. I know, we've seen each other around the Senate chambers, but haven't really had time to talk."

She smiled. "You spend most of your time over there with leadership. The peons are beneath your notice."

Hayes shrugged. "That's the job, unfortunately. But I want to set it right. I've heard good things about you."

Their eyes were locked.

"Such as?"

Hayes instantly went to the lie factory. The fact is, he had never given Susan Hopkins a moment's consideration before this morning. He had never asked anyone about her. He hadn't noticed her in the Senate, among the hundreds of people milling around. Obviously not. He would remember if he had.

Even so:

"I've heard you're hard-driving, ambitious, and smart. I've heard you surprised everyone with your first victory. And I've heard you're super popular with your constituents." He paused. So far it was all off-the-shelf platitudes. She knew that. Everyone in the room knew it. So he said the real thing, and gave her the big hint.

"I've heard you have a national following that transcends party lines."

She looked at him. She was about to say something but didn't. Then she looked at Geri Macario. Geri nodded.

Hayes put a finger to his lips.

"I am under the impression," Hopkins said, "that you and Clem Dixon are close friends and allies."

"We are. That's right."

"So he…"

"Nothing's been confirmed. Obviously, nothing's been announced. It wouldn't be your place to make any assumptions or spread any rumors, publicly or privately."

Hopkins nodded. "I understand."

The telephone on the desk behind them began to ring. Aggravating, but that was the business. Geri glanced up at David Halstram and made a little head bob toward the desk. Instantly, David complied. He caught the phone on the third ring.

"We'll need to talk more, of course," Hayes said. "Nothing is set. And I'm not promising anything."

"Of course," Hopkins said.

"But I want to gauge your level of interest, if such a thing ever came to pass."

She didn't hesitate. "A hundred percent interested. Two hundred percent."

Hayes and Geri both nodded. Already, without saying anything, this had been an interesting meeting.

"Thomas?" David Halstram said. He was standing at the desk with the phone. His face had changed. He was serious now, no longer the cat trying to choke down the family canary. "You're going to want to take this."

CHAPTER TEN

1:20 pm Eastern Daylight Time
The Situation Room
The White House
Washington, DC

"Mr. President, we're ready when you are," a serious voice said.

Don Morris was standing next to the President's chair. He had come over to say a brief hello. Clement Dixon had aged noticeably in the months since Don had last seen him. Being hijacked, repeatedly beaten, then surviving a plane crash and a shootout with automatic weapons and rockets in the streets of Mogadishu might do that to a person.

They did a good job of keeping up appearances on the television. On TV, Dixon looked the same as he ever had - ruffled, mussed with crazy Albert Einstein hair and a face that had probably looked old when he was 30. But nicely tailored suits, not too expensive - in keeping with the common touch he was renowned for - and as always, sharp eyes, and a sharp wit.

But here, in person, he looked tired.

He shook Don's hand. His grip was far weaker than Don's. Don was careful not to apply much pressure.

"Don, I'm glad you're here."

"Thank you, Mr. President. I'm glad to see you. I wish the circumstances were more favorable."

Dixon pointed at Don. "I miss our talks. Let's set a date to get together, away from these problems. Call my office, tell them I said to call, and I'll make sure it gets on the schedule. We'll do lunch in the Oval Office."

"I would like that, sir."

"So would I, Don."

Don didn't imagine it would happen. He'd already been in Washington long enough to know when they started to put distance between you and them. Clement Dixon was no longer the champion of

44

the Special Response Team. Don supposed he didn't blame him. The memories were incredibly painful. Don felt the same way.

His wife Margaret had been aboard that plane. Don himself had changed since then. He'd been sure that Margaret was dead, or worse. He'd attempted to rescue her, only to be arrested and thrown in jail by the Vice President, Thomas Hayes, who was also here today. Don could barely bring himself to look at the man.

Don was as through with all these Washington games as anyone. Dixon seemed to be on the same page with him. Not that Dixon ever would, or could, admit that. And so he put distance between himself and Don.

Clement Dixon and Don Morris had become close for a short period, two very unlikely allies, the lifelong liberal and the lifelong warrior. They had gone on a state visit to Puerto Rico together, and disaster had struck. Now the connection was tainted by bad luck and every sour thing. It was as if some evil force, a succubus, had attached itself to their relationship.

Dixon still gripped Don's hand.

"Mr. President, we're ready when you…"

"I heard you the first time, General," Dixon snapped. "You're ready when I am. But I wasn't ready yet."

Don felt Dixon release his hand.

Don took his seat at the conference table. He looked around the packed room. The place was a forest of eyes, all of them watching the President. Dixon was known for his fiery temper. But that little outburst was more consistent with a grumpy old man than with the passion of deeply held convictions.

Dixon seemed trapped in here. He looked a lot like a man who would prefer to be puttering in a garden right now or sitting on a patio with a glass of wine, or painting a watercolor of sailboats, or anything at all. This place was stifling, and Dixon was being stifled by it.

The Situation Room was shaped like an egg and was smaller than outsiders might imagine. It reminded Don of a TV show or B movie from the 1960s - not the War Room of apocalyptic Cold War dramas, but a sterile room, like an operating room where aliens from outer space might probe the minds of their human captives. There was something inhuman about this place.

Standing along the walls were the young people, the aides, the assistants, their eyes open and staring and concerned, but also serious, ready to punch numbers into their Blackberries, or whatever the latest gadget was. The technology seemed to change every week at this point.

Sitting with him at the oval table in the center were the bigwigs and heavy hitters. The usual suspects were here, including a few overweight men in suits, along with the thin and ramrod straight military men in uniform. Several of them had once outranked Don, and had been his superior officers, men who publicly frowned upon and disavowed his actions when he was running Delta Force, and quietly gave him the green light behind closed doors. Politics. While Don was out fighting wars, back here at home maneuvering, lying, misdirection and shifting sands were the order of the day.

In just a couple of years, Don had already become sick of it. He would be happier if he could somehow be reinserted into the military, and yet somehow not know the truth of what really went on in the civilian government.

Large video screens were embedded in the walls, with a giant screen at the far end of the oblong table. The chairs were tall leather recliners like the captain on the control deck of a starship might have. When the Situation Room was crowded like this, they could all be slaves crowded inside the cargo hold of a ship headed for deep space.

"Okay," Thomas Hayes said. "It looks like we're all ready now."

Don Morris glanced at him. Thomas Hayes, the Vice President of the United States. Bill Ryan, the Minority Leader of the House of Representatives and Don's old friend from the Citadel, was convinced that Thomas Hayes was a viper. A traitor. An enemy in our midst. Don tended to believe him. Certainly he would give Bill Ryan's instincts the benefit of the doubt. And Hayes had never done anything to disabuse Don of that notion.

It was even darker than Don would like to think about. Bill had hinted that he believed Hayes was behind the death in prison of the arms dealer and trafficker in teenage girls, Darwin King. King's death had been ruled a suicide, but hardly anyone with half a brain bought that story.

King had been held by himself in a decaying cellblock left over from the 19th century. Apparently, being held in isolation was for his protection. Except that late at night, the security cameras in his hallway had malfunctioned. The two guards assigned to watch over him - it was their only assigned task - had both fallen asleep that night. And King had hung himself with a bed sheet he had never been issued and shouldn't have had in his possession.

Why would Thomas Hayes want King killed? Because he had once been friends with King, that was why. And King, while still breathing, in jail, and with every incentive to tell whatever story he could think of to get out, was a much bigger danger to his friends than to his enemies. To be fair, Darwin King had a lot of friends who might have wanted him dead. But Thomas Hayes was the only such friend who was one breath away from the presidency.

And Hayes was coming. That much seemed clear. Clement Dixon was checking out of the game. Don could see it in his eyes. A crisis was unfolding, and Dixon was barely in the room. Meanwhile, Hayes was eager to get started, raring to rip in fact.

Dick Stark of the Joint Chiefs of Staff was standing across from the President, in front of the largest screen.

"In that case we'll bring it to order," he said.

Behind him, on the video monitor, and on screens all over the room, a photograph of a thin, smiling middle-aged man in black robes appeared. Beneath the photo there was a caption: *Justice Richard Sebastian-Vilar*.

"As I think everyone here must be aware by now, just after 12 noon our time, early evening in Spain, Justice Richard Sebastian-Vilar of the United States Supreme Court was abducted from the small village of Bossost in the Pyrenees Mountains, about two hours west of the city of Barcelona. The abduction was a well-planned and organized attack by between 10 and 15 men who emerged from the back of a truck. During the attack, two members of the judge's security team, including his head of security, were killed. The mayor of the village was also killed. No members of the kidnapping team appear to have been killed, and possibly not even wounded."

Thomas Hayes raised his hand. "General."

"Yes, Mr. Vice President?"

"How many men were in Vilar's security team, what agency were they with, and what happened to the rest of them? It seems at first glance that their performance was not what we might hope for when the lives of high-ranking officials of the government are at stake."

The man was grandstanding. Don nodded to himself, which to the naked eye would appear that he was nodding in agreement with Hayes. He was nodding because he saw that Hayes was already stepping into the role quietly being vacated by Dixon.

Behind Stark, a map of northern Spain and southwestern France appeared on the screen, as Vilar himself faded from view.

"Justice Sebastian-Vilar had a skeleton crew of three bodyguards with him at the time of the attack. They were all experienced officers of the Supreme Court Police, with more than 40 combined years of duty between them. The group had left Barcelona earlier in the day.

The night before, the judge had apparently requested that his much larger Spanish security detail stand down, and not accompany the group into the Pyrenees.

"As a judge, that is Vilar's prerogative, although we are investigating the details of that stand down, and who else may have been informed of it. The one surviving member of Vilar's security team appears to have saved Vilar's wife and daughter and barricaded them inside the small hotel where the family was staying. We believe that the bodyguard took this action at Vilar's request during the attack."

"Why was he even there?" Hayes said.

Stark shrugged. "It appears he went on a fact-finding mission to France and Spain in preparation for the court case next week. Both countries have large numbers of immigrants, legal and illegal, from North Africa. And both countries have been hit by terror attacks in recent years, carried out in whole or in part by North Africans. Additionally, Vilar's grandparents came from the mountain region outside Barcelona, and he apparently thinks of that region as his homeland."

Stark glanced around the room. "Any more questions?"

"What are we doing to get him back?" Hayes said.

Stark turned and ran a red dot across the map on the screen with a laser pointer. "The village in question, Bossost, as you can see here, is within a few kilometers of the French border. The borders there are porous, with no real controls. French and Spanish police and military have converged on the area."

He looked at a man sitting near him.

"Roger, can you give us those details?"

Stark's aide Roger was thin with black hair, a captain wearing a dress green uniform and wire frame glasses. The man nodded. He was a young man, perhaps in his early 30s. He didn't look up from the papers in front of him. He cleared his throat.

"More than 300 Spanish police and soldiers have responded to the incident. Forty paratroopers from the Spanish Special Operations Command have been airlifted to the region. The Spanish have employed drones, helicopters, and satellite surveillance to try to detect the movements of the kidnappers. There is some suspicion that the kidnappers are using the Linea P siege tunnels from World War Two to escape detection. On the French side of the border, the French government is moving more than 200 officers the National Police, and..."

48

"I asked what we're doing to get him back," Hayes said, interrupting the aide in mid-sentence. "I didn't ask what the Spanish and French are doing."

"Vilar was abducted in Spain," Dick Stark said. "If the kidnappers attempt to cross the border with Vilar in their custody, then this also becomes an issue for the French Border Patrol."

"With all due respect to the Spanish and the French," Hayes said, "our own military would likely be better suited to carry out this mission, wouldn't it?"

This was rapidly becoming the Thomas Hayes show. Don took a quick glance at Clement Dixon. He didn't even seem to be listening.

Dick Stark raised a hand. "Sir, not necessarily. Both the Spanish and the French have units that are familiar with that area and have trained there. We don't. We don't know the terrain at all. Both the Spanish and the French responded to the situation rapidly. It might have taken us hours to get our own troops on the ground there, after unraveling the red tape that's always involved in entering a sovereign nation with our military. And as a practical matter, it would be a bit of an embarrassment and an imposition to put our own troops in there, considering that both Spain and France are close allies of ours."

"So we're not doing anything, then?"

Stark shook his head. "On the contrary. We're doing all we can. Roger?" He looked at the aide again.

The aide turned over the next page and skimmed it before reading aloud. He cleared his throat again and breathed deeply.

"We are doing our own satellite and high-altitude drone surveillance of the region," he said. "NSA and CIA listening stations are on alert for chatter among Al Qaeda and other terrorist networks related to the kidnapping or attacks on American personnel, especially as related to Spain, or the U.S. Supreme Court. Data analysts are poring over data from recent weeks, looking for similar chatter. Known and suspected terrorists in U.S. custody are being interviewed specifically about any knowledge…"

"What else?"

Hayes had a bad habit of talking over people. That was the second time he had done it to Stark's aide in the course of five minutes.

Roger didn't even look up from his paperwork.

"There is a potential lead," he said. "We are following up on it. Justice Sebastian-Vilar's wife believes that the judge was given a watch some years ago by an acquaintance. That watch may have the ability to be tracked by the satellite Global Positioning System. She also believes he may have been wearing the watch at the time of the attack."

"That's pretty slim, isn't it?" Hayes said.

Don was tired of this show. Hayes was just as obnoxious as Don remembered him to be. In fact, he was more obnoxious. Something was going on here, and Hayes clearly thought he was the one in charge. He'd better be careful he didn't overstep.

Further, Don didn't think the watch lead was slim at all. It was the kind of thing to get some people on right away. Find the watch, and maybe find the judge. That was worth a few man hours, or even a few hundred.

Let the French and Spanish beat the bushes along the border. If the kidnappers were as organized and coordinated as they seemed, they probably left the area almost as quickly as they entered it.

That left the watch. Find out of it was real. If it was, then find it.

Don suddenly had places to be. He began to pack his things and stood. "Gentlemen, I'm sorry but I need to take my leave, if I may. This has been very enlightening, and the Special Response team stands ready to offer our services if you need them."

Thomas Hayes waved a hand as if to dismiss him. For Don, this was the hard part of being in Washington. This was always going to be the hard part. Actually, it was one of several hard parts, but one that especially stuck in his craw.

When he was in the military, he was accustomed to being treated with respect. In civilian Washington, respect was not guaranteed. And it wasn't a question of earning it. Don had given decades to this country, and risked his own life, and the lives of his men, more times than he cared to remember. But a lot of these people, they just didn't care.

Thomas Hayes was one of them.

Don glanced around the room before he left. Almost no one was even looking at him. Everyone was going through their own paperwork or whispering to aides and assistants. Dick Stark was waiting for Don to leave so he could begin his talk again.

Clement Dixon looked at Don and smiled. He made a hand gesture like he was dialing a telephone. Then he mouthed two words:

"Call me."

Don nodded. "Sure," he almost said. "We'll do lunch."

CHAPTER ELEVEN

Time Unknown
Place Unknown
In a tunnel, or a cave

Even when his awareness returned, it only faded in slowly. It seemed for a long time that he was swimming at the bottom of a deep black sea.

There was darkness, and he was part of it. He didn't have a name, and there was no sense of past or future. Nothing had happened, and nothing was going to happen. There was only now.

Then male voices seemed to murmur around him, very low, in a language he didn't understand. Gradually he became aware that he was in pain - his head hurt. And the memories came back. He was Richard Sebastian-Vilar, a very important man. He had been a prominent attorney and had even argued a case before the Supreme Court. His mother had been bursting with pride. Later, he became a federal district court judge. He had written legal opinions and had been a guest lecturer at Yale and Harvard.

No. Wait. That was all in the past. Now was the most important thing. He had hurt his head and forgotten. He hadn't just argued a case before the Supreme Court. He was a sitting judge on the United States Supreme Court. He was married. He had a daughter.

His wife…

Suddenly, he came awake. His entire body bucked. He opened his eyes but could not see. Everything was black. He had gone blind. Men had attacked.

He screamed.

The sound echoed against the walls of wherever he was.

Then a strong hand was pressing hard against his mouth

"Shut up!" a voice hissed. "Do you hear me? Shut up!"

Something smacked hard against the side of his head. His head was already in terrible pain. It smacked him again. It was a fist. Someone, an invisible person, was punching him in the side of the head.

"Unnh." He grunted in agony.

51

"Shut up," the voice hissed again. "If you make another sound, I'll kill you."

The fist punched him again. This time, Vilar kept his mouth closed. He breathed deeply, gasping.

"That's right," the voice whispered. "You understand."

A bag of some kind was removed from his head. First a hand pulled a zipper up the back, bits of Vilar's hair catching painfully in the teeth of it. Then the bag was gone. But he was still blind. He could see and feel the difference now, though. The darkness had changed - there was a lighter tone to it. He was wearing a blindfold over his eyes. He could feel the tightness of the cloth tied around his head.

Then the blindfold was gone, and the light came streaming in. It was not a bright light, though the contrast blinded him for a few seconds. He blinked, his eyes growing accustomed to sight again. He was sitting cross legged on a floor. His legs were free.

His back was to a curved wall, and his wrists were bound tightly behind him. The position pulled his shoulders up and back and stretched his arms painfully. He could feel the tightness across his chest, his shoulder blades and his neck. His teeth were gritted. If he hadn't taken blows to the head, if he hadn't already been in pain, the way he was bound would be enough to give him a tension headache.

A man was crouched in front of him. The man was dark-skinned, maybe Arab, but could also be Spanish, or Turkish. His eyes were blue. It was impossible to say what nationality he was. Except the man had a full dark beard.

Behind the man, there was a low ceiling, and rounded walls very close. The light was dim and yellow, coming from a couple of flashlights lying on the ground. Against the far wall, a group of men, maybe four or five, sat against the wall in the gloom. They were dressed in dark jumpsuits and fatigues and had rifles at their feet. A few of the men stared at Vilar. Their stares were not hostile, or even curious. They were blank. They stared at him the same way they would stare at the floor. Just something to look at.

"Where am I?" Vilar said to the man closest to him, the man who had taken off his blindfold. The man who had punched him.

The man held a finger to his lips. "Shhhhh. Very quiet." He spoke in a voice barely above a whisper, as if to demonstrate to Vilar how it was done.

Vilar nodded. He spoke again, lower this time.

"Where am I?"

The man shook his head. "It doesn't matter where you are."

"Why are we talking so quietly?"

"Because they are looking for you. We don't want them to find you. If they find you…" the man stopped speaking and began to fiddle in a satchel hanging from his shoulder.

It occurred now to Vilar that the man spoke English. He was speaking in Vilar's own language. The blank stares of the other men probably meant they couldn't understand a word he said. This was the man assigned to communicate with him. These were the kidnappers.

It was hard, after being knocked unconscious, to piece reality back together again. Vilar had never been knocked unconscious before. But now he knew what it was like. It was very, very disorienting.

The man's big hand came out from the satchel with a pistol. He pressed the muzzle of the gun to the side of Vilar's head. Vilar winced.

"If they find you," the man began again, speaking more quietly than ever. "If they find us, I have to put a bullet in your brain. Do you understand?"

Vilar's heart froze in his chest. For what seemed like a long time, but was probably only seconds, he did not breathe. Then he nodded, his eyes meeting the man's fierce gaze. There was violence in this man's eyes, and death. Vilar supposed he had never before quite understood what people meant by dead eyes. Now he did.

"So be very quiet," the man said.

"My wife and daughter," Vilar said. "They were with me."

The man shrugged. "They were not of interest to us. Your bodyguards have them, as far as we know. They are safe. But know that they could be dead, had we chosen. Your government kills women and children across the Islamic world every day."

Vilar was coming more into himself with every passing moment. He was a lawyer, first and foremost, and a champion debater in high school and college. He chose not to touch the issue of women and children being killed. Knowing, or believing, that his own family was safe was enough for this moment.

"Am I of interest to you?" he said.

"You are Richard Sebastian-Vilar, are you not?"

Vilar nodded. There was no sense denying it. "Of course."

"And you don't know why you're here?"

"No."

"You don't know anything, do you?"

Vilar didn't answer. He knew many things. There was no sense responding to accusations. He didn't know what these men wanted, at least not yet. But he wasn't a mind reader. They would have to tell him.

The man stared into his eyes for a long moment.

"You vote to retain this American abortion law."

It wasn't a question. Again, Vilar didn't know what to make of it.

"You mean, in my role on the Supreme Court?"

The man nodded.

"It is the settled law of the United States," Vilar said. "The case precedent is set."

"But when it has come up," the man said, "you have voted in favor of it, despite your so-called religious views?"

"Do you know my religious views?" Vilar said.

"I know a lot about you, my friend. You call yourself Roman Catholic, a Christian, though you support the abomination of abortion. In Islam, this is haram, forbidden. Children are a blessing from Allah. To kill them…"

He trailed off. He said something to the men behind him in their language. One of the men said something back.

"It is why we here agree that Catholic is apostasy and should be declared such." He shook his head. "This ruling breaks Allah's heart. A Catholic who supports this, and has not been cast out? It does not make sense."

It wasn't the first time Vilar had been criticized as a bad Catholic. He had been hearing it since he entered public life. This, however, was by far the strangest venue where he had ever taken up the debate.

He shrugged. "People feel strongly about this, and I understand. But it's the law of the United States, and the dispute was settled in 1973, long before I entered the court."

The man spit in his face, his eyes suddenly bright with anger.

The spittle hung there on Vilar's cheek. He could die here, he realized. His legs began to tremble at the full realization. His whole body soon followed. He had awakened in a terrible situation, and because his mind had been clouded, the fact of his complete vulnerability was only reaching him now.

"You're a pig," the man said quietly. "Your God and my God are the same."

Vilar nodded. "I know that."

"Allah, or God in your words, looks with horror upon you. I should kill you now and be done with it."

Is that what this was about? These men had risked their lives in a violent attack, people had been shot and maybe killed, Vilar had been abducted and was being held somewhere underground, all over the question of abortion?

"I am sworn to uphold the law," Vilar said, as if that would move these men in any way. It rang hollow in his own ears as soon as it left his lips.

The man shook his head. "Your responsibility is to your God, first and always."

"Why don't you kill me?"

"My orders are to keep you alive, if I can."

The man stared at Vilar for another long moment. "How would you have voted, if you were at the court next week?"

Ah. The travel ban. Of course. These men were Muslims from North Africa. That was what this was about.

Suddenly, an entire edifice in Vilar's mind came cascading down. He had been living in a dream world. He had taken a trip to two countries that had been wracked in recent years by terror attacks by people from North Africa.

He recognized now that it was part fact-finding tour, and part publicity stunt. He was of French and Spanish descent, and both countries had long-standing, difficult, and painful relationships with the countries just across the water from them. Vilar, unusual for a man in his station, had never shied away from the public eye. You might even say he had courted it throughout his career. He had given a dozen newspaper, magazine, and television interviews during his short stay in Europe.

And then he had declined his full security detail when visiting Bossost. He might die for his arrogance, and he had put his wife, daughter, and everyone in that village at risk of death.

"Tell me," the man said.

Vilar shook his head. "I can't. I never decide how I will vote beforehand. I have to hear the facts of the case first."

The man smiled, and his eyes seemed sad. "You lie. Your country, your entire culture, is a lie. It's a sin."

One of the men behind him said something in Arabic. The entire group began to work their way to their feet and gather their belongings. A signal had been sent and received, one that had been invisible to Vilar.

"We're moving," the man in front of Vilar said. "Do not resist, and do not make a noise of any kind. Your fate is not set. You may survive this, but only if you cooperate. Do you understand?"

Vilar nodded. "Yes."

55

The man put the blindfold in his pocket. It seemed that he would no longer bother with it. Instead, he took the black zippered bag, and pulled it down over Vilar's head again. Vilar felt the man's hand at the back of his head, and felt the bag tighten to his skull as the man pulled the zipper closed. The darkness closed in on him again.

Strong hands grabbed Vilar by either arm, and yanked him to his feet.

"Let's go," the man said.

CHAPTER TWELVE

9:35 pm Central European Summer Time (3:35 pm Eastern Daylight Time)
The hills near Hohensalzburg Fortress
Salzburg, Austria

Luke knew the call was coming; he just didn't know when.

He had the bright blue satellite phone on the table in front of him. His eyes wandered to it once in a while. He noticed that Becca's eyes did the same thing. It was an alien presence, that phone, and technically, it shouldn't even be there. It was late. Luke and Ed were not on the clock. He should have left it back at the hotel.

"Young people, man," Ed Newsam said. He raised his glass.

Luke raised his, as well. "Young people."

"Hear-hear," Becca said.

"I'll drink to that," Cassandra said. But it wasn't true. Cassandra was still less than halfway through her first stein of beer. She didn't *drink* beer. She hardly sipped it. It seemed that making her lips touch it was enough for her.

Cassandra had a body that only rarely encountered a carbohydrate. And when it did, it put a protective wall around itself. After the baby was born, she had melted back to her pre-pregnancy size in what seemed like minutes. Seeing her transformation was like watching time-lapse photography.

Ed made a swinging gesture with his huge fist. "Young people! Got our whole lives ahead of us. This right here is what it's all about."

Ed was a little drunk. So was Luke. The girls? Maybe. They were doing the young mother thing, being very careful. Gunner was asleep on Becca's lap, hugging her like a baby chimp would hug its mother. Jade was asleep in a sort of denim sling contraption that Cassandra wore over shoulders.

They were all sitting on the patio of a little... what was it? A restaurant? A beer garden? Luke wasn't sure what an Austrian might call it. The place served food. It also served beer.

The surroundings were pleasant, even garden-like. The place was on a tiny alley of a side street below the giant medieval Hohensalzburg Fortress, which towered behind them. In front of, and below them, was a sweeping panorama of the city, lit up and sparkling at night.

The view extended down the hillsides to the River Salzach, the architecture of the town hundreds of years old, and beyond that to the snowcapped peaks of the Alps looming in the distance. It was an incredible place. And it gave Luke a feeling. He would almost call it wistful.

He didn't want this moment to end. They were here, the group of them, and you could almost say they had the world on a string. Beautiful city, beautiful surroundings, on a work-sponsored trip with the young families. In a sense, he and Ed didn't have to do another thing. They had done it already.

They had risked death again and again. In the past year, they had saved the President of the United States. They had toppled an international arms dealer and human trafficker. It was too much as it was. No one could blame them if life just became wonderful trips with their beautiful wives to incredible places and watching and mentoring their children as they grew up.

But the phone was about to ring. Luke knew it, Becca knew it, and although they were harder for Luke to read, on some level Ed and Cassandra probably knew it too. The phone was going to ring, and all of this was about to change.

And Luke was quietly dreading that.

It had been all over the TV news. It didn't matter that the TV news was in German. Cassandra could translate, and it was easy enough to follow in any case. A Supreme Court judge from the United States had been traveling in France and Spain and was kidnapped from a village in the Pyrenees. Two of the three members of his Supreme Court Police security detail were murdered in the incident, as was the mayor of the village. The attack had happened suddenly and was carried out with precision.

Now, the judge was just gone. There didn't seem to be a trace of him. Hundreds of police and military personnel had descended on the area. Cops from the local villages were out in force. All to no avail.

The countryside there was wide open and steep, and it was after dark. There were a lot of places to hide.

Spain was what? Two, maybe three hours from here by plane? Finding and retrieving missing and kidnapped people had become a specialty of the fledgling Special Response Team. You might even call

58

it *the* specialty.   And two of the SRT's key people were already in Europe, just a hop, skip and a jump from the site of the abduction.

So what? Luke held up his empty beer stein to the waitress. She smiled and came right over with another. In an instant, Luke had a full mug of beer, and the waitress was gone with the empty.

"Luke!" Becca said.

Ed put up a big hand and smiled. It was the STOP hand.

"Cut him some slack, girl. The man only lets his hair down..." Ed shrugged. "Never, pretty much."

Yeah. Ed was drunk.

The phone rang. Its friendly face lit up and the phone itself made a very low buzzing sound. It was also set to vibrate, so it moved a little bit along the table.

For a second, it reminded Luke of that weird football game they used to have when he was a kid. You put all these plastic player figurines with metal in their bases on this long green metal football field replica. It was electric. You turned it on, the field vibrated violently, and the players moved around in random fashion. Nothing remotely like football took place.

What was the point of that game?

Luke stared at the phone and sipped his beer. Then he looked at Ed.

Ed's shoulders slumped. "Is it..."

"Yeah."

Ed shook his head. "I was afraid that was going to happen."

Luke nodded. "Me too."

The effect of the beer was already wearing off. He picked up the phone and answered. It was Trudy Wellington, calling from Washington. Of course it was. He listened to her for a few seconds, her deep, musical voice washing over him.

They had to finish up here, then walk the girls and the kids back to the hotel and get them settled. Luke could use a cup of coffee, he supposed. Ed probably could, too.

"Give us about a half hour, okay?" he said.

* * *

"This should be interesting."

There was nowhere in their tiny hotel rooms to talk, so they took the call on a wide stone pedestrian bridge over the River Salzach. The lights of the city stretched out all around them and above them. A mile away, the fortress looked down upon everything.

It was a quiet time of night. There was no one around.

Luke put the call on speaker phone so Ed could hear, but with the volume down so no one else could. He placed the phone on the stone wall. If he flicked the phone with his hand, he could knock it into the river.

He and Ed were each holding coffee in thick paper cups.

"Hi guys," Trudy said. "Can you hear me?"

"Loud and clear."

"I'm here with Don Morris and Mark Swann. We're in the conference room on speaker phone."

"Boys, I imagine you know why we're calling," Don said.

"Hi Don," Luke said.

"Hi yourself. I'll make this clear before we even start. You don't have to do anything I ask. I was at the White House until an hour ago, and even then it was apparent that you're the best men for the job. In the past half an hour, it's become even more apparent. But that doesn't mean you have to do it."

"What is it?" Ed said.

"I will let Trudy explain the situation. Wellington?"

"I'm going to assume no prior knowledge," Trudy said.

"Okay."

She began without preamble. "The Supreme Court judge Richard Sebastian-Vilar has been kidnapped."

"All right," Luke said. "You can assume we know that much. We're not under a rock over here. It's on every TV station, everywhere you look."

She continued as if Luke hadn't spoken. "He was taken from the village of Bossost in the Pyrenees Mountains of Spain earlier today. It happened right around sunset local time. The kidnappers were a well-organized, heavily armed band of at least 10 men, who emerged from the back of a tractor-trailer parked in the town. Two members of Vilar's security team were killed, as was the mayor of Bossost."

Luke looked at Ed. Ed shrugged.

Okay. Let her roll.

"The town is high on the north slopes of the mountains, right on the border with southern France. The border is porous there. There are immigration checkpoints on the roadways, but you can cross easily over open land. Further, there is a network of underground siege tunnels left over from World War II known as Linea P. Spain was technically neutral in the war, but they had been allied with Nazi Germany during the Spanish Civil War. The Spanish dictator

Francisco Franco was worried that the Allies would invade and depose him, so he had the Linea P built."

"We never did invade, did we?" Ed said.

"No," Trudy said. "Exiled Spanish communists tried to near the end of the war, but nothing came of it. In any case, the tunnels are extensive, abandoned by the government, and in a state of total disrepair. Any maps of the system were lost during the Franco dictatorship. It's well known that the tunnels are no longer sealed, haven't been for a long time, and that drug smugglers sometimes use them as way stations for overnight stays and for storing product. It's now believed that Vilar was smuggled out of Spain and into France using the tunnels."

"What if they went south?" Ed said.

Mark Swann's reedy voice came on the line. "We know that they didn't go south." They were the first words Swann had spoken in this conversation.

"They could have pulled a trick. Kidnap a guy near the northern border, and everybody assumes you're going to cross that border. Go south instead."

"It's a good idea," Trudy said. "But we have reason to believe they went north into France. And in fact, kept going."

Luke and Ed traded a look. "To where?"

"Germany," Swann said.

"Is this call encrypted?" Luke said.

Luke could practically hear Swann's smile over the phone. Swann was always proud of his codebreaking, his encryption ability, and the way he fired satellite calls around the world, masking their origin.

"Of course," Swann said.

"How do we know Germany?"

"Vilar has powerful friends," Trudy said. "Or in this case, had a powerful friend. He made many connections during his ascent, and one of those connections was a man named Anthony Margillio. Margillio inherited a large East Coast metal scrap business and a small commercial real estate empire in New Jersey and Pennsylvania from his father, the notorious Philadelphia mobster Fat Dominic Margillio. Basically, the younger Margillio kept the legitimate businesses that his father once used as front companies, and publicly distanced himself from Mafia activities."

"So a Supreme Court judge is friends with a Philadelphia mobster?" Luke said. "That sounds good."

"Was friends," Trudy said. "About 18 months ago, Margillio was found dead in the trunk of a car buried up to its rocker panels in a swamp in Staten Island. So he didn't get as much distance from the Mafia as he would have liked, I suppose.

"But the friendship wasn't quite what you think. Margillio the younger was a devout Catholic, as is Vilar. Margillio was also an activist for liberal reform of the Church. Besides his businesses, he founded and ran an organization called The New Path. He believed in allowing married men and women to become priests, and in fact recruiting them for this purpose. He was also pushing for transparency in the interior dealings of the Vatican. Apparently, he and Vilar were on the same page on these issues."

"Do we think the Vatican kidnapped Vilar?" Ed said.

Luke glanced at Ed. Ed had been pretty drunk earlier. Maybe he still was.

"No," Trudy said. "We don't think that. We're almost certain that the kidnappers are Muslims, probably North Africans, and that the kidnapping is somehow related to the Supreme Court vote set to take place next week. We think that Vilar somewhat foolishly put himself in harm's way at a sensitive time. The kidnappers saw a target of opportunity, and they took it."

"And Margillio?" Luke said, trying to keep the conversation on track, and make sense of the players.

"According to Vilar's wife, Sydney was traumatized by the events, and still is. Not much of use has been obtained from her, except one thing. Sometime in the past few years, Margillio gave Vilar a very expensive watch. It's a Breitling Chronomat and may be several decades old."

"Let me get this straight," Luke said. "A Supreme Court judge accepted an expensive gift from a mobster's son. The two of them shared an interest in reforming the Catholic Church. And cases involving the Catholic Church may or may not end up in the Supreme Court at some point in the future?"

"I wouldn't call that a conflict of interest," Swann said. "But I wouldn't call it anything else, either."

"Things like that happen more often than you think," Trudy said. "It might surprise you."

"Nothing surprises me anymore," Ed said.

"All right children," Don Morris said, a hint of annoyance punctuating his Southern drawl. "Let's stay on point."

"Anyway," Trudy said. "The point about the watch is that before Margillio gave it to Vilar, he had it retrofitted with an internal microchip that's in constant communication with the satellite Global Positioning System. Apparently, Margillio was worried about Vilar's welfare, and didn't want him to disappear."

"Because the Vatican..." Luke said.

"Something like that, yes."

"He should have worried about himself," Ed said. "Bought himself a watch."

Trudy soldiered on. "We've been hunting for the microchip embedded in that watch. Vilar's wife didn't remember much about it, other than it had a chip inside. She didn't know who or what was tracking the chip. And Margillio is dead, of course, so no one can ask him. The best guess is a private satellite communications company monitors that chip, but there are hundreds of such companies, tracking countless thousands of chips. Also, it's possible that no one monitors it, that the contract expired, that the service was never set up, lots of possibilities. So what we..."

"I found it," Swann said. "About 15 minutes ago."

Luke smiled. "Of course you did."

"It took a little bit of sleuthing. What Sherlock Holmes would call deduction. Hacked and pirated feeds from half a dozen corporate satellites,\ and obtained historical data on devices leaving Barcelona and going up into the mountains. Lots of signals, lots of noise, especially in the city. Just a forest of activity and movement. So I narrowed down the... Eh. I guess I won't bore you with the details."

Ed and Luke shook their heads. "Thanks for that."

"The watch seems to have stayed in the region near Bossost for about an hour, then it made a beeline north. At some point, it must have gotten on a plane, because then it moved very quickly, and went straight to where it is now."

"Who else knows where it is?" Luke said.

"No one. As far as we know."

"So where is it?"

There was nothing else to do but say it. Swann said the phone call was encrypted, so Luke had to believe it was. And of course Swann, Trudy and Don had talked about the location of the watch before this call. The offices there were constantly swept for bugs, but technology jumped forward in leaps and bounds. There could be listening devices planted that were impossible to detect.

"The watch is in Berlin," Swann said. "It's at a notorious squatter building downtown, near the old Checkpoint Charlie from the Berlin Wall days. If you guys jump on a plane, you can be there in an hour."

"We can," Ed said. "But that doesn't mean we should."

CHAPTER THIRTEEN

11:50 pm Central European Summer Time (5:50 pm Eastern Daylight Time)
Freedom House
Neukölln District
Berlin, Germany

"The Wall was three blocks from here."

Don was growing paranoid, that much was clear.

He hadn't told anyone they were here. It seemed that no one in American intelligence, the American military, national security, politics, the government at all, knew that Ed and Luke were in Berlin.

Don had pulled strings and hooked them up with a SWAT team from the Berlin Police. Their minder, a man who had introduced himself as Peter, was speaking. He was a tall, thick blond with wire-framed glasses. He spoke English fluently.

"Very bad neighborhood at one time," Peter said. "Red light district. Fights. Murders. Cold War spies. Many immigrants lived here and still do. Many Turks, a growing number of North Africans, and some Iraqis displaced by the war."

"And the building?" Luke said.

They were outside the metal gates surrounding a wide, old, dilapidated six-story brick apartment building. Even in the darkness, the place looked like it wasn't sure which way to fall. There were weak lights behind some of the windows. The windows on the ground floors were covered with wooden boards.

"The infamous Freiheit Haus. Freedom House in English. A squatters den. On the inside, a most unpleasant place."

"It doesn't look that great from the outside," Ed said.

Peter shrugged. "The building is very typical of the German *Grunderzeit* architecture. You would call it the age of industrialization. They built many such structures to house the rural people dispossessed of their lands, and coming into the city to work in factories. This place was constructed for this purpose in 1891. Quite a few similar buildings are very fancy, expensive addresses now.

"But after the war, many of them were abandoned, especially this close to the Wall. So the artists, bohemians, gay people, drug addicts and leftist radicals began to move into them. They restored the electricity, restored the water. This building was first occupied by squatters in 1979. The name Freedom House seems to have come into being some time in the 1980s. It has been a squat continuously for nearly 30 years. It is an illegal residence, targeted by the city for demolition, but no one wants the riots that would happen if the people were forced out."

In the gloom around them, the SWAT team was gearing up. Men were putting helmets on, shrugging into body armor, checking and re-checking weapons. These were big guys, and they looked dead serious. From here, the myth of European cops not carrying guns appeared to be exactly that - a myth.

Ed, Luke, and Peter were already armored up. Ed and Luke, because they were guests, were not empowered to carry guns. Instead, they had batons in case they needed to defend themselves, heavy flashlights, and zip ties in case they felt the need to arrest someone.

This should be fun.

Don had set this raid up through his own side channels. He wanted his people here, not to observe, but to be on hand if Vilar was found. He didn't want the information shared with other agencies because at this point, he didn't know who to trust. It made sense. And Luke believed in Don's decision-making.

But he also much preferred to go in heavy, and if necessary, with guns blazing. It felt awfully vulnerable leaving that part up to others.

"Six months ago, someone here made the bright decision to allow a group of Islamic radicals to join. The police have been called many times since then. No one has been killed yet, but it is only a matter of time. We have been working with informants on the inside who will be only too happy to see the group removed. The Muslims have no interest in so-called freedom. They have no respect for the artists and activists here. It is a dangerous situation."

Peter shook his head.

"Do you see the light inside the yard?"

How could they not see it? There was a spotlight inside the gates, in an old courtyard where perhaps a dozen cars were parked helter-skelter. The spotlight was bright and shone upwards at a blank wall of the building, an area with no windows that had been painted white. A German slogan was spray painted on the wall there in big black letters. It took up the entire wall.

"We see it. What does the writing say?"

"Translated into English, it reads: *There are no borders, no gods, no races, no classes… only brothers and sisters.* Do you think this Muslim cell cares about that? The very motto of the Freedom House where they live? I think not. I think they are offended by it. It is their belief system or nothing. How would you Americans say it? My way or the highway."

Peter smiled at the phrase.

"We need to hit hard and fast," Ed said.

Peter looked at big Ed closely. Peter was nearly as tall as Ed, not nearly as broad. He nodded. "Yes, I know. And you seem like a man who can hit hard and fast."

Ed shrugged. "It's my job."

Peter gestured behind them at the SWAT team preparing in the darkness. "These men? It's their job, too. They hit as fast and as hard as anyone. Certainly in Germany, possibly the world."

Ed smiled. "I've met some hard hitters before. That's a big statement."

Now Peter smiled. These guys were flirting. Ed never met a hard hitter he didn't like. As long it was one of the good guys.

"I stand by it," Peter said.

Suddenly, Luke didn't like it. He didn't like anything about it.

Becca had cried when he told her he was leaving. She sat on the bed in the room and wept. He had left his wife and 17-month-old son at a hotel in Salzburg and had come here to Berlin to risk his life, all because the phone rang. And he was the one who put the phone on the table.

Not only had she cried; she had lashed out at him. She had accused him.

"You're an addict, Luke. I'm married to a drug addict; did you know that? The drug isn't heroin, or cocaine; it's adrenaline, and it's death. You're addicted to death. Your own death, and the deaths of other people. Yes, I know all about it. I'm not stupid. I know it was you and Ed who went to Honduras. I know it was another bloodbath. I can read between the lines.

"Where are the rewards of your so-called work, Luke? Nowhere. You know why? Because for an addict, the drug is the reward."

There was a long pause between them. He glanced around at the hotel room. It was a beautiful room, very small, with exactly two windows looking out on the city. Gunner was fast asleep in his crib.

The place served breakfast downstairs in the morning. Simple breakfast - eggs, sausage, coffee, baked sweet rolls. It was great.

"I'm gonna go," he said. "You guys are safe here. Ed and I will be back in the morning. We'll be here before breakfast is on the table."

"No one will even know you were gone," Becca said, sarcasm dripping from her voice.

"Something like that."

"What am I supposed to do, Luke? Can you please tell me? I can't live like this. We were having a nice trip, a work trip, a vacation. Like normal people. Now this. How am I supposed to sleep? Until you turn up again, I won't even know if you're alive or dead. I'm going to be a widow, with a young son."

Then she was really crying. He knelt to hug her, but she pushed him away. So he left. What else was there to do?

Now, he was here in Berlin, on a dark deserted street, outside the courtyard of a falling down building. Don didn't trust anyone in American intelligence anymore. So Luke and Ed were about to raid this building with a group of Berlin cops.

A kidnapped Supreme Court judge might be inside here. There were no active Special Ops guys here. No Navy SEALs. No Delta. Joint Special Operations Command had not been apprised of this situation. The greater FBI, unless they were listening to Special Response Team chatter, didn't know. Nobody knew.

It was just Ed, and Luke, and a local SWAT team.

He could see the reason for a surgical strike. There were a lot of people in this building, and massing a hundred operators out here, with logistics, helicopters, loudspeakers... it could get messy very quickly. They needed to get in, find and rescue Vilar, and get back out again. Fast... hard... sudden.

Luke sighed. He just didn't know if these were the guys he would choose to go in with. Nothing against them, he was sure they were pros, but no one on this team had been vetted, no one had been specially selected for a particular expertise that he knew of, and nothing had been brainstormed or game-planned.

It was just: *Here are some cops. Enjoy!*

"We go in silently," Peter said. "Our contact will lead us up through the maze to the section controlled by the Muslims. We don't look right or left. That's the agreement. Whatever other crimes are being committed are not our concern."

"Good," Ed said.

68

"We hit hard and fast, as you say," Peter said. "Neutralize resistance before harm can come to your hostage. If he is here."

Luke stepped away for moment. He took out his satellite phone and hit the only number that was saved into it. The signal bounced around the world, into outer space, and back again. There was a delay. There was always a delay.

"Al's used auto parts," Swann said.

"We're here."

"I know. I'm tracking your phone."

"Is the signal still inside the building?"

"Yes," Swann said. "Your signal and that one are packed so close together right now, you could be kissing."

Luke nodded. "Okay. Wish us luck."

"Vaya con Dios," Swann said.

Luke looked at Peter and Ed. Behind them, the SWAT team was ready.

"The signal is in there," Luke said.

* * *

"There are people living in the cars in the courtyard," Peter said quietly. "Don't be startled by them."

Luke wasn't sure if Peter quite knew who he was talking to. Ed and Luke had seen a lot of startling things in their time. Homeless people in cars probably weren't going to make the list.

The squad started to move through the gates of the compound. Luke and Ed were in the back with Peter.

"I will go to the front now," Peter said. "The informant is my contact. Follow along, but please don't engage with opponents unless absolutely necessary. We will get your hostage out safely. I promise."

Then he was gone.

The squad were like shadows. To their right and left were more shadows, people lurking near the aging relics of cars, vans, and RVs. Eyes watched them pass. People whispered. No one moved or attempted to do anything.

Ahead and to their far left was the skylight illuminating the grand slogan of Freedom House. Luke had nothing against these people and their ideas. If anything, it was quaint. The outside world was on fast forward, surging ahead toward some unknown future, some technological ecstasy, and inside this compound, the people were being left behind. A lot of people everywhere were being left behind, but these people had decided to make a statement out of it. It was a piece of performance art.

At the double front doors of the building, Peter was quietly speaking with a young man in a t-shirt and jeans. The guy had long hair and a beard. He was nearly as tall as Peter, but very thin. With Peter's solid build, his armor, and his helmet, the two men seemed as if they were from different species.

Peter nodded, turned, and made a quick hand signal to his men. Luke didn't understand the signal. He shook his head. Great. He and Ed didn't speak the language, and they didn't even know the signs. This was going to be good.

Suddenly, the men started, moving quickly and as a unit, passing across the threshold.

"Go time," Ed said under his breath.

"Yeah."

They surged with the squad. Through the doorways and now up a central stairway, taking the steps two at a time. No one spoke. There were no lights on in the hallways. The men at the front had their flashlights out, sweeping the wide stairs in front of them.

Up one flight, then another, then another.

A thin young woman appeared out of the gloom, hair frazzled, bright white skin, dark eyes, like a ghost. She said something in German. Then Luke was past her.

They reached the top of another flight, and the group turned left, down a hallway. Weak light filtered through a translucent window at the other end of the hall. Solid glass bricks half a foot thick.

There was some kind of streetlight out there. No, it was the glow from the spotlight that illuminated the message on the side of the building.

Those glass bricks gave the only light - the overheads in the hallway were all out. The men slowed down now. They moved along the hall silently, almost on tiptoe. They were catlike for big men.

Sounds echoed through the building. Laughter. Somebody shouting. Running feet. TV sets or maybe a radio – the power was on.

Water dripped somewhere. Plunk, plunk, plunk.

The men stopped in front of a door. The door looked thick, made of solid wood. Luke thought he could hear murmuring on the other side. Anyone or anything could be on the other side of that door. Richard Sebastian-Vilar could be behind there. A bunch of skinny 20-somethings could be making finger-paintings. A half dozen guys in suicide vests could be waiting for their moment.

Two SWAT guys stepped up with a heavy battering ram. The guys looked to be the biggest of the team, and the ram was a swing-type, an officer holding the handle on each side. They didn't make a sound. Everything here in this hallway was silent. If someone coughed now, or sneezed…

Luke felt himself take a deep breath.

Peter was at the front. He held up his fist. His index finger appeared.

That was one.

Middle finger. Two.

Ring finger…

The two men reared back as one and swung the ram.

BAM!

Didn't do it. Didn't happen. The door broke, the wood splintered down the middle, and one of the hinges came apart. But it was still hanging on. The element of surprise was lost. The initiative was lost.

Luke's whole body tensed into a crouch.

Next to Luke, Ed made a quiet sound. "Aaahhh."

Peter shouted now, his voice nearly a shriek. "Mach schnell! MACH SCHNELL!" There was no sense pretending we weren't out here.

The rammers lined it up, reared back, and hit it again.

BAM!

This time, the door broke inward as the rammers dropped back. The others swarmed in, big men shouldering through the wrecked doorway, guns out. Then they were screaming, voices loud and commanding. Other men, other voices, screamed as well.

Luke reached the doorway. He and Ed were supposed to be observers, not participants. He glanced to his right and Ed was with him.

It was a big room, wide open. Candles flickered on the wooden floor. At the very back, to the far left, near an open window, a group of men stood. Maybe there were ten, maybe there were twelve. Flashlights panned over them.

They were dressed in western clothing, tracksuits, or jeans and t-shirts. Most were heavily bearded. Several had guns out, rifles, jutting outward from the circle. A couple of them were holding handguns. The men were a jumble. Their eyes were wild, like cornered animals.

In the darkness, it was hard to see behind them. Were there more men back there? Was the judge back there?

71

Around the room, the Berlin SWAT team had spread out, enclosing the Muslim men in a semicircle. The Germans were bigger, bulkier. They trained their guns in on the smaller men.

Both groups shouted at the other, a Babel of screaming voices.

Guns pointed. Guns jittered.

Luke had seen this movie before.

Oh God. Here we go again...

"Wait!" he shouted. "Wait!"

No one heard him. No one understood him.

BANG!

Someone fired. It was impossible to say who.

Luke hit the ground as gunfire broke out in all directions. It was LOUD. Luke covered his head, curled into a ball and rolled back into the hallway.

The shooting lasted several seconds. It seemed to go on and on. It slowed, and then there were a finalfew shots here and there, like the last kernels of corn popping. When it was finally over, Luke picked his head up.

Ed was with him here in the hall. Footsteps were running up the hallway behind them. They both leapt to their feet. They flashed their lights down the hall.

Artists. Activists. Wide-eyed. Mouths open. Hands up.

This was their home.

One of them said something in German.

Ed raised a hand. "Stay back."

Two SWAT guys came out of the doorway and began to push them. Now there was shouting with the kids as well. The kids pushed against the cops. There was going to be a riot, right here in the hall. Later, there were going to be protests. Luke could see it from here.

People screamed and moaned in the room behind Luke and Ed. Luke turned back to it. He looked through the doorway. The place was a killing field. A knot of people by the wall lay in a writhing pile. Some were dead, others were dying. The Muslim cell had just been annihilated.

A couple of the SWAT guys were down. They seemed okay. Shot in their body armor with small caliber weapons. Ouch. That hurt, but they would be alive tomorrow. Their own guys were attending to them. One SWAT guy was talking into a handheld radio. It was Peter, probably calling in the results.

"Messy," Ed said, his voice low.

Luke nodded. "Yeah."

"The judge?"

"I don't know, man."

They stepped through the room, past the SWAT guys who were down, and between the ones standing and looking over the Muslims. The Muslims were bloody and riddled with holes. A couple of the men had their eyes open and were gasping for air. No one was making any attempt to keep them alive. It probably wouldn't matter, but the Germans weren't even trying. A few of the SWAT team members had their helmets off.

Luke looked at the Germans. "Medic," he said.

They stared back at him.

"Medic!" Luke raised his hands as if asking them a question.

One of them shrugged. He was big, with a crewcut and a cherubic face that reminded Luke of a small boy.

"Coming," he said. "Soon."

Not soon enough. Luke glanced at the guys administering aid to the downed SWAT team members. All right. This was their show. This was how they did it. But this wasn't how the SRT did it. This wasn't how Luke Stone did it.

He thought back to the DEA bust in New Jersey he and Ed were on as observers some months ago. A young kid, 16-years-old, had shot Ed. Ed was wearing body armor and had been unharmed. The kid was gunned down by a DEA agent a second later. And seconds after that, DEA medics had gone to town, trying to keep the kid alive.

People got killed out here. That was a fact. More than that, it was practically an immutable law of nature. But it wasn't as simple as keeping the good guys alive and letting the bad guys die. You could try to be good to everybody, even the ones who might not deserve it.

And as a practical matter, the Germans were going to lose any possible interview subjects.

"Stone," Ed said.

Luke turned back to Ed. He had waded into the bodies on the floor. He was holding up the arm of a man in a blue t-shirt with white Arabic letters across the front. He wore jeans and sneakers. He had a heavy beard. His head hung bonelessly to the side, his dark eyes blank, his mouth open a slit with the tip of his tongue sticking out.

"Yeah?"

"Check this out, man."

Luke came closer and Ed shone his light on the guy's wrist. The guy was wearing a watch. The face of it was blue, and elegant. Breitling.

"That's the watch?" Luke said.   He didn't really mean it as a question.

Ed nodded. "I think so, yeah."

Luke gazed across the pile of corpses. "So Vilar's not here." They had come here for nothing. The guy with the watch had probably been at Vilar's abduction, but now he was dead, and so were the rest of them. Luke and Ed weren't going to get any information out of dead guys.

"Right but look at the second hand."

Ed was still shining his light on the face of the watch. Luke stared at it. The second hand was moving along the watch's face.

Ed glanced at Luke. He smiled.

"Takes a licking and keeps on ticking."

Luke watched as Ed removed the watch from the dead guy's wrist. Just then, one of the corpses suddenly jumped up and dashed to the window. A shout went up among the SWAT team members. But it was too late. The man moved fast, a blur of speed, dove out the open window and was gone.

"Oh, man!" Luke said.

* * *

Ed moved slowly to the window, thinking the guy had done a headfirst plunge to the pavement. It would be just like one of these jihadi dudes. On the verge of getting busted? Kill yourself.

The SWAT guys didn't move at all. They were more interested in the commotion out in the hall. They were probably thinking about how this was gonna look on the TV news. They were probably thinking about getting home to their girlfriends or wives. Maybe they were thinking about how they had just killed a whole mess of Muslim guys, and for what?

Only Jesus knew what they were thinking.

Stone was the first to the window, two steps before Ed. He looked left, he looked right, then he stuck his head halfway through the opening.

"Hey man. I wouldn't do that if I…"

The guy was right outside. He aimed a kick and caught Stone between the eyes. Stone took a step backwards, fell and landed on his butt. Rare for Stone to make an amateur move like that. He was lucky he didn't just catch a bullet.

Ed saw the guy race by outside the window, moving fast.   Ed counted.

One... Two... Three...

Then he poked his own head out.

There was some kind of ancient fire escape out here. He caught a glimpse of Abdul's head going down the stairs. And just like that, he had given the guy a name.

Abdul.

Ed clambered out onto the ironwork. It was flaking with rust. There was an alley here, and across the alley was another old building. In the darkness, that one seemed even worse than this one. It didn't appear to have any lights on at all.

Or maybe it was the same building, and this was just an airshaft.

Ed stood, went to the railing of the fire escape, and looked below. Two floors down, Abdul was perched up on the handrail like a bird on a telephone wire, grasping the stairs behind him with one hand.

The guy wore a dark tracksuit and white sneakers. He was thin, with a heavy beard. He looked up and saw Ed there. His eyes were alive and alert. He didn't seem like he had been shot at all. Somehow, he had fallen under the bodies of his friends, and they had taken all the bullets. When he thought his chance had come, he seized it.

Now he was here.

Ed dropped down the stairs, taking them two at a time. He reached the first landing, turned the corner, and two seconds later stood at the top of the next flight. It was three, maybe four stories to the alley.

"Abdul! Don't do it, man!"

The guy didn't even spare Ed another glance. He let go of the stairs behind him, balanced precariously on the railing, bent deep at the knees and launched himself out into nothing like some kind of aerial circus performer.

He flew across the alley and crashed into the neighboring fire escape. He hit it railing high, catching the railing in his stomach. He hung on, legs dangling, and yanked himself up and over the railing. He fell onto the landing and rolled over. Then he began crawling up the stairs.

Ed watched as Abdul, gaining his feet now, reached the landing across from and a little above his own. Abdul stopped and leaned on the railing, breathing hard. Right there, but just out of reach.

He looked over at Ed and flashed a smile. He shook his head and said something Ed didn't understand. Then he continued on his way. Within a few steps, he was taking the stairs two at a time.

He was the only guy who had survived the killings back there. He was the only one left who could maybe identify the guy who was wearing Vilar's watch. He was the only one who might be able to tell them what was going on.

Ed couldn't let him get away.

He leaned over the side again. It hadn't seemed like such a long way down just a minute ago, when Abdul was doing it. But now it did.

At the bottom of the alley, all manner of garbage was piled high. There was no one down there. The garbage didn't mean anything. It wouldn't break your fall. If you fell that distance, you would die. Ed gazed across the abyss. Abdul was above him, moving up the stairs and away.

Lose that guy and you may never see him again. Sure, the Germans might pick him up on the other side of the building. But they might not. He might disappear. He might have an escape route all picked out. He had jumped that gap without hesitating, like he had done it before.

Well, if a skinny drink of water like Abdul could do it...

Ed leapt up onto the railing. Precious seconds ticked by. Between his shoes he saw all that open space. The alley might as well be the bottom of a deep well. Ten miles across the alley, and a little bit below, the landing of the opposite fire escape beckoned.

Now or never.

He had done so many airplane jumps and helicopter drops, he'd lost track of them all. But this was different. It was jumping out into nothing - with no chute on your back and no rope to hold on to. It was all you, and whatever you had inside.

He bent his knees like he had seen Abdul bend, a full squat.

Do it.

He launched.

The fire escape came at him. He hit it like a meteor. The railing caught him in the stomach. He slipped down and grabbed madly for anything. The rail jammed into his armpits, his hands found grips, and he held on. The iron creaked and groaned and shook all the way up. For a second, he thought his extra weight would collapse the whole thing.

He pulled himself over the railing and fell to the deck.

"That was easy," he said.

He was alive and the chase was on. He groped his way to his feet. He needed to move fast.

He climbed, dragging up the stairs at first, then catching a rhythm and starting to hit it. One landing, around the corner and more stairs. Another landing, no idea where Abdul was now. Did he go in a window?

No. The windows were all bricked in.

Ed kept pushing, guessing the roof. He passed another landing, then another. He kicked the engine into another gear. He reached the top landing, eight floors he thought, but he wasn't sure. Some view up there. The lights of Berlin stretched away to the horizon. He had no time to look at it because there went Abdul, up ahead, racing across the roof.

Ed had sprinted in high school. He had big legs and big lungs. He was a lot faster than he looked. He had caught people asleep on that watch before.

He took off, thundering hoof beats pounding on the roof.

Ed closed the gap by half before Abdul reached the building's edge. A low brick wall marked the end. Abdul never slowed. He hopped onto the wall, launched out into the darkness, and disappeared.

Ed slowed, then came to the wall and stopped. The next building was lower and five feet across an air passage. Abdul was over there, still moving.

Ed leaped up onto the wall, hesitated for a second, then took the gap easily. He touched down on a gravel roof. They were now on a row of packed-together narrow buildings.

Abdul reached the next gap and vaulted over it. Ed gave chase, gaining again. He leaped, the chasm opened and closed below him. His eyes were on Abdul's back. They jumped from roof to roof, Ed growing closer all the time.

They reached the end of the block and Abdul turned right. He flew across a gap to a long and wide gravel roof that was lower still. It was a pretty good jump, but Abdul did it no problem and Ed was too turned on to slow down now.

He burst off the building's edge. There was a moment, out over nothing, arms and legs pumping like a long jumper. The ground was far below.

Ed landed in a starter's crouch, gravel skittering, Abdul just ahead of him. This roof opened up like a football field. Here Ed's legs would do their damage. He pushed himself up and sprinted. As he did, he became aware of the pile of zip ties pressed hard to his ass in the back pocket of his jumpsuit.

Closer. Abdul five steps ahead. Their long shadows mingled on the rooftop. Legs and arms pumping. Closer still.

Ed could hear his own breathing, loud in his ears. HUH-HUH-HUH-HUH.

You got him. You got him. Time it right.

77

Abdul made a sound like the shriek of a banshee. He felt Ed there, right behind him. Of course he did. They were so close.

Ed dove and hit his man waist high. He wrapped Abdul's legs and spun onto his back. They slid together across the roof, the tiny stones tearing Ed's SWAT team clothes, finding gaps in his armor, getting under, digging into his flesh. Ed spun again and landed on top.

This close, Abdul smelled like cigarettes and body odor. He probably hadn't bathed in a week. They wrestled. Ed was bigger and stronger, but Abdul raged in desperation. He screamed in Ed's ear. He turned over and began to crawl forward on all fours.

Ed renewed his grip, climbed up and rode on Abdul's scrawny back. The weight pressed on Abdul, slowing him. Ed reached a big arm across Abdul's front, and pulled backwards, yanking Abdul's arms out from under him. Abdul crashed face first to the gravel roof, big Ed riding him down.

Eat rocks, kid.

Abdul was still struggling. Amazing how much fight he had in him. Ed was out of breath.

"Abdul! Stop!"

He pushed the guy's head against the gravel. Hard. He straddled Abdul's back. With his free hand, he wrenched Abdul's right arm backwards.

"Abdul! I will break your arm. Give it up."

Yes, Ed knew he was speaking English. Yes, this guy probably didn't understand English. And yet, Abdul suddenly gave up. He went limp, lying flat on his stomach, and gasping for air.

Ed wrenched the man's other arm back, pulled the wrists together, and yanked a zip tie from his back pocket. He tied the man's wrists. The guy was down like a prized steer. Ed could tie his ankles now, if he wanted. But he didn't want. He was going to have to walk this guy down to the street somehow.

"Got you, Abdul," Ed gasped. "What do you think of that?"

The side of the guy's face was pressed to the roof. One baleful eye looked up at Ed. "My name is not Abdul."

CHAPTER FOURTEEN

September 23
1:15 am Central European Summer Time (7:15 pm Eastern
Daylight Time, September 22)
Police Station Alexanderplatz
Berlin, Germany

"We have the identity."

"That was quick," Luke said.

"He is well-known to both Interpol and Scotland Yard," Peter said.

"Who is he?"

They were inside Peter's cube at the police headquarters. The room was hyper modern, a sort of Lucite box stuck in a corner of a much larger bullpen of desks belonging to the SWAT team. The Lucite was blurred, so that no one could see in, but Peter could glance up at a video screen mounted on the wall and check on his minions any time he wanted. Recessed lights in the ceiling gave the sense of being in an art museum.

The office was a mess, with piles of folders and loose paperwork stacked on nearly every flat surface. Peter's filing system was very un-German, as far as Luke was concerned. A stereotypical German would have a place for everything, and everything would be in its assigned place. Peter, instead, seemed to get an idea of what his office should be like by watching American cop shows from the 1970s.

Luke was mindful of the time. He had promised Becca they would be back for breakfast. It was still early and beginning to look as if he might keep that promise. If they could board the plane by 3:00 am, or even 3:30, he would more than manage it. The best part about it was he could look his wife straight in the eye and tell her he hadn't killed anyone, or even hurt anyone, and he was never really in any danger. He hadn't even picked up a gun. All he had done was get kicked in the head.

It didn't matter. Becca wouldn't believe any of it, no matter if it was true. Ed had risked his life by jumping across that alleyway, and chasing the fugitive down, but that was Ed's problem. He could share that with Cassandra, or not.

Peter looked at both Luke and Ed from across his desk. "His name is Eza Berrada. He is 21 years old, a Moroccan national, who has lived in numerous European cities over the past five years. He is very bright and was a child scientific prodigy. He received a scholarship to study engineering in London at the age of 16, but he dropped out soon after arriving."

"When can we speak to him?"

The look on Peter's face was not a pleasant one. To Luke, it seemed like he was trying hard to present a mask of neutrality.

"He isn't wanted for any crime," Peter said. "He's merely been placed on certain watch lists because of his associations. He didn't commit any crime tonight."

"Resisting arrest," Ed said immediately. "Assaulting an officer of the law. He kicked Stone here in the head. He struggled to defeat me and escape from me."

Peter almost seemed ready to smile, but then didn't. The thought of the skinny man Ed brought back struggling to defeat him…

No.

"Neither of you are police officers in Berlin. Berrada was simply living in a squat that was raided by the authorities. Nine people were killed. He was not armed. He attempted to run because he feared for his life."

"A man in his group was wearing a watch belonging to a kidnapped American Supreme Court judge."

Peter nodded. "Yes, I know. But Berrada wasn't wearing the watch. The man who was wearing the watch is dead."

"Who was that man?"

Peter shrugged. "Your guess or mine. We are still looking for a fingerprint or DNA match. He could be anyone. He seems to be a man in his 30s, and that should mean he is somewhere in a database, but…"

Peter raised his hands in the air, palms upward, as if to say, "It's out of my hands."

Luke tried again. "When can we speak to Berrada?"

Peter's big shoulders slumped. He sighed. "I will grant you ten minutes with him. But be mindful. He is not our prisoner, or yours. Protests have already begun here in Berlin, but also in Budapest, in Warsaw, and smaller cities where there are squatter movements. We went in to help you find your kidnapping victim. And perhaps to clear out a terrorist cell. But now we stand accused of premeditated murder and human rights violations."

"You didn't do it," Luke said. He thought back to the nonchalant way the SWAT team stood around after the gunfight. "They shot first."

Luke had no idea if that was true or not. There were a lot of people shouting, and a lot of guns pointing. If the Muslims shot first, they were foolish. None of them were wearing body armor. Then again, maybe their orders were not to be captured.

"I know we didn't do it," Peter said. "But the newspapers will know differently."

Luke stared at Peter. Peter stared at Luke. Peter's eyes were bright blue, like shallow water in the Caribbean. His graying hair had been entirely blonde at one time. He was big. He was almost certainly smart.

"Come," he said. "Come talk to Berrada. But you cannot touch him. The truth is, he is in the country illegally. As you know, the Schengen Area countries allow travel across borders without presenting a passport. But he did not legally enter any European Union country, not under his real identity, so he is not free to travel within Germany."

"All the more reason to hold him, in that case," Luke said. "Wouldn't you agree?"

"I don't have an opinion," Peter said. "He's being deported to his home country. Tonight. On the first available plane. And I want him out of this building within one hour from now."

Luke and Ed stopped walking.

"You can't do that," Ed said. "He's implicated in the disappearance of a Supreme Court judge."

Peter shook his big blonde head. "According to the facts we have, he isn't implicated in anything. Anyway, this isn't my decision. It comes from on high. Central government levels. For their own reasons, which they do not share with me, they want him out of the country, so out of the country he goes."

"We need him," Ed said. "He's our only link to…"

Peter shrugged. "Then follow him to Morocco. Recapture him. Disappear him to one of your…" His hand fluttered like a bird, as if that gesture would describe the phrase in English that eluded him. "Black sites. That's none of my affair."

Luke stared at Peter. "I'm… I don't have a word for what I am right now. Surprised doesn't cut it."

"Try flabbergasted," Peter said. "That is a fun English word. And it's how I feel as well. I often feel that way. But orders are orders, so if you gentlemen will please follow me."

Ed glanced at Luke. "The kid is slippery, man. This could be our last chance to talk to him."

Luke nodded. "Agreed."

Peter walked them out through the bullpen, which was now empty except for a couple of guys standing and chatting quietly in a far corner. The desks were clean, in some cases bare. There was nothing on the conference table. The trash cans had been emptied. Peter was the sole messy one on this team.

They moved down a long corridor. At the far end was a white door. Peter gestured at the door.

"He speaks English."

Ed and Luke nodded. "We know."

"Cameras are always watching," Peter said. "Microphones are listening. You understand. He is not a prisoner. He is a temporary guest."

"Understood."

They entered the room and shut the door behind them. Berrada was a slight man, sitting on the far side of a table, as if he was waiting for them to come in so he could conduct a job interview.

His bloodshot eyes were alive and alert above his beard. He was tired, he was probably shocked and exhausted by the night's events, but he was staying on guard. His eyes followed big Ed, the man who had caught him. He said something in German as they came in.

"We're Americans," Ed said.

"And my name isn't Abdul, you racist pig."

Ed smiled. "I know your name. I know who you are."

Luke hadn't said a word yet. Berrada looked at him.

"Who are you?"

Luke decided to try a novel approach. He was going to be transparent and see what that brought him. This guy was going to be gone like smoke soon. But maybe not. If he thought he could trust them, if he thought they had something to offer him... you never knew. He was a young guy, evidently smart. He could have a different life. Maybe he was looking for a way out of this, a way out without running, without constantly looking over his shoulder.

"My name is Special Agent Luke Stone. I work for the United States FBI Special Response Team."

Berrada's skinny shoulders slumped. His head leaned over at a 45-degree angle, as if this piece of information was the final insult, the thing that would break him at last. He looked at Luke and Ed with flat eyes.

"You two are the reason for that massacre back there."

Luke shrugged. "We're looking for a kidnapped Supreme Court judge."

"I know what you're looking for. He's not here, obviously."

"Where is he?"

Berrada stared at them. "How would I know?"

"One of your friends back there was involved in his kidnapping. We tracked your friend from northern Spain to that building."

"Those men were not my friends. I barely knew any of them. I was hiding among them. That's all."

"The man practically died on top of you," Ed said.

Berrada said nothing.

"Why were you hiding?" Luke said.

"Why does anyone hide?" Berrada said. "Fear."

"That escape trick of yours. You planned it ahead of time?"

Berrada smiled, just a bit. "I assumed something bad was coming, sooner or later. Something bad is always coming. I practiced jumping that alleyway probably 20 times, until I could do it without hesitating."

Now Ed smiled. "It didn't matter, though, because I beat you." He raised a big finger at the kid. "You should know that I'll always beat you, no matter how much you practice. No matter how fast you run, I'll always be faster."

"So you caught me," Berrada said. "And now everyone knows where I am, and soon I'll be dead just like the rest of them. Congratulations. They have my location. I'm inside this police station. Wherever they send me next, I'm marked. This time tomorrow, if I'm still breathing, I'll count myself the luckiest man on Earth."

As men went, Berrada looked an awful lot like a young teenager. The beard could have been glued on his face.

"Who's going to kill you?"

"You will. Or someone just like you."

Neither Luke nor Ed took the bait. Berrada looked from Ed to Luke, and back again. He took a deep breath. "Either you guys do a good job pretending you don't know what's going on, or... you really don't know what's going on."

He paused and shook his head. "I can't decide which is worse."

"So enlighten us. What's going on?"

83

Berrada looked at Luke for what seemed like a full minute. "I'm a dead man. That's what's going on."

* * *

"Guys, we should have Big Daddy Cronin on the line in a minute."

Luke and Ed sat outside the police headquarters in their rental car. They were in a *Police Only* parking spot, the same one they had parked in when they arrived. The friendly blue satellite phone sat on the dashboard, connecting them to the SRT offices thousands of miles away.

From where they were, they had an excellent view down the block to the wide front steps of the police station. A large crowd, two hundred people or more, encircled the station, holding large banners with words in German, and chanting slogans. They were held back by a line of cops, perhaps fifty yards from the stairs.

They sat in silence. Luke stared out at the crowd. If anything, it had grown bigger in the past few minutes. Luke got it. He really did. These folks were protesting for the rights of people who would gladly see the European way of life destroyed. He understood it, and if it were just about freedom of speech, he would agree with it. But it was one thing to say, "I want to destroy you," and quite another to act towards that goal. He wondered sometimes if everyone grasped that.

"Are we on the phone here, or what? The minutes on these things are…"

"On the company dime," Don Morris said. His drawl sounded small and tinny on this thing right now. He didn't sound like he was far away. He sounded like he was at the bottom of a tin can.

"We're waiting for Big Daddy to enter the call," Trudy said. "Swann created a three-way hookup."

"What do you have on Eza Berrada in the meantime?" Luke said.

He could almost see pretty Trudy shrug, adjust her funky red glasses, and move some papers around, or maybe scroll through a few screens on a laptop.

"Things you may already know," she said. "Eza Berrada. Twenty-one years old. Grew up in Tangier, Morocco. His father was a drug trafficker to Europe, who died under mysterious circumstances when Eza was young."

"What qualifies as mysterious circumstances?" Ed said.

"His body was found early one morning near the Tangier waterfront. He was shot once in the back of the head, execution style, and left on a

84

deserted concrete dock. The crime was never solved. No one, as far as records show, was even arrested or questioned, despite the fact that he had many known associates."

"Ah. Mysterious like that. Like maybe the police killed him. Or maybe his friends did it. Or his enemies. Or maybe some combination of all of those things at the same time."

"Something along those lines," Trudy said. "Yes. After that, Eza grew up with his mother, and was recognized as highly intelligent. In particular, he was determined to have high aptitude in science and math. At the age of 13, he entered the School of New Sciences and Engineering in Tangier. At the age of 16, he received a full scholarship to the much more prestigious Imperial College of London. It's kind of like the English version of MIT. MIT across the pond, so to speak. So he went to London in the fall of 2001, and by Christmas he had already dropped out."

"Tough for a kid that age," Ed said. "A lot of pressure."

Luke glanced at Ed. This was the same guy who earlier tonight had run the kid down across rooftops.

"That's not why he left school," a deep voice said.

Luke smiled. "Big Daddy, is that you?"

"The very same. How's my favorite rogue agency doing?"

"Holding up our end," Don Morris said. "How's our favorite rogue agent doing?"

"I wish I could say the same," Big Daddy said.

Luke conjured an image of Big Daddy Bill Cronin in his mind. He was probably in his late 40s, a bear of a man, with blonde hair and beard going gray. He had been in the CIA since the dawn of time, and he seemed to know everyone and everything. There was hardly a clandestine event or incident he couldn't recall in exacting detail. Many of the operations he had been on. But it didn't matter if he was or not. Classified, top secret, things he had nothing to do with - he knew what happened.

Big Daddy had been in trouble recently, though Luke didn't know the details. And he hadn't seemed the same after his agent, known as the Meerkat, had been killed during the Air Force One hijacking. You might even say the death of the Meerkat had broken his heart.

Never mind that Big Daddy, or someone, had inserted an undercover CIA agent as the special assistant to the President of the United States. That little fact had never become common knowledge.

"How's it going, Bill?" Luke said.

"Bad," Big Daddy said. "Thanks for asking. I'm under suspension. My old friends disappeared me for a few days, I won't say who or where. But it looks like they're going to give me the golden show..., uh, parachute. I'll get out with my 20-year pension intact. If they'd let me ride a desk for another six years, I would have gotten my 30. But what can I do? I've decided to disappear myself."

"Where are you now?" Ed said.

"Uh... I'm in Greece. Athens at the moment but thinking about the islands. I like this country. I always have. It's got a slower pace of life, especially once you get outside of the city. It was a getaway for me for years when I was working the Middle East."

"We're in Germany," Luke said. "Not far from you."

"Yeah," Big Daddy said. "I knew that already. By American standards, nothing's far in Europe. Do me a favor and don't stop by. I'm not in the mood for popovers these days. Don't get me wrong, I like you guys. From a distance. But it seems like every time I hang out with people from the special operations crowd, I get accused of doing something wrong."

"Sounds like it's been a rough road," Ed said.

"It has. In spades."

"Our violins are playing for you, Bill," Don Morris said. "And I mean that in all sincerity. You're a good man, and you've been a great asset in this country's undercover wars. But we need to move this along. The judge is still out there somewhere, someone has him, and we need to know how close this kid really is to the action. The longer we wait..."

"I understand," Bill said. "So this is what I have. Eza Berrada dropped out of school because after September 11th happened, he was recruited, first by MI6, the British Secret Intelligence Service, and later by the CIA. He was identified right away, as soon as he landed in London, as a kind of useful idiot.

"MI6 watches Imperial College the same way the CIA watches MIT and Stanford. They're always looking for talent. And this kid is talent. He understands how buildings are constructed. He understands explosives. He knows how to make them portable. He knows how to disassemble them and reassemble them later. He's an Arab, and can pass for Iraqi, Syrian, Libyan, Egyptian, whatever you need. So the spy agencies put him to work."

"What did he do?" Luke said.

"You tell me," Bill said.

"I don't know. That's why I asked."

86

"Stone, you love to pretend that you have no idea what goes on; ever notice that about yourself? A market square blows up in Baghdad. A building collapses in Tehran, or Tripoli. You love to believe that these are the mysterious work of terrorists, or acts of God. Sometimes they are, sometimes they aren't. You live up to your neck in this stuff, but somehow you blithely stroll along as if it isn't happening."

"All right, Bill," Don said. "Get off your stump."

"It's fine," Luke said. "He can speak."

Bill was upset; Luke knew that. His career, and probably his life, weren't going the way he expected. He wanted to lash out at someone? Fine. He wanted to make Luke the bad guy right now? It was okay.

"We have a job to do, kiddies," Don said. "Point fingers on your own time."

"This is my own time," said Big Daddy. "It's all my own time now."

"No," Don said. "This is my time. And you're wasting it. If you don't want to help us, that's okay. Just hang up the phone. If you do want to help us…"

He let that idea sit there.

"They took the best years of my life," Bill said. "I've done things I don't care to describe on behalf of this country."

"We've all been there," Don said. "We're all at the same dance."

"Yeah, but some of us want to act like we're still virgins."

"Okay. Enough is enough."

"They've stripped me bare Don, to the bones, and are throwing the whole mess into the alley for stray dogs to eat."

"My finger is on the button, Bill. You're about to go your own way here. I'm not your shrink, son. And neither is anyone else on this call."

Bill sighed. It was a heavy, heavy sigh, like a man preparing to push a large boulder up a very steep hill. It might have been the heaviest sigh Luke Stone had ever heard.

"Okay," Bill said. "Where were we? Berrada. He worked for MI6 and the CIA. The missions are classified. I don't know what they are or were. I don't know who he works for now. At some point, he walked away. Or maybe they sent him away. Later, there was some concern he might have gone over to the other side. He's very young. Maybe he became fed up with the things he was being told to do. Maybe he had some regrets, or remorse, and wanted to even it out a little. I don't know. I do know he disappears from time to time. Drops out of sight."

"No one ever goes away," Ed said. "Not really. Once you're in, you're in."

"That's right," Bill said. "No one ever does. Not for good. Not until they die. If Berrada was in a squat with a guy who was involved in the Vilar kidnapping, then it isn't a coincidence. He's either working with the kidnappers, or he was an undercover plant working for a government, or possibly both. He may have been doing something unrelated, and this kidnapping just popped up and landed in his lap. But he knows more than he's letting on; I'd bet my house on it."

"Where do you think he'll go now?" Don said. "Any hunch?"

"I know exactly where he's going," Bill said.

"You do."

"Yes."

"How do you know that?"

Bill laughed, but it was an almost strangled sound. He was not the happy go lucky cloak and dagger spy, agent runner, and enhanced interrogation specialist he once was. He was a long way from there. He might never make it back to that place.

"You know I'm not at liberty to discuss things like that. They're putting me out to pasture, as far as we know. They're not feeding me into the bone cutter, at least not yet. And I don't want them to. But I'll tell you this. Part of the problem with a guy like Berrada is he's an open book. He's a sincere kid. It might be that he got involved too early, and never had a chance to grow up. He has patterns and habits. They were never able to break him of that. One habit he has is that when things get rough for him, and he feels under pressure, he runs home to his mommy."

Luke was refraining from talking at the moment. He didn't want to instigate Bill any further.

"So you think…" Ed said.

"Berrada is from Tangier. His mother still lives there, in an apartment right outside the medina, the walls of the old city. If the Germans are deporting him to Morocco, then he's going to go to his mother's place, go to ground. It's what he does. It's crazy, but he probably feels safe there. As I indicated, he's still a kid in a lot of ways."

"Is he safe there?" Ed said.

"Eza Berrada isn't safe anywhere."

"Bill," Don said. "Do you happen to know where Richard Vilar is right now?"

It was the question Luke would have asked. One fact about this line of work was, no matter how secret a thing seemed to be, there were always people who knew. Often enough, Bill Cronin was one of those people.

There was a long pause.

"If I did, we wouldn't be having this conversation. Because in that case, Vilar would already be back home with his family."

"You think we should have someone in Tangier pick Berrada up?"

"Sure, if you want that person to identify his corpse."

Now Luke did speak up. "What are you saying, Bill?"

"I'm saying I'm not the only one who knows where Berrada goes when it's time to hide. I'd say all kinds of people know it, on both sides of the fence. He was little more than a child with a big brain when he got involved in all this. I don't think it occurred to him quite how expendable he would become."

"So what you're saying is we need to do it," Luke said.

"Now you're catching on, Stone. Yes. That is what I'm saying."

Luke stared out the windshield at the big Berlin cops holding back the crowd. In here, with the sound muted by the car, it seemed like a little bit of a stage play. There were a lot of protestors out there. They were chanting and shouting, and shaking fists at the cops, but they weren't really trying to break through the line. If they wanted to, they could do so easily. There weren't nearly enough cops to hold them back.

Then what? What would they do if they broke the line? Rush up the stairs of the police headquarters and… what?

Stand around, probably, at the top of the stairs.

These were civilized people, these protestors. They were like a dog who loved to chase cars. The dog wouldn't know what to do with one if he actually caught up to it.

The protestors didn't want to break the police line, and the cops didn't want to bust heads to make them stop. When push came to shove, they were all on the same team.

It would be nice, Luke reflected, to play a game like that.

"We're going to miss breakfast," he said.

Ed nodded. "Yeah."

Luke shook his head. It was coming to this. The job might not be compatible with marriage. He had been trying to make it so he could have both things at the same time. Don had been married for 30 years. There must be a way. But so far, that path had proven elusive.

"Then I guess we better get going," he said.

CHAPTER FIFTEEN

**6:15 am Central European Summer Time (12:15 am Eastern
Daylight Time)**
Eurostar Paris to London High Speed Train
Nord-Pas de Calais Mining Basin
Outside of Lille, France

It was a good morning for murder.

The man in the service worker's uniform walked through the lead
Business Class cabin of the train. He carried a heavy satchel over his
shoulder. The cabin was quiet and dark, and a sign on the door leading
here indicated that it was closed for repairs.

And it was closed, but not for repairs. There was only one person
in the entire car. He was a man in a business suit, who appeared to be
passed out. In his little group of four facing seats, the table leaves were
extended, as though a group would sit there and order breakfast.

Only there was no one there but the one man, his head resting on
the table, his arms dangling under his seat. He looked like he had come
from quite a party in Paris, caught the early train for England, and gone
straight to sleep. To his left, the French countryside zoomed past the
large windows.

The service worker went by the sleepy businessman without a
second glance. That man was not his problem. Someone else's
certainly, but not his. His problem was taking possession of the train
itself.

The name stitched on the worker's breast pocket was *Francois*.
That was not his name, even though it may as well be. Many things
were not as they seemed. The drunk businessman was not a
businessman. Francois was not really a service worker, responsible for
taking food orders, attending to customer questions and concerns, and
keeping the passenger areas spotless. He had played that role for some
months, but in reality, he was well capable of driving the train.

This seemed like an ordinary morning, the early fast train on its
way to London's impressive old St. Pancras station, where it would
arrive just after 8am, its passengers disgorging to whatever company

90

office, or flat, or favorite eatery awaited them. There were many passengers on the train, close to five hundred, Francois guessed, who probably assumed that this was exactly what was going to happen.

But it wasn't an ordinary morning, and the train was not going to arrive, at least not the way they anticipated.

Francois touched the button that opened the door between this Business Class car and the foyer before the operator lounge beyond. Momentarily between cars, he was confronted with a digital keypad on the next door. He pressed the security code without hesitation, which deactivated the lock mechanism. He swiped his identification card across the reader, and just like that, the door unlocked.

Of course it did. Nothing out of the ordinary was happening. He worked here, after all, and in the course of his duties he sometimes needed access to this lounge. Those who were with him might need access as well, so he deactivated the digital lock completely. Now anyone could open the door simply by touching the button.

He passed through the doorway, realizing that his Francois identity had reached the end of its effective lifespan. In the aftermath of what happened next, Eurostar would know that Francois was the worker who entered the operator lounge at the precise moment everything went wrong. And they would pass that information to the various police departments, intelligence, and defense agencies that were soon to become involved.

Francois was going to become one of the most wanted men in Europe, if not the entire world.

The operator lounge was compact, comprised of a table with seats on either side with a large window, much like in the Business Class compartments. At the far end, there was the heavy security door to the cockpit.

There was a gleaming stainless-steel machine that could provide coffee, espresso, cappuccino, and hot water for the various teas that were on offer. There was a small glass refrigerator with milk and juice bottles, and cans of soda inside. Also inside the refrigerator were pre-made sandwiches and pastries such as croissants, Danishes, and crullers.

Backup train operators could order meals from the Business Class kitchen, but as a practical matter, they rarely did.

There was also a private restroom in here, and a place to hang jackets and coats. Finally, there was a sort of divan where backup drivers could nap during the ride. This was what they often chose to do. When a driver was assigned as a backup, they were rarely asked to operate the train. But they might be driving the train later in the day, or might have driven it earlier, so this was a good time to relax.

That's what this morning's backup driver was doing. His jacket was hanging up, the front facing away from Francois, so the name there was not visible. But Francois knew him and had traveled with him before. His name was Guy - he pronounced it like *Jee* - and he was a friendly, overly talkative chap.

He was sprawled on the divan, his legs out, his head leaning against the rest, his cap pulled down over his eyes. When he heard Francois come in, he tipped the cap to see who it was. His eyes were bleary under there.

"Bonjour, Guy," Francois said quietly.

Guy nodded and pulled the cap back down. Just a worker, here to replenish the tea bags or wipe down the table, or make sure there were toilet rolls and paper towels in the restroom.

"Bonjour."

Guy, who'd had his arms folded across his chest a moment ago, placed his hands behind his head in a sort of cradling pillow. The man's body was so open, so defenseless, so exposed, it almost didn't seem fair.

Almost.

If Guy was the entire job, then maybe it wouldn't have been fair and, to make it sporting, perhaps a warning should be issued to him. But Guy was not the job. He was just another small step toward completing the job, and one best dealt with quickly.

Francois put his heavy satchel down on the floor. He pulled a long hunting knife from inside his jacket and removed it from its leather sheath. The knife was sturdy and razor sharp, serrated on one side of the blade, long and smooth on the other. It was silent, with no bullets to ricochet and accidentally cause damage to sophisticated train equipment.

Francois tossed the leather sheath aside, and took two quick steps toward Guy. He bent, falling forward and pressing his left hand hard to Guy's mouth. In the same instant, he plunged the knife deep into Guy's chest.

Francois had trained for this moment for months. He punched through the breastplate and stabbed Guy's heart on the first try. It didn't require another one.

Guy's eyes opened wide, and his cap fell off backwards. His entire body became rigid, as if a powerful jolt of electricity was running through it. His hands came out from behind his head, and for a second it seemed as if they might try to initiate some sort of struggle. Then they fell to his sides.

Guy's eyes stared at Francois in confusion. But the light in those eyes was fading. In another moment, the light had gone out. The eyelids came down and almost, but not quite, closed. Francois's hand was still pressed against Guy's mouth.

He lifted the hand, at first just a bit in case life remained in Guy. But there was no worry. A bridge of saliva descended from Francois's hand. A small sound, like a gasp or a low sigh, came from the mouth.

It was just air escaping. Already Guy's body was settling. His head turned to the side and stopped. Some blood had spilled from his chest, but most of it was probably spilling inside the chest cavity.

Francois pulled the knife out, ripping heart muscle and flesh with the serrated edge, just to be certain.

Guy didn't respond. He was dead. The first strike had been a perfect one.

Francois took a deep breath. He stood tall and looked around the compartment. Outside the window, some fields zipped past. There was light in the sky. Francois could make out high-tension electrical wires against the horizon.

Things were flowing smoothly. There was one more hurdle: the driver. Francois knew the schedule so well he barely had to think to conjure an image of the man operating the train. Reginald Fawcett, an Englishman, who was probably in his early 40s.

The train operators were the elite of the Eurostar workers, of course, and they were a bit aloof as a result. They almost seemed to think of themselves as media stars, or fighter pilots. Aloof to the underlings, but with a camaraderie among themselves.

Fawcett was more than aloof. He was a heavyset man, with a large doughy face. Among the drivers Francois had worked with, he was the least likely to extend a friendly word, a greeting, a compliment to anyone. He rarely even made eye contact.

He wasn't aloof, Francois supposed. He was an introvert. He preferred his own company. A quiet man, a shy man, who had somehow acquired an exceptional job driving an exceptional train, a man with thoughts and feelings, and perhaps loved ones over in England…

Francois shook his head to clear it of such ideas. He went to the coat hanger, took Guy's jacket down, and shrugged into it. The fit was good.

The Fates were not kind. What the man currently in the driver's seat was like, or who was close to him, or what he preferred, or didn't prefer, no longer mattered.

Francois glanced at the food offerings. There were a few small packages of crisps he might like. A sandwich loaded with meats of various kinds. An iced coffee drink in a bottle. He was going to be in the cockpit for a long while.

He took the items he wanted and placed them on the floor next to his bag. *Take care of the driver, then come back and quickly bring the food and the bag inside.*

It was a solid plan.

* * *

A man walked by a moment ago.

Richard Sebastian-Vilar opened his eyes. It was hard to keep them open. They kept fluttering closed again. He let them rest for a moment, and then it seemed he had fallen asleep. Again.

He woke with a start. His eyes popped open. His eyelids wanted to slowly drop back into place, but he fought them.

If it was hard to keep them open, it seemed impossible to lift his head. He was looking sideways. Across an aisle from him were four seats, two and two, facing each other. Just past the seats was a window. A dim, half-formed landscape whizzed by through that window, shadows moving so fast he almost couldn't look at them. The scene made him dizzy. It made him feel like he might become sick.

Something had happened to him. He couldn't remember what. It was RIGHT THERE, just beyond the reach of his working memory. It was something bad.

I'm on a train now.

Yes. Of course. He was on a train. He could feel its vibrations. He could see that there was an aisle here, and he was on one side of it. He could see the world passing by outside the window, a ground-level world that made it clear he wasn't on an airplane. He was inside a fast-moving train. And his head was resting on a table of some sort.

The car he was in was dark. Slowly, with tremendous effort, he lifted his head. The world swam around him. He took a deep breath, in and out, faster than he intended.

Whew!

His shoulders were hunched, and he was bent over. He tried to lean back into the seat behind him, but he couldn't. There was pressure on

94

his wrists pulling him forward. Curious, he craned his head and looked below him. The mere movement almost made him pass out again.

He was wearing handcuffs on his wrists. The cuffs were fastened to the central table leg, restricting his movement. He could lean forward and lay his head on the table, but he could not lean back into the chair he was sitting on. He tried to pull on the post, but he couldn't make it budge. Even trying made him sick.

He was a prisoner here.

The chairs around him looked wide, plush and comfortable, like the chairs an executive would sit in. The appointments here were modern and fancy. Places to plug in electronic gadgets, phones, laptops. He guessed he was in a First Class or Business Class compartment.

But there was no one else here. Where was everyone? A compartment like this would normally be in high demand, wouldn't it?

Fractured, dimly lit memories began to return to him. He could barely walk, was stumbling. Barely walk? He could barely keep his head up at all. Two men were helping him walk, his arms slung over their shoulders. He was practically dangling limp between them. The group were passing through a security check.

"Oh, he's a bit drunk," one of his companions said. "Our mate's a bit drunk, isn't he? Yes, that's it, that's it. That's his passport."

Drunk? He was Richard Sebastian-Vilar. He was a Supreme Court justice. He rarely took a second drink, and never more than two. He hadn't been drunk in at least 20 years. Why would they say he was drunk?

They were lying. He hadn't been drunk, and he wasn't their mate. They were just saying that to get him past security.

They... who were they?

His kidnappers, that was who. It was all coming back to him now. He had been in the Pyrenees, and he'd been kidnapped. There was fighting. The Mayor got shot. Vilar could remember looking at his dead eyes, his body lying on the cobblestones.

"Sydney..." he said now. The bodyguards had brought her and Grace into the *pension* and slammed the gates shut. No. One bodyguard had done it. The other two were dead.

"Unh."

The sound came out of his mouth. It was a grunt, or a sigh. He had done it. By declining a large security detail, he had consigned his own bodyguards to death.

He remembered being in a cave. A man there spoke English. The man spit on him and chastised him. He told Vilar that the kidnappers weren't interested in his family. That was good, if it was true. For a moment, Vilar had thought the man would kill him over abortion rights.

Then they were moving again, Vilar with a bag or a mask over his head. Then... they must have done something to him. The next thing he remembered was being carried into the train station, and maybe onto the train itself.

They must have drugged him, got him aboard the train, and dumped him here. But why? Why go to all the trouble of kidnapping someone, just to abandon him on a train? A train worker had bustled past a moment ago, and when he came back, Vilar would get his attention. Then the whole ordeal would be over.

It didn't make sense. Unless... unless the manhunt put such pressure on the kidnappers that they simply decided to get rid of him. But why keep him alive at all?

Simple, the lawyer and judge inside him answered. Kidnapping was one thing, but pre-meditated murder was something else again. The penalties would be that much more severe.

If they killed me...

No. It was no good. It didn't hold water. They killed at least three people when they abducted him. They didn't care about killing people. And anyway, kidnapping was a serious offense with stiff prison sentences in just about any country with a legal system.

His mind drifted to the handcuffs holding him in place.

They haven't abandoned you.

No. They still had him captive. He was here on this train, and so were they.

* * *

"Beautiful," Reg Fawcett said.

The sleek, ultra-modern train hurtled along, just under 200 miles per hour.

Fawcett was at the controls. He sat alone in the cockpit, as was always the case aboard Eurostar trains. He sat up tall and alert, a cup of coffee at his right elbow, his hands on the desk, one hand on the stick that controlled speed, the other hand near, but not touching any of the other controls. He watched the landscape of northern France zip past. But that wasn't what elicited the word from him.

In fact, it could hardly be said that he was actually watching the landscape. The landscape and the tracks in front of him were going by so fast that it was hard to focus his eyes on any of it. The first light of a new day was slowly filling the sky, but it might as well be pitch dark out.

The old slag heaps commemorating when Lille was a coal mining region were clear in the distance, but they weren't something to look upon, and certainly weren't beautiful in any sense of the word. Closer, the signs - town signs, warning signs, and instructions - which were there for drivers like him to read, were nearly impossible to see.

His onboard video screen would broadcast the upcoming sign for several seconds before it appeared outside the train's curved inverted triangle windshield and keep it there for several seconds after it was gone. That was the only way Fawcett could read the signs. Not that he even needed to read the signs at this point. He'd been driving this route for five years now and knew it more or less by heart.

Most of what he did was watch the signals along the tracks. If they were green, he was free to open the train throttle up and let it do its thing. If the lights were amber, or red, he knew to apply the brakes and slow the train down, or even bring it to a stop.

Also, on a downhill, he knew to ease off the power and let the train's momentum carry it. Eurostar considered itself a "green" company, and they monitored driver energy usage. They liked it when you let the train coast at high speeds, as long as you remained on schedule. He enjoyed the challenge of keeping his energy usage down while simultaneously keeping his speed up. He could monitor the tradeoffs - energy for speed - on his digital display.

And that was where the beauty lay - within the train itself. The technology was so advanced that the concepts which created this train, and its physical presence in the world, were beautiful. The speed and aerodynamics were beautiful. The cockpit and controls were aesthetically pleasing to the point of beauty. Fawcett had been a train buff since his earliest days, collecting toy locomotives as a child. Driving the Eurostar from London to Paris and back again was his dream job.

He loved the Channel Tunnel, another technological marvel. He had studied everything about it, how it was a vision of engineers since the early 1800s, and finally realized nearly 200 years later. It almost seemed a shame that the train burst through the tunnel at nearly a hundred miles per hour and went end to end in a brief 20 minutes.

He loved that this was a true international job. The French signal operators' union refused to have their workers speak English, so Fawcett had to spend nine months learning French, and he lived for a short time with a French family, before the company would let him near the controls.

He loved the solitude of this job. Technically, there was only one driver at a time in the cockpit. There was a backup driver on every train, and often the backup might pop in for a chat in the final minutes as the train slowed down for the approach to London or Paris. But otherwise, you were on your own. And Fawcett relished this time, especially early mornings like now, alone with his coffee and his thoughts, and his wonderful train.

Behind him, the door to the cockpit unlocked. Fawcett's backup on this run was a Frenchman named Guy. Fawcett liked Guy, but Guy was the chatty type. A certain amount of fraternizing was fine. Although random conversations were against the rules, brief visits to communicate important information were okay, and the company knew the drivers were human. Guy tended to push the rulebook to the edge, though.

The door opened. Fawcett didn't turn to look. He kept his eyes on the tracks and the controls. He figured his own seriousness might send to a message to the more frivolous, rule flouting Guy. Might as well be a little friendly, though.

"Bonjour, Guy," he said. "How is your morning?"

An instant later, a strong hand clamped over his mouth and a sharp pain pierced his back. It happened so fast; he had no time to react.

His first instinct was to slow down the train, which he did.

More pain. Stabbing pains, again and again.

He pushed himself to his feet and wrenched himself away from whoever was grabbing him. He turned, and a man was there. He wore the blue Eurostar uniform, complete with sports jacket, the same as Fawcett. The man was young, dark-haired, clean-shaven with hard brown eyes. It wasn't Guy. He held a long, bloody knife in his right hand.

Who was this? What Eurostar driver would attack a fellow driver? Fawcett looked at the name stitched on the man's left breast.

Guy.

Fawcett stared at it. That didn't make sense.

The man stabbed him again, this time in the front.

And again.

"UH!"

Fawcett heard himself grunt from the pain. Then a long moment of blackness passed, as if the train had passed into a deep, dark tunnel.

When the light returned, Fawcett was on his back, looking up at the ceiling. He was lying on the floor. To his right and above him, the young man wearing Guy's uniform was sitting in the driver's seat, his hands at the controls.

Fawcett watched as the man brought the train up to speed again. To the passengers, it would have seemed a momentary slowdown, as if the train might have passed a warning signal. To signalmen and the company engineers watching the train's progress in Paris and London, it would have seemed that the driver saw something that made him wary, slowed down, then sped up again when the concern had passed.

It would seem like nothing important had happened.

Fawcett tried to speak. He opened his mouth and his throat worked. "Guh!"

Blood flowed from his mouth, and down his chin. Some of it went across his right cheek. His could see the redness of it in his peripheral vision. It was the most alarming thing he had ever seen. He realized now that he was in a lot of pain, in his chest, in his back, deep inside his body. He needed emergency medical care, and right away.

"Guh," he said again.

The man in the driver's seat kicked him absently, without turning to look at him.

"Shut up, old man. Shut up and die."

CHAPTER SIXTEEN

**7:15 am Western European Summer Time (8:15 am Central European Summer Time - 2:15 am Eastern Daylight Time)
Medina of Tangier
Tangier, Morocco**

"Tough night," Ed Newsam said. He was sitting in the driver's seat, slumped low as if he would fall asleep any moment.

Luke nodded. "Brutal."

The sun was up. They were sitting in a small car parked outside of a gate to the Tangier medina. The gate was white stone, three stories high, the tunnel through it shaped like a minaret. It was part of the walled old city that had been here for 700 years.

The modern city had long ago burst its banks, sprawling in whitewashed and multicolored stone buildings and houses, upward into the surrounding hillsides. The ancient city was still here, the tiny beating heart of larger Tangier, a warren of narrow curving alleyways, with shopkeepers and itinerant fruit and vegetable vendors hawking their wares.

Luke felt a bit exposed. He had taken a Dexie maybe 20 minutes ago, but it hadn't kicked in at all. After how long he'd been awake, it was possible that it wasn't going to kick in. It was early morning, and the vendors were coming to set up for the day. Seagulls were screeching and swooping, looking for scraps from the bakeries. This early, there were no tourists around, and Luke and Ed didn't look like any of the locals.

As Luke watched, the point was emphasized as a small man in workpants and a windbreaker walked by, escorting two women covered head to toe in black, and three little girls dressed the same way.

"This car smells like cigarette smoke," Ed said.

"Yeah, it does. I wonder where Swann got this thing."

It was a weird old car, small, green, with no obvious automaker affiliation or logo anywhere on it. It didn't even seem to have a model name. The dashboard was made out of some cheap brown molded plastic. The seats squeaked. Their springs were on the verge of being sprung. This thing reminded Luke of cars that AMC was making in the 1970s, but worse.

The car had been waiting for them at the airport, and they had chugged here in it, the tailpipe belching black smoke the whole way. So they had a big black guy (wearing dark sunglasses), and a big white guy, obvious foreigners, sitting in a smoky piece of junk car, doing obvious surveillance of a residential area just outside the medina.

Morning traffic was busy, a weird parade of bicycles, motor scooters belching exhaust, a handful of cars and many people, some pushing along carts of various kinds. Diagonally across an open plaza from Luke and Ed, maybe fifty yards away, was a small white apartment block.

Berrada's mother lived on the second floor of that building. The apartment that appeared to be hers had a small terrace, with a black iron railing that was carved into a maze of shapes, kind of like something you'd see in the French Quarter of New Orleans. A thick-bodied woman in a black head scarf had hung some clothes out on that terrace a few moments ago.

Luke gazed up and down the street. The question was if Berrada would actually show up here. If he didn't, then they just wasted hours of their lives, and missed breakfast with the families, flying from central Europe to Morocco. Luke hoped that wasn't the case, but Bill Cronin would owe them a beer if it was. At least a beer. This was his cockamamie idea.

A high-speed train, the Paris to London line, had been hijacked while Ed and Luke were flying down here. It seemed like there was a never-ending parade of madness in this world. Ed and Luke were trying to nail down who stole the Supreme Court judge, and where they took him. And while they were doing that, someone else stole a train.

Or maybe the two things were related. Luke was tired, nearly spent, and from where he was sitting, it was impossible to say. His synapses were not firing perfectly right now. Any speculation at all would be fruitless. Leave connecting the dots to the Trudy Wellingtons of the world.

"We should have gone back to Austria," Ed said.

"Let's not talk about it."

As Luke watched, a skinny young guy in a dark windbreaker came out of the minaret-shaped keyhole in the wall. He walked like someone who was tired, nearly out on his feet. He was carrying a brown paper bag. There appeared to be two long loaves of bread sticking out of the top.

Luke took the binoculars off his lap and put them on the guy.

It was him. It was Berrada. He was indeed carrying bread. Maybe his mom had sent him out for it. Or maybe he had just arrived, and this was his idea of a peace offering or a homecoming gift.

"He's here."

Instantly, Ed sat up straight. "Where?"

"Kid across the way with the bread."

Berrada was at the bottom of the white concrete steps to his mother's building, talking to a skinny old guy who was stooped over on a cane.

"Would you look at that," Ed said. "He's right out on the street."

"How do you want to play it?"

Ed shrugged. "I think we better take him now. Once the old duffer clears out. If he gets inside that building, and especially the apartment, he could barricade himself inside. What we don't need here is a long, protracted event."

Luke nodded. "Yeah. Good. Might as well start up the beast in that case."

Ed looked at Luke from the corner of his eye and smiled.

"Ramming speed?"

Luke laughed. "My thoughts exactly."

Ed turned the key in the ignition and fed the gas. The engine burped and blatted into life. Clouds of black smoke belched from the back. They watched as across the way, the oldster said some final farewell to Berrada and moved off down the street.

"Hit it," Luke said. "He's got his keys out."

Ed dropped the car into gear and peeled off across the plaza. They bounced across the paving stones, the low-slung building coming at them as though it was on a fast-moving conveyor belt. The kid was at the top of the stairs, fiddling with the door when he realized something was off. He turned and saw the car coming at him.

Luke watched his facial expression change from dull, tired concentration to wide-eyed alarm. The bag with the bread flew out of his arms.

"He sees us."

"I got him," Ed said. "I'm gonna box him in."

Instead of going into the building, Berrada leapt over the low stone wall that flanked the staircase. He dropped eight or ten feet to the pavement below, dropped to one knee, then bounced up and ran.

"Oh man," Ed said. He made a sharp left to run the car parallel with the kid and pull alongside him.

Two men who had been sitting in the shade of an awning maybe fifty feet away suddenly got up and were running after Berrada. A third man, who had been standing in the shadow of a storefront smoking a cigarette, joined the chase.

Berrada disappeared through the minaret keyhole and into the medina, moving fast. The first two men entered nearly on his heels. The third man ran by without giving the gate a glance. Luke watched him. There was another minaret-shape gate further down the street.

"Drop me here! Drop me here! He's got more friends than just us."

"I see that," Ed said.

Luke's door was already open before the car stopped. "That last guy's going for the other gate. There must be a shortcut of some kind."

Ed nodded. "Got it."

Luke jumped out and Ed roared off behind him. Then Luke was running. He passed through the gate and into the crowded alleys of the medina.

* * *

Eza Berrada ran for his life.

He was small, and fast and light. He was young, and even though he was tired, he felt like he could run forever. His youth would allow him to run, but fear was what would drive him on. He'd seen at least three, maybe four, men coming for him.

He zipped through the crowds, sliding around and between people. Strong men carried heavy boxes on their shoulders, bent under the weight. Men pushed metal dollies loaded with more boxes or piled high with brightly colored carpets.

He darted, he danced between people. The blood roared in his ears. He could hear the steady huffing of his own breath. People turned to look as he bore down on them, then ran past. The streets were very tight here.

He turned right, he turned left, he knew these ancient alleyways like he knew his own face. He had grown up here, been a small child on these very streets.

It had pained him to see his mother. It haunted him. She was growing older while he was off in the world, and she had not been happy to see him. Her jaw dropped when he appeared at her home early this morning.

The interaction played out in his mind as he ran through the alleys. He glanced behind him. He was fast, faster than the men who wanted him. He knew the medina better. He might just make it.

"I thought you were dead," his mother had said.

"No, mother. Not dead. Very much alive."

"The police were here, Eza. They said that you're a terrorist. I told them I already know what you are."

But she had let him in. What else was she going to do? He was her only son, after all. She had sung to him when he was a small boy. She had loved him once, even if she didn't now.

Eza weaved through the milling early morning shoppers. He turned left and headed along a very narrow walkway that would lead him back out to a main alley. He could see it, another fifty meters ahead, crowds of people streaming back and forth. Once he reached there…

A man in dark clothes stepped out of a doorway right in front of him. Eza's momentum carried him into the man. At the last instant, too late, Eza saw the long blade in the man's hand. The man plunged it deep into Eza's belly, then ripped upward.

The pain was not real.

"Unh."

Eza felt his mouth drop open. He heard his own breathing, very fast now.

The man leaned in close to him. He was a nondescript man, not small or large. Eza realized he hadn't even seen the man's face yet. The knife was still deep inside Eza's body. The man's hand was still on the knife's handle.

"My young friend," the man said in Arabic. He was practically whispering in Eza's ear. "You have too many conflicting loyalties. There's only one true loyalty, and that's to Allah."

The man ripped the knife out and pushed Eza to the ground. Then he was gone. Eza lay on his back in the narrow alley staring up at the blue sky between the buildings. What he saw when he looked there was his mother's face.

* * *

Luke turned right, he turned left, plunging through the crowds.

Please, he thought, *don't let him be gone.*

He cut across an intersection of two alleys, eyes ahead, scanning for his prey. Too much so, in fact. A woman in front of Luke stopped short. She wore a kerchief on her head and a long coat, and she had an old cart piled high with what looked like rags.

Luke crashed into the cart, knocking it over, but stayed on his feet. A motor scooter leaned on its horn and zig-zagged around the crashed cart. People yelled.

Luke kept running.

"Sorry!" he shouted. Probably no one understood him.

To his right was a long building. Along the side of it, people were unloading boxes from carts and small trucks, shouting at each other. He ran by them.

His head was on a swivel, waiting for Berrada to resurface. There were too many people. Berrada knew the area too well. Luke turned right, stopped running and walked along a very narrow, dismal alley. The sun hadn't reached in between these buildings yet today, and maybe it never did.

The alley was curved, so it was impossible to see what was coming. Suddenly, up ahead, around the curve, there was the sound of a woman screaming. It started as a scream, but then morphed into a sort of wailing of grief.

Luke started running again. He came around the curve, and of course here was the kid. He was on the ground, half on the narrow curb, half on what passed for the street. He was lying in a pool of blood.

The woman was still there, an old woman in a kerchief. She had thrown her head back, was lifting her arms to the sky, as though she was howling at the moon in the daytime.

Luke ran up to Berrada and kneeled beside him. He was pale and turning paler. His shirt was saturated with blood below his chest and above his pants. He was stabbed or shot, and they had gone for the guts. They knew what they were doing. Berrada would be in septic shock minutes from now.

"Eza, "Luke said.

Berrada's face was a mask of agony. His eyes found Luke.

"Oh God, you again."

Luke nodded. "Yeah. It's me."

"I want to tell you," Berrada said. "I want to tell you everything. But there's no time."

"Try," Luke said.

He didn't see the point of telling the kid there was time. There wasn't. He was hemorrhaging, and the toxic contents of his intestines were leaking into his bloodstream. They were in Morocco. Who knew where the nearest hospital was, or if it was any good? Meanwhile, the kid had information, and Luke needed it.

"A train was hijacked," Berrada said.

Luke nodded. "I know. I heard."

"It's a bomb."

"What's a bomb?"

The kid gritted his teeth and shook his head, as if he was frustrated at dealing with an imbecile. "The train. The whole train. It's a bomb. They've been making it into a bomb for weeks, maybe months. Smuggling C4 onto the train. Putting it together like pieces…"

His face became a mask of sudden agony.

"…of puzzle. It's a linked chain. It can take down the whole tunnel."

Luke stared at him. "Your idea?"

"Not my idea. But I designed it."

Terrific. This kid was hanging out with at least one person who kidnapped a Supreme Court judge. He also designed a bomb to blow up the tunnel beneath the English Channel. And now he was dying. Their only connection to two crimes was laying here in a narrow alleyway…

"There are two ways the bomb can go off," Berrada said. He was speaking barely above a whisper. "There's a detonator on board, or they can crash the train at high speed. But there's a problem. There are two controls to set off the detonator - one with the lead hijacker, one with the train driver. The lead hijacker's control doesn't work."

"It doesn't work?" Luke said. "Why?"

Berrada sighed heavily. Blood started to come out of his mouth and run down his chin. "Because I changed my mind. I made a…"

"But the driver's detonator will work?"

"A terrible mistake."

"Eza! Answer me."

Berrada nodded. "Yeah. It works." He started crying. "You have to kill him."

A shadow appeared, a darker shadow against the shadows of the alley. Luke looked up and Ed was coming. He came like a storm, moving in quickly.

He immediately kneeled by Berrada's head.

"What kind of injury is it?" he said.

Luke shook his head. "I don't know."

Berrada shook with sobs. "I don't want to die now."

106

"You're not dying," Luke said. He looked at Ed. Ed pulled the kid's shirt up, exposing the gaping wound there. It was like a long red mouth. Blood was everywhere. Ed's hands were instantly red with it. "Knife wound," he said. "Deep. Deliberate. Gastrointestinal tract. I would try to probe it, to see what's going on, but the pain alone would be unbearable."

He shook his head and grimaced.

"The driver can detonate," Berrada said. He didn't seem to be paying attention to Ed at all. "Or crash. Either way."

"Who were you working for?" Luke said.

The kid shook his head. "Guys like you will never learn."

"We're looking for the judge," Luke said.

"You found him. He's on the train."

Somewhere in the distance, sirens were approaching. How were they even going to get an ambulance in here? They wouldn't. They were going to have run down here with a stretcher, then run the kid back to the ambulance.

"Why is the judge on the train?"

"Because that's how you make a statement."

"What do they want?" Luke said. "The hijackers."

The kid was fading now. He didn't seem to see Luke anymore. He stared into space. Luke looked and Ed was holding the kid's hand. A crowd was gathering around them, solemn, staring.

"Eza," Luke said.

Berrada was still with them, at least for the moment. "I don't think they want anything," he said. "I think they just want to kill."

His eyelids drifted slowly closed.

"Tell my mother…"

Luke shook the kid gently.

"Eza," he said. "Eza."

CHAPTER SEVENTEEN

3:45 am Eastern Daylight Time (9:45 am Central European Summer Time - 8:45 am Western European Summer Time)
Headquarters of the FBI Special Response Team
Mclean, Virginia

"Don?" a voice said. "Don, are you in there?"

It was late at night, and the offices were nearly deserted. A skeleton crew was still on duty, waiting to hear from Stone and Newsam in Morocco. They had checked in when they landed at Tangier nearly two hours ago, but no one had heard anything since.

This trip to Morocco, and the trip to Berlin before that seemed more and more like wild goose chases. The squat house raid had sparked protests in Berlin itself, and in half a dozen other cities in Eastern Europe where the real estate was still cheap and kids chose to live for free in falling down old buildings.

The hijacking of the high-speed English Channel train couldn't be a coincidence. It looked right now like the kidnapping of the Supreme Court judge was exactly the kind of misdirection that groups like Al Qaeda were famous for. "See what's in this hand? Oh, whoops! The card was in the other hand all along."

Don probably should have let Stone and Newsam sleep in with their wives in Austria, then wake up in the morning refreshed and ready to go out and enjoy the sights.

"Don?"

The voice belonged to Mark Swann. He was still here because of course he was. And the situation was complicated by the fact that Don was locked here in his office, in a tight embrace with Trudy Wellington, his young science and intelligence officer.

In fact, they were pressed so close together, body to body, that he could smell the shampoo she used this morning. He breathed deeply. Her scent was intoxicating. Her tiny body was wrapped in his powerful arms, and he could feel her arms snaked across his broad back. He wanted this so badly.

He loved his wife, Margaret. She had been with him, through ups and downs, for 30 years. They had raised two wonderful daughters together. When he thought he had lost Margaret during the Air Force One hijacking nearly a year ago, it was as if a part of him had died. Now he was alive again.

He never wanted to lose Margaret, but right now *he wanted this*, so badly it was as if he was losing his head. His mentorship relationship with Trudy had taken a turn, and now they were lovers. It seemed so natural, so right, to both of them.

They pulled apart just a bit now. For some reason, Trudy was smiling, but there were also tears on her cheeks. Don realized that if he lived to a hundred, or possibly a thousand, he would never understand women and their emotions. Either way, she looked beautiful. She was positively glowing. She was like an angel.

The doorknob to the office jiggled. It was locked, but Swann was also crazy. He was liable to pick the damn thing. Thankfully, the lights in here were on.

"Yeah, Swann? What is it?"

"Oh," Swann said from the other side of the door. "I didn't know you were in there. You didn't answer."

"I'm on the phone."

That was a funny thing to say. It was nearly two in the morning. Who would Don be on the phone with at this hour?

It didn't matter. He was the boss. Was Swann going to question him?

"Sorry, Don. Stone and Newsam called in. They're ready to make their report. Berrada is dead. They told me that much."

Don sighed. Of course the kid was dead. He hoped that Stone and Newsam weren't the ones who killed him. They had already been involved in one international incident tonight. The Berlin fiasco was going to be hard enough to explain.

"I'll be there in five minutes." He paused. "Make that three minutes."

"Okay," Swann said. "Have you seen Wellington? I figure she should be on this call as well."

"No," Don said. "I imagine she's around somewhere, though."

"I'll find her."

Swann's footsteps went off down the hall.

Don looked down at Trudy's pretty face, upturned to him. In this moment, he could quit this job and run away with her. He could burn everything, toss it away, leave it all behind. All but Margaret, asleep alone in their bed, as she had been thousands of times during the course of their lives together. It was terrible, what he was doing. And yet, it was also impossible to stop.

He had stepped in it this time.

* * *

"Where are you now?" Don said into the speaker.

It was Don, Mark Swann, and a couple of others. Trudy was not here. They were sitting in the SRT conference room, around the long table. Don remembered how, not too long ago, he had thought this room was the cat's meow. He used to think of it as the "command center."

High tech, with video screens at both ends, and work-stations along the conference table where people could plug in their laptops. This room, and indeed the whole building, was networked to FBI headquarters up in DC.

It had been an exciting time putting the SRT together. Those were heady days. But the Washington, DC environment - the back scratching, the back stabbing, the leaks, the gossip, and the just plain horrible human beings running around in positions of authority - had long ago punctured his enthusiasm.

Don remembered looking at a guy like Mark Swann in the early days, and thinking *whiz kid, a maverick in his own way, just like me.* Now he looked at Swann, with his ponytail and his weird yellow sunglasses, and his checkerboard Chuck Taylor sneakers, his insane personal office with wires snaking everywhere and equipment piled on top of equipment... and he didn't know what to think.

The guy was not military issue, that much was sure. If Swann could do just one thing, and that was track down and eradicate the leaks coming out of this place, it would go a long way toward restoring Don's faith. It would restore his faith in Swann, yes, but also in the larger government. Don was becoming paranoid that the whole thing was out of Swann's hands, and Big Brother was listening to every word he said.

And who were the people who comprised Big Brother, and made it run? Some of them, for certain, were filthy, dirty degenerates. The kind of people who were friends with Darwin King, and then turned around and killed Darwin King. They were weak links in the chain. Don had spent most of his adult life out in the world, fighting America's wars, only to come home and discover that his towering

Uncle Sam had feet of clay. The whole thing could come tumbling down at any moment.

He sighed heavily. Maybe he was getting old. Maybe his perspective was bleak because he was tired. Maybe he just needed to go home and go to bed. A little sleep did wonders sometimes.

Stone's voice came over the black octopus speaker phone device sitting on the conference table. He sounded tinny and far away. There was a hum of sound behind him, like voices, and maybe machinery of some kind.

"We're in a police station in Tangier. They brought us here to question us, I imagine. But they must know we didn't kill the kid, and they haven't brought us anyone that speaks more than three words of English."

"What is that noise in the background? Can you turn it down? Or go somewhere else where we don't have to hear it?"

"It's an old Coke machine. Looks like from your time, Don. It's about four feet away from us. It hums. It's loud. Every now and then, someone comes and buys a can of soda. It gets louder when the cans come barreling out of there. It's not even Coke that they're selling. The machine says Coke. The cans are orange with Arabic writing on them. I'd move away from the whole mess, but I'm handcuffed to a desk at this moment."

Don looked up and Trudy Wellington came walking into the room with a laptop under her arm. She was wearing a white dress shirt and jeans. Her funny red glasses that obscured her face were back on. Her hair was tied up and tousled a bit.

"Here she is," Swann half said, half sang. "Miss America."

Don shook his head. "Thanks for honoring us with your presence, Wellington."

"Sorry I'm late," she said as she slid into a seat. "I was in the ladies' room."

"Stone?" Don said.

"Yeah," came the tinny voice. "We're still here."

"What do you have?"

"Well, Berrada is dead, as I indicated. He was stabbed in an alleyway. We were chasing him, but we didn't see who did it. They got him before we arrived. The kid was a jackrabbit. He was about to give us the slip. But we talked to him before he died. This time, he was willing to talk, kind of his last testimonial, but we have no idea if what he said was true."

"What did he say?"

111

"The bullet train between Paris and London that was hijacked this morning? The Channel Tunnel train?"

"Go ahead," Don said.

"Berrada claimed that Richard Sebastian-Vilar is on board. According to Berrada, the whole point of kidnapping him was to put him on the train. Now, he didn't say that when we were in Berlin, so it's not out of the question that he came upon that information later, after the Germans sent him home."

"It's also possible that he made it up," Ed Newsam said.

Don didn't say a word. He looked around the room. Everyone was staring at the black phone device.

There was no reason to ask why the hijackers would do that. It made perfect sense. If they were hijacking a train anyway, how much better would it be to have a high value prisoner on board the train with the regular passengers?

A lot better, that was how much. And yet, as far as Don knew, they hadn't announced it.

"Also, they infiltrated the train company. Apparently, they've been sneaking C4 aboard that train for months."

It was silent in the room.

"Berrada was a demolitions expert, as we know. The train is a rolling bomb. They're going to bring down the tunnel on top of themselves, and on top of whoever else is on board."

The silence went on and on. For once, Don was at a loss for words. Maybe he was tired. He couldn't think of a single thing to say.

"Don," Stone said. "Any chance you can pull some diplomatic strings and get us out of this police station? We're no good to anyone chained to a couple of desks."

CHAPTER EIGHTEEN

11:01 am Central European Summer Time (5:01 am Eastern Daylight Time)
Eurostar Paris to London High Speed Train
Approaching the mouth of the Channel Tunnel
Coquelles, France

This was the appointed hour. It was time to show the world they meant business.

"Let's go," Yasser al-Fallujah said in Arabic. "Quickly. Let's go."

The man was dressed in light gray business clothes, as though he was a Westerner, or a traitorous Arab. The clothes fit him well. He had removed his jacket, but he still wore the vest and the slacks. His shoes were black leather.

Yasser was the name given to him at birth. He had chosen the *nom de guerre* al-Fallujah to remind himself of the crimes of the Americans and other western countries in the city of Fallujah, Iraq. Their savagery would be remembered and never forgotten. It would be avenged seven times, if Allah willed it.

And Yasser, faithful servant, would carry out the vengeance, should Allah look with favor upon him. He was the leader of the hijackers. Perhaps the only one senior to him was Francois, who was driving the train. Francois was a dauntless, skilled, and fearless soldier of Allah, who had prepared himself with utmost sincerity these past months, and who had carried out his tasks this morning perfectly and without hesitation. But even Francois was subject to follow Yasser's orders.

Only one could be in charge. And that one marched back through the train cars, seized passports in one hand, his pistol in the other. Two brothers, young jihadis, trailed behind him. The complete confidence Yasser had in Francois, his abilities and his determination, was matched by his uncertainty in some of the others on this mission. Young, inexperienced, possibly afraid of death. How could a true believer be afraid of death? If the sacrifice was pure, and Allah Himself would wrap His loving arms around them and lead them through the gates to Paradise, what could they possibly fear?

113

Yasser had no idea. But when he looked at them, he saw fear in their eyes.

"Don't worry," he said to the young men trailing him. "Purify your hearts and Allah will accept your sacrifice. You will look upon his face this very day, God willing."

"Allahu akbar," one of the young men said. "God is great."

"Yes," Yasser said.

They passed through a door into a coach cabin. One of their men, Basim, was here guarding the doorway. He seemed okay. His courage was not wavering. He nodded to Yasser as he entered.

"It's time," Yasser said.

"Very good."

"The first one is here. In this car."

Basim nodded. "Yes. Seven rows down, on the right. I marked him, and I have been watching to make sure he didn't try to hide."

Yasser scanned the rows. He saw the man. He was a young man, prematurely balding, wearing a dress uniform of the French Army. His insignia suggested he was a corporal. He was wearing a ribbon on his chest, blue and red vertical stripes, a medal hanging from the bottom.

Yasser mused that it was probably during one of the recent NATO or United Nations misadventures. Or maybe the man had waded into the Calais Jungle refugee camp here at the end of the tunnel and beaten the hopeless inhabitants with a truncheon. The French would probably label that as combat.

The man was not wearing the beret typical of French troops. His uniform was ill-fitting, baggy and with creases, which to Yasser's mind was perfect for the French military. They had lost in embarrassing fashion to the Germans in World War Two, only to turn around and carry out atrocities in Vietnam in the 1950s and Algeria in the 1950s and early 1960s, only to lose in embarrassing fashion once again. Yasser would be ashamed to wear such a uniform, as this man should be.

Yasser pointed at the man and snapped his fingers twice.

"You," he said in French. Yasser spoke French and English well and had enough phrases in Spanish and Portuguese to be understood. "Please come here."

The young man's eyes went wide. He pointed at himself. The passengers in the seats around him looked upon him in something close to horror. Everyone knew what was happening here. Even if they hid the knowledge from themselves, somewhere deep within them they knew.

114

"Yes, you. Soldier. Come, please. I have a task for you. It will only take a moment. You're able-bodied, yes? Of course you are. You can lift heavy items? Please come with me."

The man rose from his seat. He seemed timid. Some combat veteran. Clearly not a true believer in whatever god he professed to worship.

Yasser gestured with his hand, come ahead.

"Yes, please. Come on. There is nothing to fear."

Now on his feet, the man moved with a little more confidence. He was a thin man, swimming in his uniform, perhaps a few inches taller than Yasser. He wore black boots, polished and shiny.

He was not armed. This had been determined in an earlier pass through, when they had taken the passports, and the phones, and the beepers, and the various devices the passengers carried with them. A treasure trove of electronic wizardry had been seized.

There were to be no communications between passengers and the outside world. Also, they had searched for weapons. This man, this soldier, was one of a handful of people on the train with guns in their luggage. He had surrendered his unloaded service revolver immediately upon being questioned.

Innocent lamb, willingly led to slaughter.

The man reached them. Perhaps he was a good-looking young man, despite the early loss of his hair. He had piercing, intelligent eyes.

"I'm no threat to you," he said.

Yasser held the man's medal between his fingers for a moment. There was a gold bar across the ribbon. The word etched on the bar was *Haiti*. So the man had been stationed in Haiti at some point, as France guided its former slave colony ever further into catastrophe.

Yasser nodded. "I know that. I'm not concerned."

"I have a wife and young son."

"Are you anxious?" Yasser said. "I assure you there is nothing to be worried about. Please come with us."

He pressed the button to open the door between cars. He presented the soldier with a sweep of his arm and an open arm gesture, as if to say, "Right this way."

The man stepped out into the foyer between train cars. There was a door to the outside here. The train was moving slowly, perhaps a few kilometers per hour. Francois, true to form, was doing exactly as instructed. He was operating exactly according to plan.

Yasser gestured at the young jihadi standing there. "Get the door."

The young man had a tool that would manually unlock the door to the outside. It was a sort of wrench, the end of which went into a slot. Several turns of the wrench would engage the manual override of the mechanism that locked the door while the train was in motion.

Yasser supposed Francois could open the door from the cockpit, but he did not want to trouble Francois except when necessary. It wasn't necessary at the moment.

The young jihadi opened the door to the outside by pulling it. It slid along a track, most of the door disappearing into a slot in the wall.

The soldier stood at the threshold. He stared at the track bed, moving past them at the pace of a snail. Beyond the gravel track bed, there were a few sickly trees and concrete infrastructure. They were near the tunnel now. The countryside was gone.

"Am I to jump?" the soldier said.

He said it in a hopeful tone. It was several feet to the ground, but a young man such as himself could make the distance easily. Perhaps he would sprain an ankle, perhaps not. Apparently, he imagined that Yasser did see him as a threat and wanted him off the train. Hijackers wouldn't want members of the great French military on the train with them. They could never rest for fear the man would lead a revolt.

The first part of that imagined scenario was false. Yasser didn't see the man as a threat. The second part was true. He wanted the soldier off the train.

He wanted him off because the uniform was a symbol of France, and French colonialism, and Yasser wanted the world to see it. He also wanted the decision makers in the western countries to witness his resolve.

To Yasser, the Frenchman was going to die anyway; they all were, so he might as well do it now.

"No," Yasser said. "You don't need to jump."

He lifted the pistol in his hand, pointed it at the back of the man's head, and without hesitating, he pulled the trigger.

BANG!

A small spray of blood went out through the man's forehead. His legs went out from under him, and he collapsed bonelessly forward and down. Yasser gave him a push with his foot, and the man tumbled out the door and onto the track bed. His body landed at an uncomfortable angle, arms and legs askew.

"There," Yasser told the world. "There's your France."

He stepped quickly back, out of the line of sight of any snipers that might be lurking outside. He looked at the young jihadi.

116

"Close it."

The sound of the gun had been loud. Yasser was sure the other passengers in the two nearby cars had heard it. The ones on the north side of the train would look out the windows and see the Frenchman there. Word would travel and would have a chilling effect on the passengers.

Yasser looked down at the next passport in his hand. This one was an American, a man from New York City named Leonard Klinefelter. He was 68 years old and confined to a wheelchair. He was sitting in an area for those with physical disabilities two cars back from here, where their wheelchairs could be secured to the floor.

Yasser took a deep breath and smiled.

Klinefelter was a Jew. Yasser was sure of it.

The old man was going to make quite an impression on world opinion. His corpse was going onto the tracks, wheelchair and all.

CHAPTER NINETEEN

11:15 am Central European Summer Time (5:15 am Eastern Daylight Time)
The Skies above Central Spain

The six-seat Lear jet flew north across the morning sky.

Ed was up front, sprawled out across the seats, sleeping. He was the smart one. It seemed like he really was out. He was on his back, and his chest rose and fell slowly. The pills he had taken must have worn off. Exhaustion would do that sometimes.

Luke had fallen into a doze soon after takeoff, then had been awakened by midair turbulence. It seemed he must have been asleep for less than a half hour. He had dreamed something, but he couldn't remember what.

A few images, or fragments of images, remained. Becca's face screaming. An explosion. Blood splashed across a stone tile surface. A crowd of people standing on a street, staring at him. He couldn't remember the rest, and that was good.

What was bad was he felt like he hadn't gotten any rest at all - none since he had left Austria long hours ago. He'd been awake, more or less, for 24 hours straight at this point. He'd spent yesterday sight-seeing in Salzburg, the evening having dinner and drinks, then the night and next morning flying across Europe to North Africa, raiding a squatters' den of radical Muslims, then chasing a kid through a warren of alleyways, and watching him die.

Luke was tired.

He sat in the back of the long narrow cabin, staring out at the bright sky. His open window shade was the only source of light in the airplane. Far below the airplane, and below some skittering clouds, a red and orange plain passed. Far up ahead, there appeared to be mountains and some lowering thunderclouds.

A new series of images flitted through his mind. Becca as a young woman, in a long spring dress with a sunhat, laughing, not a care in the world. He could see her but didn't remember the exact occasion.

There must have been a hundred occasions like that one. Before Gunner came. Before the upheavals of recent years.

He pictured a collapsed stone pillar at a very old mosque in Lebanon. Kevin Murphy was there, underneath it, after a firefight. The column was thick and heavy, and somehow Murphy was beneath it. He seemed to be embedded in the floor. His face was there, and his left arm stuck out. He still had his Uzi in his hand.

He was talking, and he seemed fine. But a suicide bomber driving a truck bomb was coming. The mosque was going to be a firestorm, moments from now.

Suddenly, Murphy started making a squirming, snakelike movement. He was undulating madly, violently. Luke watched him in a sort of dream. He whipsawed, faster and faster.

Swann, screaming in Luke's ear through the satellite phone:

"GET OUT! STONE!"

"Go!" Murphy said. "Listen to the man!" He didn't even look at Luke. He was doing some sort of crazy desperate dance under there, rhythmic, insane.

"STONE!"

Luke turned and ran for the front doors.

Outside, the headlights of the truck were approaching.

Luke was forced to run toward them. He blew through the doors, leapt down the steps and ran for the chopper. He turned and trained his gun on the van as he ran.

"Dud-duh-duh-duh-duh!"

The windshield shattered. The driver's side window shattered.

A line of explosions rained down from the sky. Drone strike.

The earth shook. The truck was on fire, still hurtling toward the mosque. The driver was on fire. The truck rammed the mosque and blew up, the explosion hurtling orange and red into the night sky.

Luke shook his head to clear it. Through some miracle, Murphy had survived that battle, though Luke never understood how. Weeks later, Murphy had turned up in the middle of a firefight on the streets of Mogadishu, helping Luke and Ed protect the President. Luke could see Air Force One burning on the ground down the block, while in the near ground, Murphy drank an orange soda and joked about Luke's idea of sleeping at the White House one day.

Murphy. Gone now, Luke had no idea where. He had gotten a cryptic postcard from Murphy months ago, sent from Cape Town, South Africa. That was the last he'd heard from him. Luke had figured Murphy would turn up again at some point, but it hadn't happened.

Murphy could be alive. He could have already struck it rich, working for criminal gangs smuggling diamonds out of the Congo. He could be in a dank prison somewhere. Or he could be dead. Luke was beginning to think he would never find out.

Memories were a hard thing for Luke. They always seemed to take strange, unpleasant turns. There were too many of them, for one thing, and too many of them were bad. Even the good ones were bittersweet in some way.

Luke glanced out his window again. Just a bright day in a small airplane, high above the clouds. They could be anywhere, and he could be anyone, going wherever.

He checked his watch. He didn't even know what good it did. The hijacking had already happened. Riders on the train were already dead. By the time this plane landed, it could already have turned into a bloodbath. If what Berrada said was true, they could have blown up the tunnel, or killed the judge. Or both.

Watching the clock gave him the sense of events surging out ahead - a familiar feeling, but one of his least favorite aspects of the job. It was a race against time. It was *always* a race against time, and they were always behind.

On the seat next to him, there was a large manila envelope. It was fat with files stuffed inside. Trudy Wellington had faxed the files to a CIA station in Tangier, then they were couriered to Luke and Ed before they left the country. There was nothing classified in them - just information that anyone could have.

After all, Luke and Ed were not part of the rescue operation for the train hijacking. They weren't even officially part of the operation for the rescue of the Supreme Court judge. They had been zooming around since last night, following a hunch that Don Morris had, which that was wherever Richard Sebastian-Vilar's fancy watch went, he was likely to be there too. Not an unreasonable hunch, but possibly an unreasonable approach to pursue the hunch without telling anyone else.

Don was playing a dangerous Washington, DC, chess game. Luke didn't understand it, and he trusted Don. Who but Don Morris could get an idea like the Special Response Team off the ground in the first place? And despite resistance and pushback from above, and an ongoing problem with either internal or external spies, by hook or by crook Don was managing to keep it going. At what cost, though?

Luke sighed. He undid the string on the envelope, ripped open the top, and dumped the contents out on the seat next to him. Photographs of Richard Sebastian-Vilar, in his Supreme Court gown, and also in civilian clothes. A short biography of him.

Not super interesting. If they found him, they found him. All they needed to know was what he looked like. They weren't going to interview him for a job. If he had any military or emergency services training, that might be good to know, but it was clear that he didn't have any.

There was a little bit here about the ongoing travel ban. Protests had taken place at the Atlanta airport and had turned into a riot. Right-wing and left-wing protestors were trading punches and tear gas canisters in Portland and Seattle. Arizona had joined the ban - Phoenix was a major airport hub. Utah and Idaho had both joined.

Michigan's governor and attorney general had joined the lawsuit against the ban, and a self-styled "militia" was now camped out in protest on the steps of the statehouse there. Trudy had kindly included a few photographs of them, about 30 overweight asthmatics in camo gear, with AR-15s slung over their chests. Ed and Luke could take down the whole lot of them in about eight minutes.

Luke had his own opinions about things like this, which he tended to keep to himself. America was a nation of immigrants, was it not? At the same time, it was a nation of laws. We needed immigrants. He had served with quite a few in the military. As a general rule, they made the country a better, more dynamic place. They wanted to be in the United States and were willing to make sacrifices to do so.

At the same time, we also needed them to be vetted as they came in. We needed to know who they were, what they were about, and where they were coming from. Was all of that really so hard to implement? The different sides in arguments like this tended to get so dug into their positions, that they rendered themselves ridiculous.

Luke looked at the other stuff. This was better. Specs of the Channel Tunnel and the train itself. Aerial photographs. Photographs from inside the tunnel. Maps of ventilation and firefighting systems. It was a lot to absorb.

It turned out there wasn't one tunnel; there were three. There was a southbound tunnel that left London on the south side, a northbound tunnel that headed toward London on the north side, and a service tunnel in between the two. Small firefighting and service trucks operated in the service tunnel.

There were doorways between the train tunnels and the service tunnel at intervals of every 350 meters or so. The doorways were pressure locked. There were miles of smaller ventilation tunnels that ran both above and below the tunnels, entire spiderweb networks of them. Air vents were mounted above and below the trains. Fresh air was pumped in from stations at either end of the tunnel. Air already in the tunnels was sucked into exit vents and pumped out to the surface. It was an incredibly elaborate setup.

He glanced at specs of the trains themselves. They were super-fast, super modern, the latest in ground-based aerodynamics. Part of the need for the exit vents came from the sheer speed of the trains themselves, which knifed through the tunnel at about 100 miles per hour and displaced a lot of air. Without air being pumped out, the pressure inside the tunnel, and on the train itself, would become untenable.

Outside the tunnel, the trains tended to top out at about 200 miles per hour in the French countryside, and 140 miles per hour when they crossed into England, which was more densely developed. The theoretical top speed of the trains was approaching 300 miles per hour. Prototypes had reached these speeds during safety testing.

Luke didn't know what any of this could mean for attempting a rescue. He would have to talk to Trudy and Swann about it, if it ever came to that. But a train that could travel that fast, and which was already at the mouth of the tunnel when Ed and Luke got on this plane, could be in London less than 45 minutes from now.

Whatever was going to happen probably already had, or was happening right this minute, and without Ed Newsam and Luke Stone.

CHAPTER TWENTY

11:45 am Central European Summer Time (5:45 am Eastern Daylight Time)
Eurostar Paris to London High Speed Train
Near the mouth of the Channel Tunnel
Coquelles, France

"Mike, we need to talk," Benjy Morgan said.

His name wasn't Benjy Morgan, any more than it was Simon Higginbotham, or Stephen Ross, or any of a dozen more aliases he'd been living under for years. Benjy Morgan was a role that he played, and he was good at it. He was so good at it in fact, that for all intents and purposes he might as well be Benjy Morgan.

But not anymore.

The train was stopped again. One of the hijackers was up at the front of this car. He was standing at the doorway to the next car, peering through the window from time to time, looking to see where his partner was.

The guy was young. He was clean shaven. His roving eyes told Benjy he was uncertain at best, possibly even afraid. He had a gun in his right hand, a matte black Glock. He had a knife in his left hand.

He also looked like he was getting tired. This thing had been going on for five hours now. The guy could be running out of gas.

Like most of the hijackers, he had apparently come on board dressed in a suit, like a young businessman headed to London for work. He had removed his suit coat and was down to a dress-shirt, vest, and slacks. He was not wearing a bulletproof vest or any kind of body armor. He didn't seem to have a suicide vest anywhere nearby.

He was taking orders from his partner, who had temporarily moved up the train. He looked a little bit lost when he was by himself. They spoke English and French to the passengers, but between themselves, they spoke the Darija dialect of Arabic that Benjy associated with Morocco.

Something needed to be done about these guys. Benjy had been sitting here, running calculations through his head. There were two hijackers visible to him. There were probably several more in other parts of the train. Ten, twelve, maybe twenty. How many men with small arms would it take to control a train, and a population of passengers, this size?

They had already killed, as far as he knew, three or four or five people. Innocent people. Murdered and thrown out onto the tracks like so much trash for the world to see. They would kill more. Of course they would. They might kill everyone on the train.

Benjy could only see the people in his train car. Most were in shock. The murdered ones were for their benefit as much as anyone's. The train had rolled very slowly past the corpses at the side of the tracks. An old couple, one of whom had apparently been in a wheelchair. That burned Benjy. It burned him with fire.

His own grandparents were that age. It wouldn't stand.

So these were his calculations. Yes, most passengers were normal people, and they were in shock. They were mostly helpless, or somewhere on the fence between helpless and... helpful, let's say.

But there would be others. People like Benjy himself, and Mike here sitting next to him. People who were not in shock. People with fighting skills.

Benjy and Mike could take this train car back, maybe. The hijackers had taken cell phones, beepers, Blackberries, whatever, at the very beginning. They had come through with a lot of energy. It was early morning then, and most of the passengers were half asleep. Benjy had been no exception.

The hijackers had smashed any laptop computers that were visible. There were no communications with the outside world possible. This made it difficult for Benjy. His bosses would know more about what was going on than he did. Maybe, if he was in contact with them, they would tell him to stand down and just wait it out.

Even so: that old couple.

And he wasn't in contact with anyone. He would have to make his own decisions. He'd been waiting long enough. Too long. He tended to have a bias toward action.

"So talk," Mike said. "Give me something to take my mind off our current predicament."

Benjy looked at Mike. Mike was in the aisle seat. He was a big kid, long hair, scruffy beard, late 20s, an American. He had a background story he had given Benjy, something about growing up in the near suburbs of Detroit, being a high school football star, hurt his knee. Not the football that everyone on Earth played, but American football, the baffling game where they dressed in suits of armor and crashed into each other at high speeds. Mike's knee injury meant he lost his chance at a scholarship to university, so he lit out for the territories instead.

Maybe some of it was true. Maybe none of it was true. What Benjy knew for sure about Mike was the kid was calm in tight spots. Like now, for example. His eyes were open, he was alert and watching for possibilities, but he was not afraid.

The hijackers had passed Mike and Benjy, taken their telephones, but evidently decided they were not much of a threat. A couple of backpacker types, hiking boots, cargo pants, t-shirts - scruffy, with unkempt hair and three-day growth of beards.

Who were they really, though? For the past six months, they'd been successfully running bricks of hash out of the Rif Mountains of northern Morocco, down to the docks in Tangier and Ceuta, and across to mainland Spain. They'd put together a team of mules and had just started making real money. But the word was out that a crackdown was coming, so they had decided it was a good time to head to London and lay low for a bit. Their networks were still in place, and it would be a relatively simple matter to get them going again, say three weeks or a month from now.

They were riding in coach and had come on unshowered and ragged like *Lonely Planet* travelers. This was to disguise the fact that they were carrying more than 100,000 Euros in cash and diamonds in their luggage.

Mike looked at Benjy. "I'm all ears, man."

"I'm not who you think I am," Benjy said.

Mike shrugged. "Not surprising. I'm not, either. In this line of work, it hardly makes sense to confess everything, does it?"

"But I'm really not," Benjy said.

Now Mike looked at him with hard eyes. "What is this? Some big reveal because you think we're about to die? Like, you're gay or something? I don't care. And I think you should save it for another time. I've been in tighter spots than this. I think we're going to walk away without a scratch."

Benjy shook his head. "I don't think so."

He had done this before, and he always felt bad about it. It was his job, but it always seemed like a betrayal. He would never forget the first one, a Greek guy named Theodor. They had run heroin together from Afghanistan into the Midlands. The look on Theodor's face when they busted him, and he finally put two and two together. Theo just couldn't believe it. They were friends. He didn't believe it even after he was cuffed, and they were taking him away.

He turned back, and said, "Call me. We must talk. I can't believe what you're doing to me."

Okay, that one was bad. This wouldn't be nearly as bad.

Probably not.

"I'm a cop," he said.

Now Mike smiled. His shoulders slumped. "A cop? You? Come on."

Benjy shrugged. "Not like you imagine. I was Special Air Service. They recruited me out of there. I've been doing drug trafficking interdiction for Interpol for the past five years. But technically, I work for the Secret Service."

Mike was staring at him.

"Yes. Like James Bond."

Mike shook his head and laughed. It occurred to Benjy, not for the first time, that Mike had a pretty good size to him. His neck was thick. His shoulders were wide, and his chest was broad. His legs were powerful. He covered it up by dressing like a wanderer, but he could really have been an American football player.

He was good in a brawl. Benjy had seen it in the British and Irish pubs of southern Spain and Portugal. Mike had no problem throwing his weight around. He could take a punch and deliver one.

"You have to be kidding me, man. Why? I can't believe you did this to me."

"I haven't done anything to you."

"You set me up," Mike said. "What were you going to do? Have them arrest me straight off the train?"

That wasn't the plan at all - it was too early. This was a long game, and Mike was only a bit player in it, but he didn't need to know that.

"I need your help."

"With what?"

Benjy gestured with his head. "I'm going to take the train back."

Mike shook his head. "Good luck with that. These guys have guns."

"Look," Benjy said. "They've already killed hostages."

"I know."

"They'll kill more if we don't do anything. I've seen this type of thing before. Once they kill a few, it gets their blood up. The ice is broken. Each one is easier than the one before. We have to put a stop

126

to it before it goes out of control. It isn't right to allow it to go on if we can end it."

Mike looked away across the aisle. "We don't have any weapons."

Benjy raised his hands. He balled them into fists. They were smaller than Mike's fists, but he was better with his hands than Mike was. After all, he had been trained by his government to use them.

"Next you're going to tell me your hands are registered as lethal weapons."

Benjy grunted. He almost smiled. "That's a fairy tale. But yes, I'm trained for hand-to-hand combat. You're not bad yourself. I've seen you knock a few blokes out before."

Mike ran a hand through his dirty hair. He made a face. He sighed. It was almost a groan.

"Easy, mate. Don't make a spectacle of yourself. The last thing you want is our friend's attention."

Mike nodded. "Okay. You're right. You have a plan of some kind?"

Benjy shrugged. "Not much of one. We rush our man there now that he's alone. If we reach him, we get his gun and knife. Then we're armed. You follow my lead. We waylay his partner when the man comes back. Then we're doubly armed. We fight our way up through the train. Maybe someone will join us. There have to be others like us on here somewhere. In the end, if we make it, when this is over, we get off the train and go our separate ways. Maybe we're heroes, maybe we aren't. But you walk away a free man. I never met you before today."

Mike was staring at him.

"You ever kill anybody before?" Benjy said.

Mike scowled. He shook his head. "Man, I'm not telling you anything. After all this? Forget it."

Benjy nodded. And a smile came to his lips. It was genuine. Soon it took over his whole face. "Okay. Either way, it was a lot of fun, mate. A time to remember."

Now Mike smiled in turn. "Yeah. It was."

"You ready?"

Mike took a deep breath and sighed. "As ready as I'm ever going to be."

Up ahead, at the front of the car, the young hijacker was still standing by himself. He peered through the window of the door again.

Benjy guessed it was about 15 meters from here to the hijacker. They would have to move very, very fast. Mike would be in the lead. Once they were standing, it might take them five seconds to reach the door. Five seconds was more than enough for the hijacker to squeeze off a couple of shots.

But two big men would be running at him. Perhaps he would panic and miss. Perhaps he wouldn't get a shot off at all. Perhaps he would try to escape. Perhaps he would shoot them both dead before they reached him. There were a lot of possibilities here, and a lot of variables at play.

"Don't hesitate," Benjy said. "Once you commit, you're committed all the way. Use your size and speed and your strength. Intimidate him. When we reach him, show him no mercy. He won't show us any."

Mike nodded. His eyes were very hard now, very determined. That was a good sign. "Okay," he said. "I'm ready."

Benjy nodded. "Then let's roll."

* * *

Mike went first.

He was in the aisle seat, so it made no sense to stand aside, wait and then let Benjy go. Anyway, he was bigger and faster than Benjy.

He simply slipped out of the seat and into the aisle, got low and ran. The high school football thing was true - not the injury part, but all the rest. He was a good high school level linebacker on defense, tight end on offense. He could hit hard.

He picked up speed as he went. His arms and legs pumped. He felt the acceleration. It felt good. He was going to cream that guy.

He had no idea if Benjy was behind him or not. Wouldn't it be funny if Benjy decided to stay in his seat?

For a moment, the hijacker didn't realize he was coming. The guy was there, a young, clean-shaven guy, staring right at Mike, but not seeing him. He couldn't believe it. His mind couldn't absorb it. It was system overload.

Then a woman, some passenger, screamed, and the hijacker keyed in. His eyes went WIDE. This bull, this beast, was bearing down on him, coming full bore.

He had his gun. He whipped it around. Mike saw the barrel of it looming there, like a cave. It wasn't the first time.

He took another step. He seemed to move in slow motion now.

The man shouted something at him. He was barely more than a kid. He was very skinny compared to Mike.

Mike saw a flash of light, like a small flame, appear from the muzzle of the gun. He dove at the same instant.

128

People shouted and screamed, all in slow motion, as he flew through the air. The gun fired again, bucking in the guy's hand.

Mike hit him waist high. He drove the guy backwards into the door. They both crashed into it, hitting HARD. The impact went through the guy's upper body, like a wave. Then they were on the floor, Mike on top.

He reared back and punched the guy in the face. BOOM! As hard as he could. Blood appeared there. He reared back and did it again. The kid held up his hands, trying to block Mike's punches. It was no good.

Mike hit him again.

Where was the gun?

BOOOM! Mike hit him again. He would punch this guy's head through the floor. He would...

A hand touched him on the shoulder. He stopped. That was all it took. He turned and Benjy was there. His face was pained. He had the gun in his right hand. His left hand was on his shirt, an area just above his left pectoral muscle, near his shoulder. Blood was coming out of there. It was a lot of blood.

"I have the gun," Benjy said.

"I know. Are you hit?"

Benjy nodded. "Yeah."

"Jesus, Benjy."

Mike looked down at himself. There was no blood. He wasn't hit anywhere. He didn't feel any pain. The terrorist had fired the gun and missed him entirely. And somehow hit Benjy. Ah, no.

Benjy gazed down at the guy on the ground. He pointed the gun. The guy's eyes were crazy wide, rolling like a madman. His hands were up.

"No. No."

BANG.

Benjy shot him in the face. The sound was loud. Instantly, Mike's ears were ringing.

The guy bucked with the force of the shot. A hole appeared in his forehead, just above and between his eyes. Blood started to pool behind his head. His eyes were dull and staring.

"One down," Benjy said.

Mike looked at him again. There was blood all over Benjy's shirt. His face began to look flat, and vacant.

Mike climbed off the dead hijacker. He stood and turned back to the passengers.

"Is there a doctor in the house?" he said. "A doctor, a nurse, any medical person?"

Wide eyes stared at Mike from both sides of the aisle. A few people shook their heads. Next to Mike, Benjy suddenly sat on the ground. Mike kneeled next to him. There was blood everywhere.

"We did it, man," he said. "We took over the train car."

Benjy gritted his teeth. "It's good. But I feel a bit woozy, mate."

* * *

"Yasser!" the voice squawked over his radio. "Come quickly!"

The voice sounded panicked, which was not a good sign. Yasser didn't like these young men to use the handheld radios. The signal was likely being intercepted by the police and military outside the train, and they would use the slightest hesitancy, the slightest confusion or fear, to gain an advantage.

"Come where?" he said into the handset. "Come where?"

"Car 5. We are in Car 5."

"Okay, don't say another word. We are returning."

As he was about to ring off, the sound of gunshots came over the radio. There were shouts of the believers and screams and moans from passengers. Something was happening.

Yasser had been headed up to the first car in Business Class to speak with the American judge. His men had told him that the man was still sleeping. The drugs he had been given to quiet him before they boarded the train were quite powerful, but usually not this powerful. Yasser was going to see for himself, shake the man from his slumber, but now it would have to wait.

"Come on," he said to the young man with him.

The man was tall with a two-day growth of beard. He was dressed casually, in a blue, open-throated shirt. and tight. brown slacks. He had a gold chain around his neck, and a gold watch loose around his wrist. Yasser couldn't say what his cover story had been. Was he supposed to be going to a disco?

"What's your name?"

"Najem."

"Najem, follow me."

"What is it?" Najem said. His eyes were large now. "What's happening?"

Yasser did not know these men. Were they real believers? Were they ready to forsake the life of this world? They had come on this

130

mission, so they must have been willing to die. And the Moroccans, who set this up and had set up successful missions before, certainly knew their own.

Even so, wide eyes indicated fear to Yasser. What was there to be afraid of? Nothing. The gates of Paradise awaited.

"Something is wrong," Yasser said. "So we will go and fix it."

He stalked back through a passenger car, the people wide-eyed and staring in their seats. They'd heard the gunshots, that seemed clear. It was something they wanted no part of. The believer minding this car, another young one, this time from Tunisia, seemed skittish. He looked to Yasser for direction.

"Courage, my brother," Yasser said as he passed. "Allah is with us." For a moment, he changed the language he was speaking to English, and spoke in a loud voice, so the passengers would overhear. "If anyone acts against you, kill them."

The young man nodded. Instantly, his face changed. He'd experienced a moment of doubt, but Yasser's strength became his strength, and Yasser's faith became his faith. Yasser had seen this countless times in the heat of battle. One strong man could loan his courage to those around him, without losing any himself.

Up ahead, the guns were still firing. The sounds were muffled by the walls and doorways between here and there.

Yasser passed through another doorway, and another foyer. He stepped into the next train car. This. This was the problem. At the other end of the car, the window of the far door was shattered. Two believers were by that doorway. One was on the ground, sprawled out. The other was crouched, gun in hand.

BANG! BANG! BANG!

Someone was firing into this car from the next foyer.

"Hurry!" Yasser said to Najem. He broke into a run, up along the aisle, passengers staring at him as he came.

He clipped the head of a passenger with his thigh as he passed. The man's head was too far into the aisle. The man had been wearing black framed glasses, and the glasses went flying.

"Watch it! Stay in your seats!"

Yasser slowed as he approached the scene of the fighting. He crouched low, so whoever was out there could not see or get a shot at him. He glanced behind him. Najem was here. Good.

One of the believers was clearly dead. He lay at an odd angle, eyes open, in a spreading pool of blood. He was not moving. Yasser checked the man's pulse at his neck. Nothing. Gone.

131

The other believer, crouched against the door, looked to Yasser. His mouth hung open. "Is he…?"

Yasser shook his head.

"He's my brother," the believer said. "My youngest. I told him not to come."

"His sacrifice is complete," Yasser said. He had seen many younger brothers die during his time. "Allah will reward him."

The man nodded, but the agreement didn't reach his eyes.

"Our mother…"

Yasser raised his free hand. "We came here to die."

The man nodded again. "Okay."

"Are you wounded?" Yasser said. The man had blood all over him. It was impossible to tell if it was his own, or someone else's.

"I was shot in the arm. The bullet seems to have gone through."

Yasser nodded. He didn't ask the man if he was in pain. Of course he was, or soon would be. He didn't try to comfort him in his grief. There was no time for that, and there might never be time. Instead, he asked the most important question.

"What is going on here?"

The man nodded his head backward. "Two men in there. They attacked the brother standing guard. I don't know if they're police or soldiers, or what they are. They killed the brother and took his gun. One of them seems to be wounded or dead. The other attacked us here. My brother… my brother was dead before he knew what hit him."

A single tear rolled down the man's face. Then his eyes went wide at something behind Yasser. He pointed.

"Look! Wait!"

Then he stood, as if to fight.

BANG!

The second he stood, the man on the other side of the door shot through the window. A spray of blood went out from the believer's forehead, and he sank straight to the floor, mouth ajar again, eyes suddenly blank.

Yasser stayed low. He turned.

A passenger had crept up behind them. He was a black man, very dark, like an African. He wore a blue business suit, and he was perfectly bald. He was on top of Najem, battering his head in with a fire extinguisher.

Once. Twice. Three times.

Najem lay on his stomach, beyond any attempt at resistance. His head cracked apart and bled like a river.

Yasser raised his gun and...

BANG!

He shot the black man in the top of the head. The man collapsed on top of Najem. Someone in the passenger compartment, a woman, began to scream and did not stop. She was ranting. It was in a language Yasser didn't understand. Perhaps it was the black man's wife.

Yasser sighed. There was a pile of bodies back here now. Three of them were his own men. Apparently, there was another believer dead in the next car. That was four gone in one incident. They only came aboard with 12, and one of those was Francois, who had to drive the train. That meant Yasser was down to six fighters besides himself.

These numbers were not good. There were nearly 500 people on the passenger manifest.

He looked back at the doorway. Whoever was behind there had a strategy. He was not going to reveal himself. He would simply stay low and shoot anyone who appeared in the window. It had worked for him so far.

It was going to stop working now.

Yasser glanced at the nearby passengers. They were watching him. They were looking in horror at the bodies on the ground. Or perhaps they were looking with pleasure at the dead hijackers, and simply masking their emotions.

Somewhere, the woman was still shrieking.

Yasser's eyes fell on a young woman. She had brown hair and was very pretty. There was a small child, a baby, in her lap, dressed all in light blue. The Western-style makeup the young woman wore accentuated her features in a way that was an advertisement to men who were not the father of her child. This was immorality, of course, but there was no time to deal with that now. It would take a thousand years to undo the degeneracy of the Western world.

He pointed at her. "You," he said in French. "Come here."

She shook her head.

He gestured to her. "Come. It's okay. I will not hurt you."

Her whole body began to tremble. People began to shout at him, and at her. It was a Babel of voices and languages. Yasser could barely hear anything through the cacophony, except for the one word, loud, like a mantra.

"No! No! No!"

He pointed the gun at her.

"Come here. Bring your baby. Now, or I will kill you both."

The young woman rose on unsteady legs, and floated toward him, as if she were in a dream.

"No!" went the screaming mantra. "No! No!"

Yasser watched them, to see if there were any more heroes like the African man. So far there were not. Just shouters and onlookers, spectators at the arena.

The woman reached him, hugging the baby tightly to her chest. She was a petite woman, and it was a big baby, Yasser guessed a boy from the color it was wearing. The woman's eyes were squeezed nearly shut, and she was weeping now. She tried to hold the baby away from him.

"NO! NO! NO!"

Yasser didn't care about the baby. That's what they didn't understand. The baby was a prop in a stage play, and so was the woman. He seized the woman and spun her around toward the shattered doorway. He stood and crouched behind her his gun pressed to her head. With his free hand, he grabbed a big chunk of her hair.

"Nobody move, or I'll kill her!" he shouted in English.

He moved toward the window, the young woman in front of him. Now, the man in the foyer was in his line of sight. He was a young man with brown hair and a short beard. His hair was long, with a few strands tied into braids, and he wore the clothes of a drifter, a backpacking tourist. T-shirt, cargo pants, and boots.

He was on one knee, aiming his gun through the window.

They faced each other.

"English?" Yasser said.

"American."

Of course an American. What else would he be? He had wreaked havoc single-handedly, which raised another question. "Soldier? CIA?"

The man shook his head. "No."

That was good. Some of these so-called black operators were trained to shrug off death and disaster, and to keep fighting regardless of the loss of life. Yasser had seen it in the field before. You almost couldn't convince them to stop. There was no price they seemed unwilling to pay. But civilians?

"Drop the gun or I am going to shoot this woman, and this baby."

The man stared. His gun didn't waver.

"Drop it! I'm going to shoot them right now."

Yasser glanced behind him. The cacophony was ongoing, but no one was rushing him from behind.

This was the moment. The moment of truth.

"NOW!" he screamed. "I'm going to shoot her right now!"

He jabbed the woman in the head with the gun three times in rapid succession. "BANG!" he screamed. "BANG!"

The woman went nearly limp. He still had her by the hair. In a moment, he was going to have to hold her under the arms to keep her standing.

He jabbed her again. "BANG!"

On the other side of the window, the man dropped his gun. It made a solid CLUNK as it hit the metal floor of the foyer.

Yasser didn't hesitate. He shoved the woman and the baby aside and shot through the window.

BANG!

This time the sound was real, the crack of a pistol firing.

Across the way, the young man's head snapped back, and he sank to the floor.

Dead.

Yasser stood to his full height slowly, his middle-aged knees popping. He glanced around. Bodies all over the floor. It was carnage here.

He looked at the young woman. She stared up at him with wide, terrified eyes. Her whole body shook with silent weeping. Her baby was crying now too, it's face a grimace of baby unhappiness. The baby didn't know what was going on, but whatever it was, he knew he didn't like it.

Yasser waved the woman back toward her seat.

"Go. Go sit down. Take the baby. Comfort him."

CHAPTER TWENTY ONE

6:20 am Eastern Daylight Time (12:20 pm Central European Summer Time)
The Situation Room
The White House
Washington, DC

"I heard the number was three," a voice said.

"Three?" another said. They were making small talk.

"Three more bodies, dumped on the tracks."

David Halstram glanced at the talkers. They were two young guys in suits, interns or aides or assistants to someone, probably. They looked tired. They should. It was just after six in the morning.

They were new, and David didn't know them. He didn't care to know them. He was moving too fast to get to know all the new aides to people halfway up the ladder between somewhere and nowhere. It didn't matter.

They were all riding in the ultramodern elevator down to the Situation Room. It was crowded in here, maybe a dozen people. There was a smell. It wasn't a bad smell, necessarily. It was the smell of people who had been awake for a long time, who were wearing the same clothes they put on 24 hours ago, who had been drinking a lot of coffee, and who had probably stopped in the bathroom at some point and slathered on more cologne.

David had to key into what was happening right now; he knew that. There were present-tense crises spiraling out of control everywhere you looked. A train in Europe was hijacked by terrorists. A Supreme Court judge was missing, with a crucial vote on a poorly conceived and hastily-implemented travel ban coming up next week. There were riots and protests about that travel ban going on all over the country, and there was chaos at the airports.

The larger and more important the airport, the more chaotic it seemed to be - Atlanta, Charlotte, and Dallas-Fort Worth were all practically at a standstill. With major hubs out of commission, domestic air traffic had slowed to a crawl. There were currently

136

thousands of delayed and canceled flights, more being added all the time.

But it was hard to think about these things. He was badly distracted, jazzed from the second meeting he held privately with Susan Hopkins. She was the front runner, as far as he was concerned. She was the perfect Vice-Presidential candidate. If she was only a little older, and a man, she'd be the perfect Presidential candidate. To David's mind, Susan Hopkins was the future of America.

The elevator door opened, and David stepped with the group into the Situation Room. The crowd was pretty sparse. It was early, after all. David noticed right away that Clement Dixon wasn't here. That was a good sign. He was already telegraphing the transition to Thomas. It was subtle, but it was there.

David glanced around before taking his seat behind Thomas and to his left. General Richard Stark was ready to preside over the meeting. There were a few other dress greens from the Pentagon. The National Security Advisor. A couple of people from NSA and the CIA. There were aides and assistants lining the walls, though several seats were empty.

Don Morris, the head of the FBI Special Response Team, sat across and down the conference table from Thomas. He was an older man, very powerfully built, with a crew cut turning gray and white. He wore a blue dress shirt which hugged his chest. His sleeves were rolled up one quarter turn each. His blue eyes were hard, but they also looked tired.

"Dick, whenever you're ready, "Thomas said.

Richard Stark nodded. "Thank you, Mr. Vice President."

Behind him on the screen, an image of an empty railroad track with three corpses appeared. A second image appeared next to the first of the same three bodies from the opposite angle. This showed their proximity to the entrance of a train tunnel. They were very close to it.

The appearance of the images made a small burst of quiet chatter break out across the room. General Stark raised a hand to quiet it.

"As many of you already know, the hijackers dumped three more bodies onto the tracks just moments ago. They then proceeded to move the train into the Channel Tunnel. They went a few hundred meters into the tunnel and stopped."

He paused for a second, then began again.

"Intelligence reports indicate that a gun battle began on the train while the leader of the hijackers was talking on the radio to his men. Listening stations monitoring the radio transmissions overheard the shooting, and the leader quickly broke off all communications. The leader has since identified himself to us, and we will come to that in a minute. The thing to know for now is that he is a savvy operator with extensive combat and undercover operations experience. He was well aware that we were monitoring their internal communications."

"Do we have an ID on the victims?" Thomas Hayes said.

Stark shook his head. "We're working on that."

"Were any hijackers killed or wounded?"

"We believe so, but that number is unknown at the present moment. The hijackers have not dumped any bodies of their own people on the tracks. They are concealing the number of personnel they have, and the extent of their casualties. After a brief statement to us from their leader, they are now maintaining radio silence."

"And what was that statement?" Thomas said.

David liked it. Everyone in the room was looking to Thomas Hayes for leadership. Everyone was letting him ask the probing questions. Thomas was one of the few in the room who looked fresh and alert. There was a man in charge right now, and that man was Vice President Thomas Hayes.

"For one," Stark said, "he revealed his identity, or claimed to. He said he is Yasser al-Fallujah. He said he was revealing this information so that we, meaning France, Great Britain, and the United States would know who they were dealing with.

"Yasser Al-Fallujah is the *nom de guerre* of a man believed to be a 43-year-old Sunni from Saudi Arabia who has gone by many names over the years. It's believed that he left Saudi Arabia as a teenager in the late 1980s and went to Afghanistan to fight the Soviets. He was with thousands of other mujahideen joining the earliest incarnation of Al Qaeda. He is thought to have tangled with the Russians again, in Chechnya, during the 1990s and into the early 2000s.

"If it's the same man, he's believed to have fought the US during the invasion of and subsequent occupation of Iraq. He may have been involved in the bloody Battle of Fallujah two years ago. He also may be one of the masterminds of several market square suicide bombings in Shiite cities across Iraq."

"That's a lot of unknowns," Don Morris said.

Stark nodded. "Yes, it is. But if he is who he says he is, his presence confirms that this operation was sanctioned and possibly organized by Al Qaeda. Whoever he is, he issued a demand. The demand is to release a roster of over 3,200 men of Moroccan, Algerian, and Tunisian origin, currently being held in French and Spanish jails

138

and prisons. This list was separately telexed to European police and intelligence agencies from a machine located inside a building in the oldest part of the ancient city of Sanaa, Yemen. No western countries have a significant intelligence footprint there, and there was no identifier on the Telex machine, so we have no way of knowing who sent it.

"The men are to be transported to their home countries by airplane or ship, depending on where they're detained. The timeline is very quick. They want all prisoners released and on their way home by 6 pm London Time, today, less than seven hours from now.

"Intelligence agencies in Spain, France, Britain, as well as Interpol, and intelligence agencies in Morocco, Algeria, and Tunisia have begun scrambling to vet the list. Early indications are that the men the hijackers want released are common criminals held in detention for offenses ranging from murder and rape to theft and trespassing. They aren't Islamic radicals with ties to terrorist organizations. And the ones charged with minor crimes, who would have eventually been released, would have been deported anyway."

"It's very smart," Thomas Hayes said. "The terrorists, if the West agrees to their demands, will get criminals released unpunished, and then set them loose in their native countries. It's a clever move."

"Agreed," General Stark said. "I'd like to add that al-Fallujah also issued a list of... I wouldn't call them demands. They're more like instructions."

"What are they?" Thomas said.

"Well, he was angry, or acted like he was. He seems to believe that the passenger uprising was organized by some force outside the train. As far as we know, this isn't true. In any event, he seems to think a similar attack could be imminent. His instructions are short and to the point. I quote: Do not attempt to board the train. Do not attempt to enter the train tunnel. Do not block the forward path of the train.

"Any attempt to interfere with the train will lead to the complete destruction of the train, and the tunnel above it. It will also lead to the loss of 481 passengers and staff, in addition to those already lost."

There was quiet in the room. It went on for a long minute.

"Do they have the ability to do that?" someone said.

"May I speak now?" Don Morris said.

Thomas Hayes waved a hand at him as if to say, "The floor is yours." The gesture was accommodating and dismissive at once. David watched them both. Thomas seemed to sit up taller, as if gathering himself to his full height and strength. Morris's jaw line almost imperceptibly tightened.

These guys didn't like each other, that much was clear. Thomas hadn't said much about Morris, but David knew they'd had their run-ins before, and he also knew that Morris was a favorite of Clement Dixon. David couldn't picture a scenario where that relationship continued under a Thomas Hayes presidency. The interaction they'd just had was enough to get the full picture in an instant. Morris's prominence, his access to meetings like this, was on life support.

"Don Morris," the man said. "Director of the FBI Special Response team, for those here who don't know me." Morris glanced down at a sheet of paper on the table in front of him. "My agency has intelligence that suggests two things I haven't heard mentioned here yet. One is that Justice Richard Sebastian-Vilar is a prisoner on that train."

A sound like the wheeze of old machinery, went around the room, followed by a burst of chatter.

"That's for starters," Morris said. "The second thing our intelligence suggests is the hijackers have explosives, likely C4, enough to blow apart the train and bring the tunnel down on top of it, just like their leader indicates. The entire train may be wired with it in a sort of daisy chain. And the leader of the hijackers, as well as the hijacker driving the train, apparently both have access to detonators that can set off the explosives."

"Where did you come by this intelligence, Don?" Richard Stark said. "We have people from CIA and NSA here. I'm sure our listening stations have been wired into whatever chatter is out there. We are getting reports from Interpol, and from British, French, Spanish, and German intelligence. Nothing consistent with what you've just said has come across my desk."

Morris shrugged. "I'm not at liberty to reveal the source at this moment. I have two agents who were in Morocco this morning, and who are on their way to Calais by airplane right now."

"Why are they going there?" Thomas said.

Don Morris and Thomas Hayes eyed each other for a moment.

"To see if the Special Response Team can be of assistance in taking back the train and rescuing the hostages."

"Director Morris," Thomas said. "With all respect due..."

Morris began to say something, but Thomas raised a big hand as if to say STOP. "Please. Give me a moment. Don't talk out of turn. I'm the Vice President of the United States, and I'm the one who called this meeting. I'm also the one running it."

140

Morris nodded. "I understand." His eyes seemed to suggest that he didn't understand… not really.

Thomas raised a long finger. "First and foremost. President Dixon has spoken privately with the prime ministers of Spain, France, and England, and has assured them of our total cooperation, and the complete transparency of our intelligence efforts. Withholding information makes our diplomatic efforts worthless."

Morris smiled. "Intelligence agencies aren't exactly known for their transparency."

"Wait," Thomas said. "Stop. Is it funny to you that the President of the United States is working to manage this crisis with other heads of state, and that your behavior undermines his hard work?"

Morris shook his head. "No. Of course not. I just don't think that…"

Thomas went on: "My office, and the Oval Office, received a report that there was an incident in Germany last night, in which the Berlin Police SWAT, what they call the SEK, were working with an American intelligence agency. A number of Muslims living in a squatters' den near the old Berlin Wall were killed by a SWAT team in what the newspapers over there are calling a heavy-handed raid. Protests are ongoing in over a dozen cities, mostly in Eastern Europe, the old Soviet Bloc countries, where other dilapidated buildings have been taken over by squatters."

"My understanding is that the Muslims were harboring at least two men with known terrorist affiliations," Morris said.

Thomas's hand went back up. "Wait. Please."

He said the word *please* in such a way that it was dripping with exasperation.

"My office also understands that personnel from the Special Response Team were in Austria as of last night and used FBI resources to travel from Salzburg to Berlin. Do you happen to know what American intelligence agency was involved in that raid? Was it yours? Berlin is going to release that information sooner or later. You might as well come clean now."

"I have nothing to report about that," Don Morris said. "As you say, information about that raid is likely to come out eventually. We can inspect the details of it then."

The whole room was looking at Don Morris now. Why couldn't he just admit it? The FBI Special Response Team had a reputation for doing things exactly like this.

"Don," Richard Stark said. "It would be nice if you could share your sources, or at least include a few of us in your loop when you decide to go rogue to obtain intel. We could be sharing this with other countries, if we had corroboration on it. But we don't have any, because this is the first we're hearing of it."

Morris shook his head. "We don't go rogue, Dick. We do what we need to do. This government is like a boat with a thousand leaks in it. The data security situation these days makes it almost impossible to safeguard the information we get, and when it gets leaked, we don't know where it goes. In short, it isn't always easy or wise to share information. We often have to be tight-lipped about it, even amongst ourselves."

"In what sense is there a data security situation?" Thomas said.

"Sir, I think you well know."

Thomas shook his head. "No. I don't. Please tell me."

"Our secure data is constantly being breached," Morris said. "No matter what we do. I'll give you an example. A good friend of mine, a very great American from the special operations community, was murdered some months ago by an American working for another intelligence agency, as a result of stolen classified information. If you want to talk about rogue elements, people at the highest levels of government appear to have been trying to protect an international weapons dealer and human trafficker."

Don Morris and Thomas Hayes were staring directly at one another now. Their eyes were locked on like laser beams. David had never seen Thomas look this way at another human being before.

"Is it possible you simply have an in-house leak?" Thomas said.

Morris continued to stare at him.

"No, Mr. Vice President. I don't believe so."

"Well, be that as it may," Thomas said. "You have a history of running your operation like a law unto itself. You know this is true. As of this moment, I'm ordering you, in my capacity as a surrogate for the President of the United States, to surrender whatever intelligence you've obtained to General Stark and his aides, so it can be vetted quickly, and if need be, shared with our allies in Europe."

He paused and took a breath.

"I'm also ordering you to stand your agents down. There's no sense sending them to Calais, or anywhere near the Channel Tunnel. Our allies are the ones most affected by the situation…"

"Sir," Morris said. "At least two Americans that we know of have already been killed, and had their bodies unceremoniously dumped on the train tracks. We believe the Supreme Court judge…"

"Don," Richard Stark said. "Don."

"And so agencies from France and England, and the combined Channel Tunnel Safety Authority, are taking the lead on negotiations with the hijackers."

"I'm not talking about negotiating," Morris said. "I'm talking about going in there."

"You're not talking about anything," Thomas said. "Your agency is sidelined from this moment forward. Do not send your men to the hijacking site. Other than surrendering your documents, do not attempt to participate in this situation at all. As a matter of fact, I'd request that you leave this meeting now, so we can continue to plan the American response to the crisis."

Don Morris stared and said nothing. Morris's mouth seemed to hang half open, as if he were in the middle of saying a word but had forgotten how to pronounce it.

"It's good that you go now," Thomas said. "I imagine you're going to be busy. I'm expecting a report from your agency detailing the intelligence you've gathered, submitted to General Stark within the next hour."

CHAPTER TWENTY TWO

2:15 pm Central European Summer Time (8:15 am Eastern Daylight Time)
Approaching the Channel Tunnel
Calais, France

"I don't see how we're gonna get through here," Luke said.

The traffic was backed up for miles. The road was a narrow ribbon, two lanes in each direction. But on this side, one lane was entirely closed. The police and military had the place blocked off. Flashing sirens were everywhere.

"Maybe we should just ditch the car and walk," Ed said.

Luke shrugged. "Maybe we should just go back to Salzburg."

Ed shot him a look. "After all this? What? Give up and go home?"

Luke smiled. He was tired. He had gotten a little bit of sleep on the plane, but not much. Ed, on the other hand, had snored the whole way.

"I think you know I'm joking. I would, however, like to get back to my family, and my working man's holiday at some point."

Up ahead, the cops had set up a checkpoint. They were demanding the identification of everyone in every car. If they didn't like what they saw, they turned you around. On the other side of the road divider, a steady stream of cars and trucks were moving away from the area. At the rate things were going, even though the checkpoint was visible from here, it was probably close to an hour away.

Luke and Ed had flown into a small airfield on the far western edge of the Paris suburbs, because commercial air traffic to this region was shut down. The sky was full of military helicopters, like a swarm of buzzing insects. Swann had gotten them this little Renault, parked at the airfield with the keys in it. They had driven out here, and it had taken over two hours. It had seemed more like ten hours.

Luke was wondering, not for the first time, what they were doing here. They had obtained intelligence that they had passed on. Maybe it was important, maybe it wasn't. Maybe it would help thwart the hijacking. But whatever that intelligence meant, whether it was true or false, he and Ed were clearly not invited to this party.

The satellite phone was on the dashboard, plugged in and charging. Suddenly, it began to ring. The ring was a pleasant series of chimes, rising and falling. The phone itself was a pleasant-looking simple blue phone with big buttons. Luke liked satellite phones such as this one. You could get them super-complicated with a million bells and whistles, but he really didn't see the point.

Ed answered it and tapped the speaker phone button.

"Tell me something good," he said.

There was a momentary delay, as the caller's voice bounced around the world, up into low Earth orbit, and back to the ground.

"Ed? It's Trudy Wellington."

Ed smiled. "I think I probably guessed that."

"I'm here with Swann," Trudy's tinny voice said.

Luke glanced at his watch. "Banker's hours, huh?"

"We don't have much to tell you. Don isn't here, and we can't seem to get in touch with him. He's not answering his cell phone. I called his house. Margaret said he came home for maybe an hour last night, then got called to a meeting at the White House after the hijackers dumped more passengers on the tracks and issued their list of demands. That was the last anyone heard from him."

"You think he's all right?" Ed said.

"Who, Don?" Trudy said.

Luke laughed and shook his head. Yeah, Don was all right. Unless an atomic bomb had just been dropped on DC, and even then...

"Guys," Swann said, interjecting. "It's Mark Swann."

Luke and Ed looked at each other.

"Go on."

"You guys still have Vilar's watch, I'm guessing."

Ed held up his wrist. Luke glanced at the light blue steel watch. It really was a beautiful piece of equipment. "You planning on giving that thing back?"

Ed shrugged. "Do you think I'm going to steal it? If I find Vilar, I promise I'll hand it right to him."

"Anyway," Swann said. "I'm tracking the watch by satellite. You guys are about 15 miles from the mouth of the tunnel. Also, the train went deep inside the tunnel and stopped. It's about ten miles in, almost halfway to the other side. So you are pretty far from there."

"The way things are going, we might as well be a thousand miles," Luke said.

"You're never going to get there by car," Swann said. "I'd suggest you get off that road at the next turn off you find. Dump the car if you have to. There is an open soccer field about two miles to your north, a little less, but that road won't take you there. They're using the field as a staging area. There are dozens of military vehicles and at least 200 personnel. There are choppers going in and out of there every five minutes. Most of them are just flying out over the Channel, but a few are bringing troops to a helipad right at the mouth of the tunnel."

"What good does it do us if we're not on the guest list?" Luke said.

"I'm watching it in close to real time," Swann said. "Looks like they've got a food tent set up there, with some kind of catering service. Whether they put you in the game or not, at least you can grab a bite to eat."

Ed looked at Luke now. His eyes had lit up. He nodded.

"Not bad," he mouthed.

That was one thing about Ed. He was either hungry, or about to be hungry. There was no other gear.

"Did you guys look at the specs I sent you?" Trudy said.

"Of the tunnel?"

"Yes."

"Yeah, I studied them pretty close," Luke said. "Looks like you can get right up next to the train from that long roadway service tunnel."

"It did look that way," Trudy said. "But the hijackers issued some threats with their demands. If anyone opens a door from the service tunnel, or attempts to approach the train from any direction, they will start killing passengers again."

"What about the explosives?"

"Right, they also threatened to blow it up, and bring the tunnel down."

"Why haven't they?"

"My gut?" Trudy said.

"Yes."

"They've demanded the release of over 3,000 North African prisoners from jails in Spain and France. Those prisoners are being vetted by the relevant authorities. Some of the prisoners have already been released and are being sent to their home countries. Some of the prisoners are violent felons, and probably can't be released. If I had to guess, I'd say the hijackers will wait until as many of the prisoners are released as possible, and then they'll do whatever they're planning next."

"Which would include?"

"I don't know. Your guess is as good as mine. Publicly execute Richard Sebastian-Vilar? Blow up the train, and the tunnel? Kill the hostages one by one? Make more demands? I'd say they have a lot of options to choose from right now."

"And we have none," Ed said.

"So far, not a lot of good ones."

The traffic gasped and wheezed, and a few cars moved up. Luke could see a little turnoff area to his right maybe 50 yards away. He signaled. He was going to take that spot. Then he and Ed could make their way on foot to the chopper pad.

He pulled the car into the turnoff.

CHAPTER TWENTY THREE

9:30 am Eastern Daylight Time (3:30 pm Central European Summer Time)
Base of the Washington Monument
The National Mall
Washington, DC

"Hayes is in on this," Bill Ryan said.

The spire of the Washington Monument rose high above their heads, thrusting heavenward into the pale blue sky. From where they stood on the flagstones at the base of the giant megalith, Don Morris gazed out across the grassy mall at the neoclassical columns of the Lincoln Memorial in the distance.

The workday was beginning. Office workers in suits and light jackets streamed across the width of the mall in both directions. They were making their way to the federal office buildings, museums, and cultural organizations that lined either side. It was a cool morning, but it was shaping up to be another beautiful September day.

"I don't trust him."

"I don't either," Don said. "But in on it? On what? The kidnapping? The hijacking?"

Ryan nodded. "All of it."

Don looked at him, taking him in seemingly for the first time. Bill's hair was going white. The constant quiet backstabbing, punctuated by open warfare that went on in the halls of Congress would make any head of hair turn white. Other than that, Bill looked good. His eyes were awake and alert. His face was lined with experience. His chest, shoulders and legs all looked broad and strong.

He wore a sharp blue pinstriped suit, beautifully tailored to his body. There was a small American flag pin affixed to the left breast. Just below that was a POW/MIA pin. And just below that was an NRA pin. Bill was a regular pin cushion today. He was wearing his affiliations on his heart. If these were the old days, when they were young, he'd probably have a John Birch Society pin on there somewhere.

Don himself was tired, and he imagined he must look it. It seemed like a long time since he'd had any sleep.

"Why would Hayes do that?" he said. "And how would he do it?"

"As for the how, they have their people, you know that," Bill said. "We have ours, they have theirs. This society, this government is splintering into factions, as I'm sure you are well aware. That's the why. To get a leg up. To manufacture a crisis."

Don looked into Bill's eyes. Everything going on around them, the early morning, the people hurrying to their offices, faded away to a blur.

"That's pretty vague, Bill. I'll be honest. It's quite an accusation based on no evidence at all."

Ryan shook his head. "You brought this information to me, Don. Your men tracked down the young boy in Morocco. Why would a British and American intelligence asset be involved in hijacking and blowing up a train, killing hundreds of people, and possibly destroying one of the greatest engineering achievements of the past 50 years?"

"Former intelligence asset," Don said.

Ryan smiled. "You know there's no such thing."

Don smiled in turn. He thought of Buzz MacDonald meeting his doom at night on an island off the coast of Honduras. The smile became bittersweet. Bill Ryan knew of these things, not through personal experience, but because he was on the House Defense and Intelligence Committees. He was close with men who knew these things all the way inside their bones. Men like Don Morris.

Okay. That was okay. It was better than not knowing it at all. A lot of people in government held the purse strings of efforts and organizations and people they knew nothing about.

"No," Don said. "There's no such thing."

"So you ask me why," Ryan said. He pointed at Don. "And I'll tell you I don't know for sure. But I wouldn't put anything past Thomas Hayes. Try this on for size. Unless the Almighty Himself intervenes, Hayes is going to be the next President. In secret, he probably wants to go along with the travel ban in Southern states. He probably wants to expand it nationwide. He knows it's the right thing, but he can't say it publicly. His political base would crucify him if he did. So what does he do? He invents a reason, a false flag attack.

"If tragedy strikes, if the hijackers blow up the train, kill a Supreme Court judge, kill hundreds of innocent people, it plays into their hands. Dixon is the most popular President we've had in decades. He stands up there with Hayes; they can claim they're standing for right. They can shore up their own power and people will fall in line. Patriotism goes through the roof in a time of crisis.

"So they create a new crisis, maybe even a new war, and the whole country goes along with them. By manufacturing a crisis, they manufacture *consent* - consent of the governed, consent for their activities, consent for their entire agenda. They will sweep aside opposition, and ride high into the next presidency. They will walk away with the whole thing. It'll be a stroll in the park."

Don didn't know how much of this, if any, he was willing to believe. Dixon was going to step down. Sure, he could believe that, and he did. But the rest of it? The Clement Dixon he knew, and the one Margaret had described as courageous in the face of his own kidnapping... Don slowly shook his head. He had differences of opinion with that man, certainly. But the man himself? No. He was a patriot as much as Don was, just in a different way. He wouldn't put innocent people at risk for political purposes.

"They are vetting vice-presidential candidates," Ryan said now. "It's gone further than you think."

"How do you know that?" Don said. He asked, even though he already knew the answer.

"I have spies everywhere," Bill said. "I do favors. People do me favors in return. I'm close to the intelligence community. I'm close to the Pentagon. It's important that people in critical positions know what's going on."

Favors. That's what it was all about here in Washington.

"I need something from you," Don said.

Ryan nodded. "Name it."

Don raised a finger. "Now, I don't consider it a favor. I want to make that clear up front. This is not a budget issue. This is not getting the FBI proper off my back. This is the best thing for everyone involved. The two best special operators in the United States arsenal, and maybe the world, are on their way to that tunnel, but Thomas Hayes has boxed me out. The SRT is sidelined."

He paused. He and Bill Ryan stared at each other.

"I wonder why he did that," Ryan said.

"It's the one thing that makes me lean toward believing these conspiracy theories of yours, Bill. I don't think Dixon is involved, but Hayes?"

Don shrugged. "Maybe he's the one who has gone rogue. Maybe he's sold out to our enemies. Maybe he thinks a disaster abroad will improve his chances here at home. Maybe none of these things are true.

In any case, if you want to stop this train wreck from happening, which I believe you do, then you need my boys in there. If there's some way to overrule Hayes at the operational level, or go around him..."

Don trailed off. It was a sentence he didn't need to finish. Bill Ryan knew exactly what he was talking about. Ryan was a politician. But he also must know that sometimes it was best if the politicians remained in the dark about what activities were happening, and who was carrying them out.

Ryan seemed to think for a long moment.

"You want to put your boys in harm's way like that?"

"Not for glory," Don said. "And not for the prestige of the Special Response Team. Not for our budget. Not for any kind of rewards. Simply because it's the best chance we as a country have. It's the best chance our friends have. It's the best chance the innocent people on that train have. If my boys want in, and I'm almost certain they do, then I want them in there."

Ryan no longer hesitated or thought about it. He just nodded.

"Consider it done."

CHAPTER TWENTY FOUR

4:25 pm Central European Summer Time (10:25 am Eastern Daylight Time)
Zone Blue - Channel Tunnel Emergency Staging Area #3
Calais, France

"This field is wrecked, man," Ed said.

Luke nodded. "Yeah, but the food isn't bad."

Ed shrugged. "We're in France."

They sat at a fold-out table under a vast, dark green tent, on what was normally a soccer field, or as the Europeans might call it, a football pitch. There were easily a hundred similar tables set up here. Dozens of emergency vehicles, including Humvees and heavy BearCat style armored personnel carriers, were parked on the grass.

A swarm of personnel from various military units and police departments arrived and departed on a schedule that was impossible to decipher. The large soccer nets had been pushed to the sides of the field. An area at the far end had been carved into two helipads, the perimeters of the pads etched in black and white and red paint. Choppers landed and took off every few minutes.

Behind Luke and Ed, a large field kitchen had been put together, with about 20 staff preparing food for the people who were coming and going. Luke had eaten ham and Swiss cheese on a croissant, with a spicy mustard that was startlingly delicious. It made the sandwich, quite frankly. He would like to go back there and ask those guys in the kitchen what that mustard was.

He had pocketed a couple of energy bars from a table laid out with hundreds of them. And now he was drinking a lovely dark roast black coffee out of a paper cup. The good meal had been a nice twist in a day that had otherwise been almost perfectly unpleasant. It was rare that you got decent food in the field. They'd been sitting here for a long while, and Ed had gone back for more food twice so far. The big man could eat.

A young guy approached them. He was bespectacled, with a blond crew cut and wearing a dark blue uniform of some kind, walking this way from the helipad. He was carrying a clipboard. Something about the way his eyes had scanned the crowd and settled on Ed suggested that he had found the people he was looking for.

Luke watched him come. When he reached the edge of the tent, Luke said:

"Can we help you?"

The kid looked at Luke, then glanced down at his clipboard again. He spoke with an English accent.

"Are you agents Luke Stone and Edward Newsam of the FBI?"

"Yes, we are."

"I'm Lieutenant Smith of the Channel Tunnel Safety Authority. I've looked all over for you blokes. Can you come with me, please?"

"Where are you going?" Ed said.

"I'm taking you to a meeting regarding a possible rescue attempt. Nothing is decided yet, so I caution you against making any assumptions."

Luke was tired. He recognized that about himself. The coffee he was drinking wouldn't do much but awaken his taste buds. But he had other ways of snapping himself into alertness. If there was really a rescue attempt in the offing, and they were bringing Ed and Luke into it…

…that meant someone had pulled strings to do so.

Luke and Ed stood from their seats almost as one.

"Follow me, please," the young lieutenant said, and turned back toward the helicopters.

* * *

"You're both quite large," the man in the suit said.

His voice echoed off the stone walls, which appeared to be wet with moisture. He spoke English fluently, with a slight accent Luke took as French. "The first thing to determine is if this idea can even possibly work for you."

Luke and Ed were in a sort of anteroom in a cinderblock building near the entrance to the service tunnel. Besides the man in the suit, who had not identified himself or his purpose, there were two men in jumpsuits with badges on their shoulders indicating they were from the Channel Tunnel Safety Authority.

A five-minute chopper flight had brought them to this place. The flight was instructive. Ground traffic was at a dead halt for miles in every direction. Nothing was moving out there.

The two Safety Authority men carried what appeared to be an aluminum length of industrial air conditioning ductwork. It was a cube-shaped cutout about three feet long. They first brought it to Ed, probably because the result was obvious before they even reached him.

"Please raise your arms," the suit said. "And bend at the waist a bit."

Ed did as instructed, no questions asked.

The men tried to slide the ductwork over and down his arms to his shoulders. They almost reached his shoulders before the cube wouldn't go any further. Ed was just way too big for that ridiculous piece of metal to slide over his body.

The men looked at the suit and shook their heads, almost in unison. They pulled the ductwork back up.

"This cutout represents the narrowest tunnel you might encounter as part of the mission we're recruiting for. Unfortunately, there is no chance you will fit through it. If you became stuck in an underground tunnel, there would be no convenient way to rescue you, or retrieve your corpse, for quite some time."

"Really?" Ed said. "That's it?"

The man nodded. "I'm afraid so. I'm sorry. In a moment, the men will show you out. As you must understand, the mission is top secret, so to safeguard its integrity you may not learn anything more about it. I'm sure you can find transportation to wherever you need to go, either through your own agency, or through the many first responders and military units that are in the vicinity. Please do not repeat or describe anything you saw or heard in this room."

The two men came to Luke.

"Please do the same as your friend," the suit said.

Luke raised his arms and bent at the waist. The men slid the aluminum cube down along his arms, over his shoulders, and across his upper body. It was a very close fit, touching him on both sides, but he was inside the tube.

"How does it feel?" the suit said.

"It's tight," Luke said.

"Do you think you can crawl through a space that narrow?"

Luke thought about it for a few seconds. He took a deep breath, which nearly made his body fill up the entire cube.

He nodded. "Yes."

"Would you still want to volunteer?"

This time he didn't hesitate. "Yes."

The men were already removing the ductwork length from him.

The suit nodded. "Very good. Come with me, please."

Luke looked at Ed. The two guys in jumpsuits had taken up positions on either side of him, as if they were ready to forcibly remove him, should that become necessary. Good luck with that.

Ed's jaw was open a little bit. He had that wounded puppy look that Luke had seen once or twice, most recently when Luke had pulled him at the last minute from an operation on an island near Honduras.

"Ah, man," he said. "Unceremoniously dumped. Again."

Luke shook his head. "Sorry, big boy. I'll see you around."

Ed nodded. "Yeah, I guess. Good luck." He turned to go.

Luke followed the suit through a big iron door to a different, larger room. Another man in a Safety Authority jumper closed the heavy door behind them as they came in. There were a handful of wooden folding chairs in this room, facing a white screen that stood on a sort of tripod. There was a folding table with a couple of laptop computers and a projector on it. Wires snaked across the floor. There was no other furniture in the room of any kind.

Another man was in the room. He was a small man, in a black unmarked jumpsuit and heavy black boots. Although he was small, his jumpsuit seemed painted on to his muscular frame. His face was all sharp lines, and he was completely bald. His blue eyes were hard and cold. A pair of aviator sunglasses were perched on top of his head. Luke could see it already. The aluminum tube fit easily over this guy's body.

"Agent Luke Stone of the American Special Response Team, this is Agent Alain Clouseau of the French Special Operations Command. Because of the classified nature of our work, we will refrain from further introductions. There will be no time for team building exercises, or ice breakers. This is not an organizational retreat. Please rest assured that your opposite number here is a combat veteran, and highly accomplished in secretive missions. If you choose to work together, you can rely completely on your partner's competence and professionalism."

The two men shook hands.

"Is that understood?"

Luke understood it, but he couldn't be sure if he believed it. The guy looked fit and hard as nails, and that was good. But it didn't always mean what it appeared to. A guy like Kevin Murphy, his old Delta and sometime SRT teammate, who Luke had now lost track of, didn't look anywhere near as hard as this guy. But Murphy was a

155

killing machine, and Luke had total confidence in him, whatever the mission. This guy? Luke supposed he was going to find out on the fly.

He nodded. "Yes."

The other nodded as well. Perhaps he had similar thoughts going through his head. "Of course."

"If you gentlemen will follow me."

They went to the folding chairs and sat down. The man who had closed the door went to the laptop and began to scroll through a number of screens. Each in turn would appear on the white screen mounted on the tripod. The first image was a drawing of three tunnels in a row, the westbound train tunnel, the eastbound train tunnel, and the service tunnel between them. Luke had reviewed a similar image on the plane.

"Right now, we are near the entrance to the service tunnel of the Channel Tunnel. The train is currently stopped approximately five hundred meters into the westbound tunnel, on this side of the border between England and France. The hijackers have threatened to explode the train and the tunnel, and kill every passenger, if any attempt is made by rescuers to access the train through either the train tunnel itself, or the service tunnel."

A new image appeared. It showed a bewildering network of what looked like ductwork, electrical wiring, piping, and other systems, superimposed over the earlier image of the tunnels.

"This is a representation of the mechanical infrastructure serving the tunnels. As you can imagine, for an engineering feat such as the Channel Tunnel, a vast service system is required to keep oxygen flowing into the tunnel, waste air flowing out, air pressure low, electricity delivered, and any accumulated water eliminated."

A new image came up on the screen. It was similar to the previous two, except it erased most of the infrastructure. Now it just showed the ductwork superimposed on the tunnels.

"The air handling system is an engineering feat in itself. Air is pumped in and out from this building and a few others on this side, as well as a series of buildings on the far shore of the Channel. Without getting into its intricacies, know that it has been determined that a man, or men, could crawl through the system, and appear in the westbound train tunnel, either below or above the train. It has been determined that the best method will be to appear beneath the train, and access mechanical vents in the train chassis from below."

The next image was of the ductwork running directly below the train tracks. Vents in the ductwork were highlighted in red. An image appeared next to that one. It was a photograph taken from inside the tunnel, of the tracks themselves. There was a bright yellow air vent embedded in the ground between the rails.

A new image appeared. It was a photograph of the undercarriage of a train. It seemed to have been taken from inside a well at a rail yard, where a mechanic would stand when working on a train from underneath it. A large panel had been opened and removed, showing an open space within the inner workings of the train.

"Is there room to crawl up below the train, and then enter it? I mean, if we come out of the ground, how much space should we expect between the railbed and the bottom of the train?"

The suit nodded. "It's a good question. There is ample room, perhaps a full meter between the railbed and the train itself. And entering the train from below gives the terrorists less opportunity to detect your presence. If you drop down below, there is always the chance that something falls onto the train, and they hear it. Also, coming down from the top gives you nowhere to hide once you enter the passenger compartment."

"How do we hide coming in from below?"

A new image appeared. It was a drawing, and it showed what appeared to be a hollow space inside the machinery of the train.

"It is possible to enter the train, and maneuver your way up through its guts, and into a narrow mechanical service area behind the restrooms along the south side of the passenger compartment. One entire wall of the restroom is essentially a large, removable service panel, though it would not appear this way to the passengers. I've heard it said that sometimes, hungover mechanics are found inside this area, taking a nap during the workday."

Luke could see it. He could see how it might work.

"Your mission," the suit said, "if you choose to accept it, is to crawl through the air handling system, up and into the mechanical works of the train, and appear in the passenger compartment from inside a restroom.

"Our understanding, from intercepted radio transmissions, and from cell phone calls and texts made by passengers before the terrorists seized all communications devices, is that there are perhaps a dozen terrorists in total, and they have arranged themselves one man per train car to oversee the hostages in each place, with individuals used as communications runners moving between cars.

"One of you, Alain, will appear at the front of the train, and work his way backward. The other, Luke, will appear near the back, and work his way forward. You will both appear to be ordinary passengers,

157

you will both be armed, and your task is to quickly and quietly eliminate the terrorists by any means available and meet somewhere in the middle of the train."

He gestured to the man in the jumpsuit.

"Louis, will you demonstrate the spring-loaded pistol, please?"

Louis nodded. Without saying a word, he held his right arm out in front of him and made a snapping motion with his wrist. Suddenly a small pocket pistol appeared in his hand. Luke noticed now that the right sleeve on the man's jumpsuit was a bit looser than the left one, in order to accommodate the gun.

Luke smiled. "Neat trick. I'll take one of those."

The suit nodded. A ghost of a smile appeared on his face. "Of course."

Alain wasn't asking questions. This seemed to indicate that he had already heard this briefing, or at least knew what the instructions were. He'd gotten here before Luke.

"What about the driver?" Luke said. "My understanding is he can detonate the explosives from inside the cockpit."

The suit nodded. "As you probably know, since the September 11th attacks, security on all forms of travel has undergone significant upgrades. The cockpit door is steel-clad, poured concrete, similar to a bank vault door. The driver has locked himself inside and implemented electronic safeguards that will make the door very difficult to open from the outside. You will not be able to open it or destroy it with any weapon you can carry on board.

"The objective is to keep the driver in the dark as long as possible. Alain is fluent in French, English, and Arabic, so whatever the driver speaks, he should be able to communicate with him. The hope is that you will be able to commandeer the lead hijacker's radio set and bluff the driver into standing down."

"And if that doesn't work?" Luke said.

The suit shrugged. "If you eliminate the other hijackers, and secure the hostages, you can radio us. The British Special Air Service is lining up sniper teams to attempt a takedown of the driver through the windshield of the cockpit. But before that is attempted, we need to know the other hijackers are neutralized."

"What if the train goes into motion? Can you cut off the electricity and stop it?"

The suit shook his head. "The terrorists have forbidden any cuts to the power system. An attempt to cut power will be met with an extreme response from them. Moreover, cutting power through the existing infrastructure is not a one-step task. There is no simple ON/OFF switch. It can take 20 to 30 minutes to effectively cut power to the rail system."

"That train goes very fast," Luke said, "does it not?"

"Yes. If it comes to that, there will be no time to stop the train through ordinary methods. A last resort is to initiate an electromagnetic pulse, or EMP weapon from the sky above the rail line. For obvious reasons, this is not a preferred outcome. It is highly experimental, and in testing does not always work the way it is intended. But there will be jets in the air with a weapon such as this available."

Luke grunted at that idea. He'd have to be about as desperate as possible to call in an airstrike with an experimental weapon, one that didn't always work as intended. What did that even mean? That it didn't work at all? Or that it did work, but in some way that was unintended?

There was a long moment of quiet. Luke was beginning to suspect that his partner Alain was actually a mute. But then the man spoke.

"I'm ready," he said.

He turned and smiled at Luke. His bald head was framed by the empty cinderblock walls of the surrounding building. Somewhere water was dripping. For a split second, that sound reminded Luke of the trillions of gallons of water of the English Channel sitting on top of the tunnel.

"How about you?" the Frenchman said.

Luke looked at the suit. "Can I call my wife?"

CHAPTER TWENTY FIVE

5:55 pm Central European Summer Time (11:55 am Eastern Daylight Time)
Near the mouth of the Channel Tunnel
Coquelles, France

It was getting late.

Ed stood outside the gaping maw of the service tunnel entrance. The entrance was two stories high, framed in corrugated metal. A steel door retracted into the entrance way. A two-lane roadway entered the tunnel. Several odd-looking vehicles were backed up at the entrance checkpoint, waiting to go in. They were like some combination of garbage trucks and golf carts.

Behind Ed, on the far distant side of the English Channel, the sun was moving away. The light was already changing, growing dimmer. He didn't know what to make of that, if anything. Would night coming on change this equation at all?

Crowds of people milled around. Ed didn't try to make sense of who they were or what they were doing. He assumed that if they had gotten this close to the tunnel, they had been vetted.

He was locked out of the action again. It was an odd feeling. Yes, this time it was because his body was just too big to fit in the ventilation system. Even so. Stone was a tight fit himself, and they took him.

Ed needed to do something. He needed to get off the bench and back into the game. He pulled out the satellite phone and dialed a number.

He waited for the phone to shake hands with the satellite, then for the bounce down to her location. Beep... Beep... Beep... Satellite phones still made him a little leery. He knew it was silly. It was a holdover from his combat days. In the field, drones often used satellite uplink signals to lock on ground targets. Not too long ago, in combat, a man holding a satellite phone was painting a big red target on his back.

That didn't matter so much anymore. Technology moved quickly, and drones could lock onto just about anything these days.

Far away, in Salzburg, Austria, she answered the phone.

"Hello?"

There was a strange echo effect. It was as if five Eds had just said hello, one right after another, their voices overlapping.

"Babe? It's Ed."

A moment of silence stretched out between them. Then Cassandra spoke.

"Ed, what is going on? Becca is in the other room, weeping. She spoke to Luke, but he couldn't tell her anything about what's going on. I don't have any idea how to console her. Is Luke okay?"

"He's fine."

"I just want to remind you that you guys left in the middle of the night and were going to be back before breakfast. Do you remember that little story?"

"Baby…"

"I also want to remind you, before you do anything stupid, that you have a baby daughter here, who is currently in my arms. Her name is Jade."

Ed rolled his eyes. "I know that."

"Do you? You sure don't act like it. Neither does your friend. He also has a wife and a child and seems to have trouble remembering that."

"I want you to know something," Ed said. "I love you."

"I've heard that song before, Ed. That's the song you sing right before you do something unbelievably stupid. I'm beginning to think the only reason I don't go straight to breakdown city like Becca is because she and Luke have been together longer than you and I have. The effects of this are cumulative, and wear people down over time."

"Cassandra, you have nothing to worry about it. I've been sidelined. I don't fit into their plans, if that makes sense to you."

There was another long pause. For a moment, Ed nearly thought the call had gone dead. Then Cassandra came back on again.

She sighed. "That's good, babe. I'm glad to hear it."

Ed stood and stared up at the sky as the blue color faded out of it.

"And Luke?" she said.

Ed shook his head. "Can't talk about that. He's fine right now. And I'm sure he will continue to be fine."

Ed had no idea if he meant that. He'd never met anyone with faster reflexes than Luke Stone. He might never have met anyone who could make sense of raw data on the battlefield as quickl, or come up with a more devastating response to that data. Combine that with being strong, well-trained, with incredible stamina, perfect vision, and complete confidence in his own abilities. Stone was damn near superhuman.

But it didn't mean anything. Ed had seen men like Luke Stone cut down before. It tended to happen without warning. Here was a guy, seemingly impossible to kill, and a split second later he was dead. It could happen to anyone and did.

And Stone had made that bone-headed move last night, sticking his head out the window. If it had been someone other than the kid, a real killer instead, Stone would have gotten more than a foot between the eyes. Even the very best had lapses of judgment, and sometimes it cost them their lives.

Nobody was perfect, and one rookie mistake could...

Ed shook his head to clear these dark thoughts. Stone was going to be fine. It was just that... he shouldn't go in by himself. The last time he did that, he would have died if Ed hadn't come falling in from the sky to save him.

"Can you maybe take Becca out for dinner?" he said now. "It might take her mind off the situation."

"Take her mind off the situation? Ed, she doesn't know if her husband is going to be alive or dead later today. And she's been living this way for years. I doubt some sausage and sauerkraut and a beer is going to put a dent in that."

Ed nodded. "Well look. I need to get off the phone, but just know that I'm on the sidelines at this time."

"Edward, that's the best news I've heard all day."

"I love you," he said.

"I love you, too."

He hung up. Behind him, the odd -looking service trucks were still entering the tunnel one by one.

He took a breath and dialed another number. He waited a long beat as the call bounced around the globe again.

"Donuts, hot and ready," Mark Swann said.

"Swann, it's Ed."

"I know who it is, my friend. I got you twice, by phone and by watch. What can I do for you?"

Ed felt a little safer speaking plainly on this call. Whatever was going on inside the SRT offices, Swann's satellite encryption tended to be excellent. "I need a plane. I need a jumpsuit, and a parachute. I need a couple of door poppers, maybe two or three guns, knives, whatever. Can you get me all that?"

"What? Why?"

"I can't ride the bench for long. If that thing happens to come out the other side, and there's a need for me in the game, then I'm going in."

"Ed, the call went out 15 minutes ago. All air traffic is now grounded everywhere around you. No more choppers are going up, and all the ones in the air now are being diverted, re-routed, or forced to land. All planes have to give the area a 50-mile radius. There are fighter planes at the edge of that airspace, escorting everyone out. You won't get anywhere near the target from the sky. You won't even get up in the air."

Ed thought for a long moment. His brain, like a computer, searched through data, raising possibilities, then rejecting them. He thought about the jump he and Stone had done just a couple of mornings ago. That was from a mountain.

"What about a bridge?" he said. "Any high bridges along the way?"

There was a long moment of silence. Ed could hear Swann's fingers racing across a keyboard. Swann's voice came on.

"Ah… oh yeah. There is one. And I think you're going to like it. It's high. But you need to get across the water somehow. Can you do that?"

Ed nodded. "Yeah. I think I can."

"Well, get moving in that case. And I'll see what I can put together."

"Thanks, Swann. You're a peach. And Swann?"

"Yeah?"

"Don't tell anybody, especially not a particular white-haired gentleman. I'm not supposed to be in this game."

"Understood," Swann said. "Give me an hour to put it together."

"Do we have an hour?" Ed said.

"Who knows? I guess we might as well try. What else are you doing?"

Ed nodded. "Fair enough."

He hung up and approached the line of service vehicles waiting to go into the tunnel. A man in a dark blue Channel Tunnel Safety Authority jumpsuit was sitting at the wheel and holding a lit cigarette out the window.

"Hey mate," Ed said. He held up his badge. "Ed Newsam. America. FBI. You happen to be going back across?"

The guy squinted at the badge. "Sure am, mate. Need a lift?"

"How long will it take?"

163

The guy shrugged. "Day like today, all these tossers around? Forty-five minutes end to end, if we're lucky."

Ed smiled. He was in business.

"I'm with you," he said, as he walked around to the passenger side.

CHAPTER TWENTY SIX

6:40 pm Central European Summer Time (12:40 pm Eastern Daylight Time)
Air transfer system beneath the Channel Tunnel
The English Channel

"Radio check," a voice said. "Radio check."

The voice was quiet, with a subtle English accent.

Luke grunted. He reached into the breast pocket of his dark blue jumpsuit. It took a long moment to work his arm into position to even do it. He was flat on his stomach, crawling forward inside the ventilation system, his small LED flashlight in his mouth.

The flashlight lit his way, but it also cast eerie shadows. And its reflection on the aluminum sheet metal surfaces causes a harsh glare that reflected back into Luke's eyes.

It was hard to move. It was hard to breathe. At one point, they had asked him if he'd ever had any episodes of claustrophobia. Now he could see why. A man could go crazy inside here. His body barely fit. His shoulders touched either side of the tunnel he was in. If he lifted his head too high, the back of it scraped along the ceiling. His legs and feet trailed behind him, all but useless in the cramped space.

All of that, plus he was a full story below the train tracks, deep underground, at the bottom of the English Channel. There were trillions of gallons of water somewhere above his head. There was also a train above him, with hijackers on board, who had wired the train to explode and bring both the water, and millions of pounds of rubble, down on top of him. It was a lot to absorb.

So he preferred not to think about it.

"Stone?" the voice said. "Radio check. Please reply."

Luke took a deep breath. It was also getting hot in here. They had turned the air off to this section, and he was wearing two sets of clothes.

His sweaty fingers found the tiny radio, pulled it from the pocket, and immediately dropped it onto the metal surface of the ventilation tunnel.

"Ugh."

"Stone, if you're in trouble, there is a small red signal button on the radio. Press it once now, if you can."

Luke shook his head. The only trouble was they had stopped his snail-like forward progress to check his radio. He understood the point - he was deep inside the tunnel system now, and maybe the radio wouldn't work.

He wouldn't want that, but even so... even so.

His hand found the radio transmitter again and slid it out in front of him. It went a little further along the smooth surface than he expected, so he slithered along to catch up to it.

"Stone?"

His finger pressed the black TALK button.

"Here." His voice sounded a little breathless.

"Everything all right?" came the radio voice. The man's voice was pleasing, with the deep timbre of a musical instrument. The accent made it even better.

"Yeah," Luke said, his breath still sounding a little short. "Everything's fine."

"What took so long?"

"Well, it's a little bit tight in here."

"Alain answered straight away."

"He's a bit smaller than I am."

"Ah. Quite."

There was a brief pause.

"Radio all right?"

Luke shrugged. "Seems okay so far."

"If you won't mind, please tap the signal button, so I can verify if it's working."

Luke glanced at the transmitter. SIGNAL was right there, next to TALK. He did as he was asked. He didn't mind at all.

"Very good. How are you feeling?"

Luke seemed to unconsciously pick up the man's cadence and relaxed demeanor. "Splendid. I'm a little cozy at the moment, and the air is a bit close, but otherwise I feel fine. Tip top, really."

"Brilliant," the man said. "Have you reached the vertical section yet?"

"Not yet."

"Oh. Well then, carry on. If you need anything, you know where to reach us."

Luke crawled forward again. Instead of trying to put the radio back in his pocket, his simply nudged it ahead of him as he went. He wasn't

166

sure what he could possibly need at this point, other than extraction. He didn't know how they might accomplish that if he did need it.

He crept along, following the glare of the flashlight. After another moment, he turned the light off. There was nothing to see anyway, and the reflections off the metal were jarring. It was giving him a headache.

He lay on his stomach in total darkness for a moment. He couldn't see anything. The darkness was better than the glare of the light, but in the underground silence, his breath began to sound monstrous to his ears.

"Huuuh…. HUUUH… HUUUUHHHH."

Your mind played tricks on you down here.

The tunnel seemed to be getting narrower as he went. Why would it do that? It wasn't covered in the briefing. If anything, they seemed to suggest that these ventilation shafts were a uniform size all the way through. The passage was so cramped now he could just about squeeze his way along.

He went on and on, fifty meters he thought, then maybe seventy-five. His hand hit a wall. He had gone forward as far as he could. He reached left and right. Walls there, on both sides. It wasn't possible that the shaft had come to an end, was it? He extended his arm upward, and of course that was it. He had reached the vertical.

With some effort, he forced his shoulders around and turned over onto his back. He took the flashlight out of his mouth, turned it on and pointed it upward. He took a deep slow breath. Okay. He was here. The vertical.

It was hard to say how far up the shaft went. Maybe ten or fifteen feet. It didn't look bad. Not bad at all. Getting himself into a standing position would be the hardest part. The opening above him only came to just below his chest. He couldn't just sit up and fit the turn like an L. He lay there and pondered this for a moment.

"It's like a coffin in here," he said.

He slipped the radio back into his pocket. Now he had it. Using his core strength, he raised his upper body about 45 degrees. He held that, then pushed himself along until the back of his head touched the wall behind him.

He bent his head all the way forward, pushing his body further along, shoving it, the back of his neck squashed against the wall now. He rounded his back and pushed with his feet.

"Aanh."

There was a moment, a split second, where he thought that was it, he had pushed it as far as he could, and he was stuck. But then he was through. His upper body was upright, and his legs were flat.

He took a deep breath. The air was very tight in here. The walls pressed against his shoulders. He would have to force his lower arms, elbows to hands, to the walls, and slowly inch his way upward until he could get his legs out of the lower shaft.

A feeling passed through him then. It seemed to start in his chest, a tightening, a constriction, and then work its way up through his face and head. His hands started to tingle. His breathing became shallow and rapid. Was there enough oxygen in this place?

This is what it feels like when people start to panic.

"Whose idea was this?"

That other guy, Alain, was a lot smaller than Luke. He probably crawled through these shafts with no problem. They had offered Luke the chance to back out, but of course he had refused. He wanted in. The look of disappointment on Ed Newsam's face when they kicked him out was all Luke had needed to see. He did not want that.

No one was coming to help him. No one *could* help him, even if they wanted to. They would have to dig this aluminum shaft out of the bedrock to reach him. At this point, there was no way out of here except forward.

He thought back to Becca's words when he told her he was leaving. She had accused him of being a drug addict. Was it true? Was he addicted to this? Here he was, slithering like a worm, deep under the earth. What was the reward, besides this surge of helpless adrenaline coursing through his body?

He could drop dead right here, right now. No one, outside of a handful of people closest to him, would even know.

Special operator dies in classified mission.

That would be the long and short of it. No further information available, or even necessary.

"All right, all right, all right."

He made himself stop and take a moment. He forced air deep into his abdomen, and then forced it out again. There was plenty of oxygen.

He took a few more forcible deep breaths. Then he pushed against the walls with his hands and forearms. He jerked his right arm a touch higher, then his left. Then he jerked his right a bit higher. And again with his left. In this way, he rose inch by inch, and pulled his legs behind him.

After a moment, he had enough leverage with his feet that he could force his way to a standing position. He did it! He was standing in the vertical shaft.

His breathing was still hard, but the rest was easy. The boots they'd given him had exceptional grips on the bottom. He took another moment's rest, then went straight up the shaft, pressing his arms and legs against the walls for leverage.

Within a few moments, he was at the top. The vent was just above his head. He braced himself with his feet. His legs were strong, and he was like a statue. He could stay in this position forever.

He took out the electric screwdriver they had given him, found the six screws in the air vent, and undid them one by one. He pocketed each one in turn. The screwdriver made a tiny buzzing sound, but it wasn't much.

He pressed the vent out and up, raised himself another six inches, and carefully and silently put the vent aside. He poked his head up. He was here. He was beneath the train. The bottom of the chassis was a good three feet above his head.

In the deep gloom under the train, he could see the tracks extending out ahead of him. Sparks snapped and crackled along the entire line. It was hot, and there was a war of competing smells - electricity, oil, plastics and rubber, braking pads, the smell of wear and tear on machinery. He turned and looked the other way. From here, it seemed there was only one more train car besides this one.

That was good. He was near the back of the train, right where he needed to be.

The smells were fetid, but even bad air circulating was better than the sterile nothingness of the shaft. There was an actual breeze blowing through here, as rank as it was. He felt it cooling the sweat on his forehead and face.

The ventilator shaft was the hard part.

That's what they had told him. Mechanics crawled in under these trains all the time, entered them from below, and even snaked their way through the machinery and up into the passenger compartments. No one crawled through those air shafts.

He pushed himself up and out, slithering onto the tracks. He lay on his back, and just above his head was the next plate he had to remove. It was much larger than the vent he had just crawled through. There would be plenty of room inside there.

The plate is heavy.

That's also what they had told him. Don't let it fall on top of you. But also don't let it fall next to you, clang against the railway, and alert the hijackers to your presence.

"This one will be easy," Luke whispered to himself.

CHAPTER TWENTY SEVEN

7:50 pm Central European Summer Time (1:50 pm Eastern Daylight Time)
Eurostar Paris to London High Speed Train
Inside the Channel Tunnel

"Yasser."

Yasser al-Fallujah looked at the young brother who had just entered his cabin from the front. Their numbers were less than before. There was Yasser and seven other men left. The surprise passenger attack had taken quite a toll.

These brothers were not highly competent to begin with, so having fewer made things more challenging. Yasser had told them to stay off the radio unless there was an emergency. There were six long passenger cars on the train. Without use of the radio, and with only two runners to move between cars, it was now almost impossible to watch every car and maintain open communications between them.

There were hundreds of passengers on this train. They seemed docile now. But three of them had wreaked havoc before, and it wasn't even a coordinated attack. The third man could not have known the first two, and simply attacked because the opportunity presented itself.

This brother, Salaam was his name, was very slim and young, though he seemed less fearful than a few of the others. Perhaps he was a true believer.

"Why did you leave your post?" Yasser asked him in Arabic.

"Ibram is still in there. He is watching over the sheep. But we may have a problem. I would like you to look."

"What is it?"

"There is someone in the restroom," Salaam said.

"Yes?"

"I monitor everyone. Everyone must request to use the restroom. No one requested. I know this for a fact."

Someone was in the restroom. Someone who did not request to be there.

"Show me," Yasser said. "Quickly."

171

The two men marched up the aisle, went through the cabin door, and passed through the foyer between cars. The next young man, Ibram, watched Yasser enter with wild eyes. His gun was out. He appeared ready to begin shooting.

"Ibram!" Yasser said. He gestured behind him. "Watch my car."

Ibram nodded. "As you command." He darted past as if he was reluctant to touch Yasser.

The doors to the restrooms were here by the door to the foyer. There were two restrooms at each end of this cabin. Salaam pointed a finger at the door to Yasser's left.

"You're certain of this?" Yasser said, very quietly.

Salaam nodded silently.

Yasser listened. Sounds came from inside the restroom. They were furtive sounds, as if someone in there were doing things, accomplishing a task of some kind, without wanting to be heard. Salaam, or Ibram, whichever one had detected these sounds, was very observant. Yasser must give the man credit for that, and he believed Allah would as well. A faithful servant must remain vigilant.

Several nearby passengers watched them with feverish eyes. Yasser stared back at them blankly. The passengers were cowed, but they must remain that way. Perhaps the best thing was to make an example of this mysterious person in the restroom, whoever it may be.

Yasser reached out and gently touched the door. He ran his hand along it. The door was somewhat flimsy. Whoever was in there had not engaged the lock. If he had, the red OCCUPIED light would have activated, and the air blower would have turned on. The person in there was holding the door closed with his hand.

Yasser took his handgun out and pressed the muzzle to the door at about chest height for the typical man.

An older woman in an aisle seat watched him and began to cry. He raised the forefinger of his left hand to his lips and shook his head. He breathed in, and slowly released the air.

Then he squeezed the trigger.

BANG!

Again.

BANG!

He moved the gun lower, then fired again. Again and again.

BANG! BANG! BANG! BANG! BANG!

The reports were loud, as he intended them to be. After many years of warfare, his own ears were damaged, so the sound had very little effect on him. But the effect on the passengers was immediate and visceral. Several people cried out in fear. A woman shrieked. A baby began to cry.

Yasser gestured at the door with his head.

"Open it."

Salaam nodded and went to it. Yasser stepped back, gun still trained on the doorway. Salaam glanced at him with big brown eyes, and Yasser nodded. Salaam pushed the door open. He had to shove it hard because a body was blocking the way.

A dead man lay there, slumped on the toilet seat, and half on the floor. He wore a dark coveralls uniform, which he had peeled down to his waist. Beneath it was the jacket of a pinstriped business suit. The man had been in the process of changing from a workman to a businessman when Yasser shot him.

Worse, a tall panel, which made up nearly one entire wall of the restroom, had been removed and placed standing up against the adjoining wall. The guts of the train were exposed behind this missing panel.

It took Yasser just a few seconds to understand what had happened here. The man had come out of that wall dressed in coveralls, likely to protect his business suit from grease and oil and was trying to remove the coveralls when he died.

They were sending commandos in! He shook his head at the treachery. Of course they were treacherous. Of course they were false.

"Watch them!" he said to Salaam. "Watch the passengers! And watch this restroom! Shoot to kill. Do not let another one come in this way."

Yasser burst out of the car, through the foyer, and into his own car. Poor, doe-eyed Ibram watched him come. Yasser didn't hesitate. He kicked in the doors of the restrooms at this end of the car. A woman screamed. A man shouted.

"Out!" Yasser shouted back at them. "Get out now! Back to your seats."

The man emerged from the bathroom, an older man, with gray hair and wearing the yellow shirt and green pants of a tourist, a golfer no less. He was no threat to anyone.

Yasser shoved him. "Go!"

He looked at Ibram. "Move through the entire train. Tell the brothers to open all restrooms. Remove all the passengers from them. Watch for commandos. Watch for anyone suspicious. Kill anyone suspicious on sight. They are coming through the walls."

Ibram turned and ran back along the aisle toward the next car.

173

As Yasser watched him go, he realized that he had a decision to make. If not at this precise moment, then very soon. The crusaders had disobeyed his orders. It was coming time to decide when to destroy this train and everyone on it.

* * *

Luke silently finished screwing the panel back into the wall. He had to be quiet, so he didn't use the battery power of the screwdriver for this. He just manually drove four of the screws in, just four, the ones at the corners.

There were four more, each in the center along the edge of the panel. But there was no time for that. He didn't have all day to stand here, fastening screws.

He stepped back and looked at his handiwork. It was good enough. As instructed, he had dumped the coveralls inside the wall panel.

He glanced at himself in the dim metal mirror above the sink. He looked okay. A man in a dark gray pinstripe suit. His dress shirt was open at the collar, as if he had dispensed with his tie during all the fuss.

He looked like he hadn't shaved in a couple of days. He also looked like he hadn't slept. Both things were true. He could pass as a guy who boarded a train, and whose day went completely wrong after that.

About the only thing that didn't pass were the dark boots sticking out the bottoms of his pinstriped pants legs. They didn't look right, but it would have to do. He took a deep breath and stepped out of the restroom.

He crossed into an alien world.

The passenger compartment smelled. The people had been on here a long time now. They were planning on a two, maybe twoand-a-half-hour trip, but that was early this morning. There was a smell of sweat. There was a smell of body odor. There were deeper, more rank smells.

People in the seats eyed him. They were afraid. Afraid of dying, and afraid of him. He didn't belong, and they knew that. They'd never seen him before. He began to walk up the aisle, looking for an empty seat.

There weren't any.

At the far end of the cabin, a man was standing, staring into what looked like the other bathrooms. He turned and saw Luke.

Suddenly, the man was racing down the aisle toward him.

"You! You there!"

A woman gave a long wail. She'd seen this movie before. The people on this train were at their breaking points. Other passengers had been murdered, and these people had witnessed it.

Luke put his hands up. He was a normal businessman. He crouched down a little bit. The hijacker was a young man in a blue windbreaker jacket and jeans. He was smaller than Luke, and skinnier.

He attacked, punching Luke. Luke caught a shot in the chin, then one on the cheekbone. Good enough. He stumbled backwards, and onto the floor. He worked his way back to his knees. He was kneeling in front of the hijacker.

Around him, people groaned in terror.

The hijacker was angry. His eyes were wild... insane. His face was turning red. He hit Luke again, and then again. He kicked Luke in the chest.

"Where did you come from? Where did you come from?"

He kicked Luke again. Luke felt it and didn't feel it. He didn't fall back.

He held his hands up. "Please! Please!"

The man reached inside his jacket and pulled out a gun. At the same instant, Luke reached inside his own jacket and came out with the knife strapped under his arm.

The hijacker's gun hand was coming around to point in Luke's face.

With his left hand, Luke caught the man's wrist. With his right, he drove the knife into the man's abdomen. He drove it low, on the right side. The knife was razor sharp and plunged in easily.

The young hijacker's eyes opened wide. So did his mouth.

"Unh!"

Luke pushed the knife in, all the way, to the hilt.

He and the hijacker stared into each other's eyes. Luke felt nothing for the soul behind those eyes. It had come here to kill helpless people.

And now it was going to die.

Luke ripped the knife across, from right to left, cutting the man open deeply. He could have disemboweled the guy, if he wanted. He stood, towering over his quarry. He pulled the knife out. There was blood along the shaft.

Every move Luke made elicited a sound from the crowd. The people were not on his side. They were not on anyone's side. Every action that took place was more horrible than the last. They didn't know who to root for. They just wanted this day to end.

Luke flicked it out and zipped it across the guy's throat. A slice opened there, from one side across to the other. Blood jetted out. The young man put his free hand to his throat. He was still standing. He was dead but didn't realize it yet.

Luke took the gun from the guy's right hand, then pushed him to the ground. The body jerked and bucked, blood spreading around it. Then it began to subside.

Next.

Luke took the tiny radio out of his jacket pocket. He pressed the TALK button. "Stone here. I'm on the train. I'm in the fight. One down."

"Copy that," said the chipper English voice from before. "Have you encountered Alain?"

"No," Luke said. "I just got here."

"We haven't heard from him. Proceed as planned. Clear the train from back to front. Assuming he's alive, he will be clearing from front to back. Meet in the middle and join forces as needed. Step lively. They can initiate destruction at any moment."

"Roger," Luke said.

This car should be second to last. He put the radio in his pocket again, turned and headed toward the rear car. As soon as he turned, he saw another young man in the window of the doorway.

The guy spotted Luke. He held a gun in his hand. He raised it and...

BOOM!

Luke ducked just as the window shattered. It sprayed inward, showering him with tiny nuggets of safety glass.

Am I hit?

Luke was in a crouch, the glass all over him and around him on the floor. There was no pain, no blood. The guy had missed him, but he needed to act NOW. There was no place to hide, and no time. Luke leapt up, gun out.

BANG!

He fired at nothing. The hijacker had dropped back into the next car.

Luke followed him. He passed through an open foyer between cars. He entered the final car. There were fewer passengers in here. But fewer didn't mean zero.

The hijacker had pulled a young woman up from her seat. He was crouched behind her, his gun to her head. He was murmuring something into a handheld radio. It was a big one, like an old-style walkie-talkie. He finished whatever he was saying and tossed the walkie-talkie aside.

Luke saw the woman clearly, every detail of her etched in his mind. She was very pretty, with startling green eyes. Her hair was brown, very straight, and long. She wore a dark blue long-sleeved t-shirt. On the front was a caption in white, written in a language Luke didn't understand or even recognize.

The young woman was crying. She closed her eyes and began to whisper to herself. She was probably saying her prayers.

Luke pointed the gun at the hijacker.

"Let her go. This is over."

"I kill her!" the guy screamed. He spoke English. Not perfect, but well enough. "Put gun down!"

"Don't kill her," Luke said. He tried to keep his voice calm. "You can walk away from this. You can live or die. It's up to you."

He took another step closer.

"Drop gun! I kill her in three seconds!"

Luke watched him. The guy meant business. He was freaked out and ready to kill.

"Don't you do it."

"Two seconds!"

"Don't..."

"One!"

Luke held the gun out in front of him and let it go. It fell to the floor in the aisle with a THUD. He breathed deep. He and the hijacker watched each other's eyes.

Would the guy try to shoot Luke now? Luke watched... waited... looked for an opportunity.

BANG!

The guy shot the woman in the head. Luke saw it all. The grimace on her face at the instant of the gunshot. The way her face suddenly went blank as the bullet entered her skull. The tiny spray of blood and bone and brain out the side of her head.

Someone screamed, a long ululating wail. It sounded like a police siren, the cops racing to the scene of a crime, the siren rising and falling, rising and falling.

Luke flicked his wrist and the pocket pistol zipped out of his sleeve and into his hand, just like they showed him at the briefing.

The guy shoved the woman's body aside and turned the gun toward Luke.

They pointed at each other.

BANG!

A red dot of blood appeared in the center of the guy's forehead. His eyes seemed to cross for a second. An instant later, he was on the ground. Luke walked to the spot where the two bodies lay. There was nothing he could do for the woman. She was already dead, her eyes open and staring.

The hijacker was the same.

Luke shook his head. So this was how it was going to be. His skin broke out in goose bumps. These guys were cold-blooded murderers. He steeled himself for the effort ahead.

He scanned the train car. Lots of frightened eyes stared back at him. It might be possible to begin a rescue here. Just break open the rear door and start getting people out onto the tracks. Have them walk back to the nearest service tunnel doorway.

Suddenly the train lurched. Then it smoothed out. It was starting to move. Outside the rear window, a tunnel light dwindled slowly into the distance.

Scratch that idea.

His best bet was to kill the hijackers. He pulled out his small radio transmitter and pressed TALK.

"Two down," he said. "Train is in motion."

"We have not heard from Alain," the voice crackled back.

Luke sighed. "These guys are serious. I'm guessing Alain is dead."

"Good luck in that case," the voice said. "Godspeed."

Luke nodded. "Yeah."

He looked out at the terrified passengers. He raised his voice to them. "Everybody just stay in your seats. It's going to be okay. I need to go up front for a little while."

He turned to leave, then stopped.

He projected his voice to everyone in the car. "Whatever you do, don't touch this man's body. He's a terrorist. He could be booby-trapped."

Blank eyes stared at him. Some people understood him, some didn't.

He had to move fast. These guys just didn't care about human life. They would blow up this train. They would kill every passenger they could get their hands on. There was no time to waste. There was no time to take a breath.

There was no time at all. Luke took his first step, and so began his assault straight up the middle of the train.

CHAPTER TWENTY EIGHT

1:55 pm Eastern Daylight Time (7:55 pm Central European Summer Time)
The Situation Room
The White House
Washington, DC

"The train is in motion," Dick Stark said at the front of the room.

An aide had come in a moment ago, a thick-bodied major who appeared to be about 40 years old and had whispered into Stark's ear for several seconds. It seemed that the military had an update on the situation.

Vice President Thomas Hayes watched Stark from the other end of the table. General Stark was not particularly tall, maybe a hair over six feet. He was thin like a razor blade, but in a way that looked strong. His dress greens fit him exceptionally well. He seemed like a man who could walk out of here, run ten miles, come back in, resume his remarks, and he wouldn't have broken a sweat or missed a beat.

A razor would be a good metaphor for him. Razor thin, with a haircut done by razor, and a face that always looked like he had taken a straight razor to it five minutes ago. Stark was composed, quietly competent, as you'd expect that any four-star from the Pentagon would be.

It was just that this crisis had gone on and on, more than 12 hours now, and Hayes had yet to hear a single decent idea from anyone in the American military. Richard Sebastian-Vilar had been gone for 24 hours, and Hayes hadn't heard a decent idea from them about that little problem, either.

Clem Dixon, seated to Hayes's right, tended to give these guys the benefit of the doubt. Hayes had noticed that. Dixon's stance toward men like Richard Stark had softened during his time as President.

Hayes didn't really foresee that for himself.

"Do we know what's happening?" Hayes said.

Stark shook his head, slowly, almost imperceptibly.

"We know there were shots fired on board. A commando team of two men was inserted. They are thought to be special operators from France and the United States. At least one of them is dead."

"How were they inserted?" Hayes said.

"We don't know. The plans were tightly controlled at the site of the staging so nothing could leak, nothing would be broadcast, and nothing could be intercepted. Right now, we know there was a gun battle on the train, possibly two, and there were radio communications between hijackers. A moment ago, one broadcast to his leader that he was under attack near the back of the train. And now the train is in motion. It's a very dangerous moment."

"What happens next?" Clement Dixon said.

Stark shrugged. "Two possible scenarios that I see. One, the worse scenario, is that the hijackers detonate the explosives now, inside the tunnel, killing themselves, everyone on board, and possibly destroying the tunnel itself."

"That's a fairly dark scenario," Hayes said.

Stark nodded. "Yes. But we knew that was a possibility from the beginning. They positioned the train for this eventuality."

"And the other scenario?" Dixon said.

"They make a fast run for St. Pancras Station in Central London, in the hopes of bombing it in a manner similar to the Madrid bombings from two years ago. The train station has been evacuated, as has the neighborhood directly around it."

"Central London is a mess," a young, brown-haired aide in a suit said from a seat along the wall. "My office has been following the evacuation. It's a mass exodus, a million people. People are desperate to…"

Stark raised a hand to the young man. "Okay. Not relevant at this moment."

Hayes looked at the aide. He was little more than a kid. His face turned red from being admonished by the general. Hayes had no idea who the guy was. He must belong to somebody around here. He was everything that David Halstram wasn't. Cocky, too eager to speak out of turn, and presenting useless information when he did.

Stark had done a decent job shutting him down.

"Why this is the better scenario, is there are British Special Air Service snipers positioned at the mouth of the tunnel. If the train comes out of there, they will take their shot to kill the driver through the front windscreen. The train has safety features that will kick in if the driver dies. The train should then roll harmlessly to a stop. There are SAS units standing by to storm the train in case this happens."

"What if the snipers miss?" Hayes said.

Stark's eagle eyes stared at him for a moment. Hayes got the sense sometimes, like right now, that these military types would kill him if they could. Hayes didn't mind that look from Stark. He welcomed it. These jokers needed to understand, once and for all, that they were under civilian leadership.

"Mr. Vice President, I think that's an unlikely scenario. The British Special Air Service is among the…"

"Humor me," Hayes said.

Stark shrugged. "In that case, the train will continue on to London. The tracks are wide open. As you'll recall, the hijackers threatened to blow up the train if the tracks were shut down or blocked in any way. I imagine the English will make some attempt to thwart this type of attack, put another sniper team further along, but I'm not privy to that intelligence."

"How long would it take the train to reach the station?" Dixon said.

Stark shook his head. "At the speeds these super-fast trains can run? Not long at all. Fifteen minutes from the time it comes out of the tunnel."

"Well, they'll have to turn off the electricity at that point," Dixon said.

"Yes," Stark said. "It would take several minutes to do so, but yes. And as soon as they do, they once again risk the deaths of everyone on board. But at least the tunnel won't be destroyed."

Thomas Hayes felt his irritation rising, as was usually the case in these briefings. America was like a deer in the headlights. There were 57 American passengers known to be on board the train, plus there was also the possibility of Richard Sebastian-Vilar being on there somewhere.

Clement Dixon says, "What are our options here?"

Stark shook his head. He had a sheaf of papers in his hand, and he half lifted them as if they would indicate something. "There really are none. Our allies run the show. As I said, there is a sniper team waiting outside the tunnel. They will try to take the driver out. If they can, the train should stop on its own. Units from the Special Air Service stand ready to storm the train in that case. But it might not even come to that. The train might be destroyed inside the tunnel. Our hands are tied."

"Who is the American?" Hayes said.

"The American?"

"The special operator. The one who was inserted."

Stark shook his head. "We don't know."

Thomas Hayes didn't like the sound of that. He didn't like the sound of anything he had heard in the past five minutes, but especially not that. All of these clandestine missions, these secret identities. Why was it that so often there were Americans in sensitive places, and we didn't even know who they were?

He looked around the room. Don Morris of the Special Response Team was conspicuous by his absence. Yes, Hayes had banished him. But he would like to have Morris here right now.

He'd bet anything that Morris would know exactly who the American was aboard that train.

CHAPTER TWENTY NINE

7:01 pm British Summer Time (8:01 pm Central European Summer Time – 2:01 pm Eastern Daylight Time)
Eurostar Paris to London High Speed Train
Inside the Channel Tunnel
England

BANG! BANG! BANG!

Bullets whined over Luke's head.

"Dammit!"

He was pinned down, three cars up through the train. Everything behind him was his territory, as far as he was concerned. And everything ahead was territory to be conquered. Taking that territory was going to be hard.

He had moved the passengers backwards through the train, told them to take seats where they could find them. He needed them away from the fighting. There were still some at the back of this car, on either side of the aisle, heads down. They were good, fairly far back from the fighting. There wasn't much further they could go, and the speed of the train was increasing every second.

But now he couldn't move forward, either.

He was at the front of the cabin, hunched next to the door to the foyer between cars. The window above him was shattered. The window of the other train car was shattered as well. There was a dead bad guy on the ground in the foyer. Luke had shot him in the head maybe a minute ago. It was a no man's land inside that foyer.

There were two, possibly three hijackers across the foyer from him, on the other side of the door. Once in a while, one of them popped up and took a few shots from window to window. They had probed this door with gunshots, and their bullets had made dents from the other side but, so far, the door had held. Now they just fired through the window. There was no way to make it across the foyer without getting killed. There was no way to even stand up.

Once in a while, Luke stuck his hand over the top and took a few shots, just to keep those guys honest. So far, they hadn't managed to shoot his hand off. This attack plan would have been a good idea if the French guy had made it to the dance. If he were coming the other way, they'd have the bad guys in a pincer. But now?

They could blow up the train, and there was no way to stop them.

They could execute passengers, and there was no way to stop them.

The train was accelerating, they had evidently decided to make a kamikaze run at London, and there was no way for Luke to stop them.

Call in the EMP strike.

If he did that, these guys would blow up the train. It was that simple. C4 was easy to detonate, did not require electronics, and it was wired throughout the train. At this moment, they thought London was the more destructive option. But as soon as they stopped thinking that…

Luke gritted his teeth and shook his head.

"I need to get moving somehow."

* * *

"We are under attack," Yasser said over the radio. "Enemy commandos are aboard."

Inside the cockpit, Francois glanced at his handset in surprise. A moment ago, Yasser had told him to begin moving the train up the tracks. He had done that; now they were moving forward, crawling along at an easy snail's pace, about 20 kilometers per hour.

Yasser was generally calm, unless he was angry. Right now, there was an edge, a shakiness to his voice, that did not seem like anger. It didn't seem like fear, either. It sounded like he was in battle and holding off an onslaught, one that he didn't expect.

"Commence counter-attack plan."

This was good. It was time to deliver the killing blow. The French and the English were untrustworthy and were bound to try for a double-cross at some point. That it came now was perfect timing. Francois almost couldn't ask for better.

The sun had set probably 15 minutes ago. Outside this tunnel, the full darkness of night was just coming in. Francois's signals were green all the way to St. Pancras Station. One of the original demands was that the enemies not try to block the route ahead of the train. Spies had been watching, and if the route had been cut off or tampered with, Yasser would have known.

It was a straight shot directly into the heart of central London, and this train was a rolling missile.

"Driver!" Yasser shouted.

He was very good, Francois reflected. Yasser was a credit to the cause, and a valuable servant of Allah. He could be dying. He could be in his final throes. But he would not reveal Francois's name.

"Do not worry," Francois said. "I'm working on it. Just another moment."

Their enemies could hear them, of course. But they couldn't know what Francois and Yasser meant. There was a chance they would think that the train would blow up right here, in the tunnel.

"Driver! There is a problem with my controller! Activate yours now! I repeat, activate controller now."

Francois's so-called "controller" was sitting on the flat part of the dashboard. It had been in his bag, and he had taken it out some time ago. He looked at it for a moment. It was a rather simple looking detonation device - a glass ampule containing a tiny amount of a very powerful and highly unstable, explosive, with a sparking device attached. The sparking device was like a metal trigger - squeezing it would send a spark into the explosive. One spark would be enough.

There was a small utility panel near the floor to Francois's right. It was built into the wall. The screws that normally held it in place had been loosened. Francois could see that they were sticking out from the panel. It would be very easy to remove them and open the panel. His instructions indicated that there was a small block of plastic explosives within that panel.

The simple detonator would click in and attach to that block. If he were to spark the detonator, it would set off a small burst of energy that would detonate the local C4, which was linked to more C4 all the way through the train. A long chain of explosions would occur, blasting the train and everyone aboard it into oblivion, beginning with Francois himself.

Hmmm. That wasn't going to happen.

Was that why Yasser's voice was shaking? Had he already tried to blow up the train? Had he been ready to be the first to die? It seemed that he had.

Francois looked through the windshield and peered carefully into the gloom of the tunnel ahead. There was no movement that he could see. If they were massing more soldiers or another commando squad to attack, it wasn't coming from the front.

"Driver!"

Francois looked about the cockpit. Everything was as it should be. The dead Eurostar driver, Fawcett, was slumped heavily in the driver's seat. He was tied there with sturdy ropes, which Francois had wrapped around him again and again. The ropes held his body somewhat upright against the seat back, although his head was slumped sideways at what would have been an alarming angle if Fawcett were alive.

It had taken a great deal of effort to drag Fawcett's fat body off the floor and wedge him onto the seat. But it was necessary. The dashboard had a sensor which would read whether the pilot was in the chair or not. If it detected an absence there for more than 30 seconds, it would shut down power to the wheels, and gradually apply the brakes. It was a failsafe that the drivers called the "dead man sensor."

There were other failsafe measures here as well, redundancies that took into account nearly every possibility for a driver health crisis. A small pedal on the floor had to be depressed at all times by the driver's right foot while the train was in motion. It was a circuit connector. If the pedal was not depressed, the circuit was broken, and electricity would once again stop being delivered to the wheels. The broken circuit would begin to slow the train immediately.

Francois had beaten this failsafe easily simply by sneaking a brick from a construction site onto the train three days ago and stashing it in a maintenance compartment under the floor in the service workers' area. Then he had brought it up to the cockpit with him this morning in his satchel. He wedged it onto the pedal, and it worked fine. The pedal was depressed. All systems were go.

"Driver! Will you respond?"

Yasser was nearly screaming now. In the background, during the moment the line was open, gunfire was clearly audible.

What was going on back there?

"We're going," Francois said into the radio. "Don't worry." Then he clicked it off entirely.

His heart skipped a beat at that. That time it very nearly did sound like Yasser was worried. When a war hardened believer like Yasser al-Fallujah, a man prepared to die at all times, sounded like that, then you knew there was trouble.

Francois reached and slowly pulled the lever that controlled speed toward him. He'd had it going at half speed, but now he pulled it all the way. The train was moving forward at a very good rate. Francois watched outside the windshield. There was still no activity on the tracks that he could see. Allah only knew what these devils were planning.

There was one last failsafe to deal with. The speed lever itself. You could not simply let go of it. If you did, it would gradually return to its original start position, and not deliver any power to the wheels. It required a small amount of constant force, pulling it towards you, to keep speed up.

And in Francois's case, he needed to keep the speed all the way up. This train was capable of traveling quite a bit faster than the highest speeds it reached on a normal run. The train could top out very close to 500 kilometers per hour, what some would think of as 300 miles per hour.

At that speed, when it hit the terminus at St. Pancras Station, the explosives would go off with tremendous force, destroying the train, much of the station, and hopefully at least some of central London. It would be an attack directly into the belly of the beast, if Allah willed it. An attack that would strike terror into the hearts of these unbelievers - these usurers, whoremongers, and crusaders. It would be an attack for all times, written in the history books, and remembered centuries from now.

When this train roared out of the tunnel at 300 miles per hour, the crusaders were going to be faced with a difficult decision, one that they would need to make quickly. At top speed, central London was maybe 15 minutes away. The southeastern suburbs of London were just a few minutes away.

If the crusaders cut power to the railroad tracks, the brothers could simply decide to detonate the explosives, taking all of the passengers and surrounding residential areas with them. If they waited to see what happened, the train would land like a bomb in the middle of their city, taking all the passengers, and many more people, and perhaps a few of their beloved landmarks.

But Francois needed some way to keep the train traveling at top speed without doing it himself. The painful truth was Francois did not plan to be on board when the train hit St. Pancras like the sword of Muhammad.

He was a believer, of course. But he was not a suicide fighter. He was getting off the train just as soon as it exited the tunnel. He had neglected to tell Yasser this, of course, but Yasser would never understand.

Yasser had that strange light around him. He had been a warrior for decades, and one who had forsaken the life of this world a long time ago. And yet, he was still not dead. The man could fight surrounded by his enemies, ride the train until it was seconds from detonation, step off at the last instant, and somehow survive. More than survive, he would likely walk away uninjured and disappear into the midst of the carnage, only to turn up halfway across the globe months from now.

That wouldn't happen to Francois. If he stayed in this cockpit, or on this train at all, he was going to die. So he was leaving. He liked this world. He would see Allah soon enough, and he believed that the work he had done would be found pleasing. Perhaps there would be a punishment, or a delay entering Paradise. That was okay. For now, Francois wanted to stay here.

Was he hedging his bets? Was it possible that he didn't believe in Allah at all? He didn't like to think about things like that, and now was not the time.

He was wearing a light parachute on his back. There was a vent at the back of the cockpit, above his head. The vent opened to the top of the train. It was there in case of an emergency, if firemen or rescuers needed to enter, or if the pilot needed to exit. In this case, the pilot did need to exit.

Moments after the train came out of the tunnel, the tracks crossed a wide river. Francois intended to be on the roof of the train when it reached the river. He would throw his parachute out, and at nearly 500 kilometers per hour, it was going to pull him up into the air and deposit him in the water. He was an excellent swimmer and by now it was dark out. No one knew he was here. No one knew who he was. No one would even think to look for him. In the aftermath, they would assume that Francois, the service worker turned hijacker, had been killed in the devastating explosion.

He glanced at the speedometer; 380 kilometers per hour, or nearly 230 miles per hour. The train was really moving. And it was still accelerating. It would leave the tunnel at any moment. He had to get going.

He pulled the lever all the way toward Fawcett's dead body. At the top of its length, the lever had a knob like a video game joystick would have. It made it easy to hold the lever with your entire palm.

He wrapped the knob with a line of rope he had already tied around Fawcett's heavy bulk. He pulled the lever all the way, as far as it would go. Then he tied the line off and knotted it.

He looked out the windshield. The green lights were flying by in a blur. They were all green. Up ahead, he saw the change in atmospheric light that meant the train would leave the tunnel. The exit was a dark hole in the fabric of reality ahead of him.

He gave one more glance at the readouts. Power was still 100%. Whatever the crusaders were going to do, they hadn't done it yet. If they waited too long, momentum alone would carry this train to the terminus.

The tunnel exit was coming. It was time to leave.

* * *

"Here she comes, mates," the spotter said. "Prepare to fire."

The sniper patrol from the Special Air Service lay on top of a serviceman's bridge over the railway. The bridge was just 100 meters from the end of the tunnel.

The three shooters lay on their stomachs, carbines extended in front of them, and tilted downward at a slight angle. The leader of the men, Bruce Redding, was a captain, 33 years old. All three shooters in this patrol were qualified marksman, the highest shooting rating in the British military. Times like this were what they trained for.

"On my mark," he said quietly.

He took a deep breath and closed his eyes for two seconds. When he opened them again, he re-sighted on the target. His scope was zeroed in on the end of the tunnel. The powerful scope made the opening seem bare inches away.

He could see the lights of the train approaching. They were coming very fast, but to Bruce, they seemed to come almost in slow motion.

He could see everything. The cockpit was lit up like a shop at Christmas time. There were two men in there - that was news.

"Two men!" he shouted.

"Aye!" the Scottsman to his left, McMurry, said.

"Got it," the man to his right, Dolan, said.

The set up was simple. Bruce was firing a heavy .50 caliber rifle, powerful enough to take out the windscreen on the train. He would take the first shot, destroying the windscreen, and leaving the cockpit open to his two men. They would fire an instant later, taking out the driver. Or in this case, both of them.

"Steady," Bruce said.

"Steady…"

Here came the train, moving like a burst of lightning. It was out of the tunnel.

"Now."

Bruce squeezed his trigger. BANG went the shot. The rifle kicked against his shoulder.

BA-BANG the next two shots went, almost as one.

Then the train was beneath the bridge, passing under them, and behind them in a flash. Bruce stood and watched its lights disappearing into the darkness. After a moment it rounded a slight bend in the track and was completely gone.

It was still moving very fast. Bruce was under the impression that it shouldn't do that. If the driver was dead, the train should begin to slow right away.

"Did you lads hit anything?" he said.

* * *

The windshield shattered inward.

There was no warning. One moment it was quiet in here, the train was flying along at what seemed an impossible speed; the next instant the dense plastic shield exploded into a million tiny fragments.

Francois's first thought was there must be a design flaw. The windshield hadn't been designed strong enough to withstand these speeds. The pressure was too much, and the structure had failed. But that wasn't it.

A split second after the windshield crashed in, he felt the bullet pass through his throat. It was a high shot that never would have hit a seated pilot.

His hand went to his throat. Blood was spurting there.

"Ugh…" he sputtered. "Uh… uh."

He found himself lying on his back. He looked up at Fawcett. The man was still there, body tied back against the seat, head slumped forward and to the side. The wind shrieked through the demolished windscreen. The train wasn't slowing down at all. Francois could see the digital readout of the speedometer from where he lay.

475 kph. Very nearly the theoretical limit of the train's speed.

He was dying. Of course he was. He was lucky that the shot hadn't taken his head clean off. Or unlucky. He gasped. He clucked. He was drowning in his own blood. He coughed, and felt the dark, hot liquid expelled from his mouth and all over his neck.

Allah. Allah would want him to commit suicide now. Blow up the train. The detonator was still on the dashboard. He could see it from here.

He couldn't move. His vision was growing dark. Everything faded into a deep, black nothing. Francois lay on his back, staring blankly upward. He thought about the detonator, but realized he had no idea where it was.

He couldn't remember anymore. And he no longer cared.

CHAPTER THIRTY

7:05 pm British Summer Time (2:05 pm Eastern Daylight Time)
Margaret Thatcher Memorial Skyway
High above the Eurostar Tracks
England

"Good luck mate," the driver said as he dropped Ed Newsam off at the bridge.

Ed nodded. "Thank you. I think I'll need some."

He exited the car with his big gym bag. The car turned around where the cops had removed the lane barriers and went back the way he came. The bridge was closed. The only traffic on the eastbound side of the M20 motorway was cars that had turned back at the checkpoint.

Ed walked to the makeshift blockade and gave the police there his FBI badge to scan. Ed supposed he looked like any other agent out here. He wore a dark jumpsuit with a thick utility belt, boots, and he was carrying a big bag. He had a tiny speaker lodged in his left ear, with a wire dangling to the satellite phone on his belt. The wire had a small microphone along its length.

It took a moment for Ed's identity to come up on the cop's laptop screen. It was full dark now, and the glow of the screen changed when Ed's information appeared.

"Newsam," the cop said. "Impressive resume. 82nd Airborne. Special Forces. FBI. Why are you up here?"

Ed shrugged. "My superiors sent me. I'm supposed to take surveillance footage of the train if it passes by. Training footage for later."

"We just heard that it's in motion. It's on its way."

That made Ed's heart skip a beat. He had gotten here just in time. He might even be late, depending on how fast that train was moving.

The man gestured at Ed's gym bag. "What's in there?"

Ed patted it. "Video equipment. Photography equipment. Telescopic lens. Lighting."

"Any weapons?"

Ed nodded. "Service weapon. I just threw it in there."

He was expecting a whole process now. The cops would want to check his bag, go through everything. Then they'd quickly realize he wasn't here to take photos or video. There were two loaded guns in the bag, one Glock semi-auto, but also an MP5, four fully loaded extra magazines for the guns, a knife, and a small stack of round explosive charges backed with adhesive. They were designed to blow doors and hatches off their hinges. You stuck them on whatever you wanted to blow, lit the fuse, and ran for cover.

Oh yeah. There was also a parachute in the bag. That could be a little hard to explain - guy with airborne training walks out onto a high roadway bridge carrying a bunch of weapons and a parachute.

I don't know. He said he was gonna take some pictures.

But the cop just nodded. "Okay. Pass."

Ed picked up the bag and walked through. There wasn't much time now. Once he was 20 feet from the checkpoint, he hit the green CALL button on the satellite phone. Swann and Trudy were on autodial. Ed kept walking as the signal bounced around low Earth orbit, shaking hands with satellites, encrypting, decrypting, doing whatever magic Swann required of it.

"Come on," he whispered.

There was a small crowd of military personnel and more cops on the roadway. The bridge itself seemed rusted and decrepit, something that the local government should seriously be considering for chopping block status. He walked out onto it, feeling the sway as crosswinds hit the structure.

It's designed to do that.

Why it was this high above the railroad bed was anyone's guess. To the west, the lights of the city of London and her suburbs shone against the sky. Ed positioned himself near the barrier above the railroad.

The barrier wasn't particularly tall, and not much of a barrier. It was a sturdy railing that came to about Ed's chest. Ed supposed there was no need for much else in normal times. This was a narrow ribbon of road with no shoulder. It was probably rare that anyone without engine trouble stopped up here. And the ones that did were probably afraid to get out of their cars.

On the other side of the barrier, there was about six inches of roadway that formed a sort of ledge. Beyond that, there was nothing but God.

"Ed?" a female voice said in his earpiece.

Trudy Wellington. Her voice was nearly blown away by the wind.

"Yeah," he shouted. "Trudy."

He glanced around. These cops weren't listening to him. Nobody could hear anything more than ten feet away up here.

"The train is already in motion, Ed."

"I know. I heard."

"It's coming fast," a male voice said. Mark Swann. "I'm dialed in to the railway processors. The data I'm getting suggests over 250 miles per hour and gaining speed."

Oh, man.

"Ed, this is crazy," Trudy said. "You don't have to do it."

Ed took a deep breath. He knew that already. But the last time Stone went on one of these things by himself… it was no good.

"Already decided," he said. "No more debate. I just need your help. There's a bunch of cops and whatever near me. If they see me go over this railing, they're going to lose it. So it all has to happen fast. One, two, three."

"I've calculated your speed of descent from that height, about 200 feet above the railway, and I'm estimating the speed of the oncoming train at 275 miles per hour when it reaches you. It's based on a…"

"Trudy. You're the math major, not me. Just tell me when to go."

"I will. But I'd get ready now. It's coming."

"It's coming very fast," Swann said. "Did I mention that?"

"You do not want to go splat," Trudy said.

Ed nearly laughed. He knew that much already. "Thanks."

"Throw that chute as soon as you're airborne. Don't wait. I calculated that the…"

"Okay," Ed said. "I got it."

Ed glanced around him. It was dark on the bridge. The overhead lamps were old sodium arcs, from another era. They gave a weak yellow light. A few of these cops had flashlights, but they weren't doing much with them. These guys were just here to keep the road closed. They weren't interested in Ed. They weren't even paying attention.

Ed opened his gym bag and took out the chute. It was like a large backpack, and he shrugged into it. He hooked the gym bag onto his belt, then climbed out over the barrier. He went low on it, slithering over the top of it like a snake, so as not to draw attention to himself. He turned sideways at the top, then put his feet down on the narrow ledge.

He pressed his back against the barrier. There were two railings, a high one and a low one, and a space between them. He could sort of slide his butt down and take a seat on the lower one. He did it. Okay. He was perched here like a bird on a wire.

He glanced around again. Good. No one was looking.

"Ready. Just tell me when."

In the distance far below him, he thought he could see the lights of the approaching train. Something on the ground was coming, and it was moving very fast. He watched it for a couple of seconds. The thing began to resolve into an eel, a snake… a train.

It was. It was definitely the train.

He took another deep breath. There was no sense doing a lot of thinking about this. It would either work or it wouldn't.

"Trudy?"

"Hey!" someone shouted from behind him. "Hey! Wait! Get off there!"

Now there were a bunch of shouts. People were alarmed. He could hear their footsteps running toward him.

"Now, Ed! GO NOW."

A strong hand grabbed his shoulder. Two arms slipped through the space between railings and tried to lock around his midsection.

Now people were screaming. They thought they were looking at a suicide.

He fought them. He knocked the hand on his shoulder away and wrenched open the fingers of the hands gripped around his waist.

"AAAAaaaahhhh!" the guy shouted. Ed might have broken his fingers.

He had to go. If he stayed another second, these guys were going to knock him off and kill him by accident.

He planted his legs, pushed as hard as he could, and leapt off the bridge, out into nothing. Instantly, he was dropping very fast.

One second passed. Two.

Three.

Trudy's voice in his ear: "Ed! Pull the chute! Pull the chute!"

He reached inside the backpack with his right hand, fumbled for the chute. It wouldn't come out! There was no time for this.

Come on! Come on!

He looked down between his feet. Everything was a blur. He saw the lights of the train. The lights of the ground. Darkness. He had no idea. He couldn't make sense of it. All he felt was his own speed. He was plummeting. The ground was coming fast.

The chute was stuck. He pulled. It wouldn't…

He wrenched it out. It went up.

Open! Please!

The chute opened above him, white against the dark of the sky. It didn't seem to fill. The pull was not hard, not like what he was used to. There was a sense of slowing down, decelerating. He looked down again - the surface was coming...

Very fast.

Fast.

Slowing now, just a bit. A moment to look, and to think.

Okay. He glanced ahead for the first time. The train was coming. It was below him, still out a ways, zooming like a missile. It didn't seem possible how fast it was traveling. And he was going to land right in front of it.

He had jumped too soon. The calculations were off.

Oh my God. No!

For a split second, he caught a glimpse of a shattered windshield, lights on in the cockpit. It seemed like a grinning skull. What did that mean?

No time to think. Here it came.

He was going to hit hard. He was going to land on the tracks ten feet in front of the train. There wasn't going to be any time. He was falling...

The train whooshed by directly below him. He gasped. The front of it had gone by already. Then another car. Then another.

He hit. He hit like a meteor.

The crash was jarring. Bone-rattling. He landed on bent legs, trying to displace the impact. He fell to his butt and bounced, his entire body folding in the middle. He went head over heels, hit the train a second time, and rolled.

"Ungh!"

He banged over the top of the train, his momentum carrying him toward the back. His hand found some sort of railing or handle. He grabbed it. The force of his movement nearly wrenched his shoulder out of his socket. He swung his other hand around, and now he was grasping the metal railing with two strong hands.

He could hear himself, gasping or shouting or breathing; he didn't know which. It was all the same right now.

"Ah. Ah. Ah."

The wind whipped around him. The train was zipping along, everything passing in a flash. His eyes couldn't make sense of it all. Green lights went by overhead, leaving dazzling impressions on his eyes. He blinked to clear them, but the streaks were still there, inside the darkness.

He groaned.

Brutal.

And on the heels of that thought:

That was loud. Did anyone inside hear that?

He nodded. Yeah. He weighed about 250 pounds, plus gear, and he had crashed into a train going over 250 miles per hour, from above. Probably everybody heard it. They probably heard it in New York.

He lay in the dark, hands gripping the metal. He didn't want to move. He just wanted to stay here for a moment and get his wind back. He wanted to do a body scan and see if he could sense any injuries. It would be hard to sense anything. His adrenaline was off the charts right now.

He was trembling. He could feel that. It was good. It meant he was still alive. Now, he felt a pull, tugging him from behind. It began to pull harder. His body was being yanked upwards. He looked back.

His parachute! It was still on. He had almost forgotten about it.

It had filled again. The train was flying, the chute was full, and pulling him back up into the air. It swung crazily in the blast of air coming off the top of the train. It nearly ripped his grip from the railing.

Unh. He was tired. That chute was trying to kill him. He had to cut it loose, but he couldn't let go of the railing.

One hand. You can do it with one hand.

He let his left hand, his weaker hand, release its grip on the railing. He was on his feet now, crouching, gripping, being pulled backwards. He held tight with his right hand.

He reached into the bag clipped to his belt. He felt around inside. Guns, explosives - where was the knife?

"AAAAHHHH!"

He screamed in frustration. Everything was flying past him. Tiny pieces of debris strafed his face like shrapnel. He couldn't stay here.

His hand found the knife. He pulled it out and hacked at the cords like a crazy man. There was no rhyme or reason to it. No logic, just slash, slash, slash.

Suddenly, he was free. The chute flew away, and he crashed back to the surface of the train again.

"Uh. Oh boy. Oh mother."

He had no idea what he was saying. He groped his way to his feet. He needed to move fast. If he got hit by anything now - a discarded soda can, a flying rock, anything at all - he was going to be knocked into oblivion.

He stumbled to the nearest air vent. It was just a few feet away. He fell to his knees. Everything was dizzying. Everything was moving too fast. The train passed through a dark tunnel of some kind. It could have been a hundred meters long. It went by in what seemed like a split second.

Ed dug the small adhesive-backed explosive charges out. He placed two of them on the square vent door. These things should blow that door to kingdom come. They should blow a nice hole all around it.

What about the C4?

Good question. If the C4 was wired through the ceiling, then Ed was going to blow this train to bits. Even if it wasn't in the ceiling - and it probably wasn't because the floor and the side walls were so much easier - he still had no idea where the detonators were hidden, or how sensitive they were.

Okay. This had been a risky idea from the beginning. There were a lot of unknowns. But he did know one thing: if he stayed out here much longer, he was going to die. It might be dangerous to blow that vent, but…

What else was he going to do?

He set the charges, reached into his bag, and pulled the sparker that would light the fuses. It didn't even need a flame. Just a spark. He hit one, the fuse caught, and started moving. He hit the second one. Now they were both moving.

"Oh God," he said.

He fell backwards, spinning as he did so. He crawled on all fours, as fast as he could. Then his body gave up. He slipped and fell on his face. He began to wriggle along like a worm. He would be the fastest worm on Earth.

Any second. Any second now.

If they didn't know he was up here yet, they were about to find out. He covered his heads with his hands.

BOOOM! The first explosive blew, lighting up the night behind him.

BOOOM! The second one blew an instant later.

He lay where he was for a long second, waiting for the whole train to explode. When it didn't, he glanced back. There was a gaping hole of ruptured steel and burning fiberglass back there, flames licking the edges of it, embers being driven howling into the night air by the speed of the train.

He could hear the screams of the terrified passengers from here.
He was in business.

CHAPTER THIRTY ONE

7:08 pm British Summer Time (2:08 pm Eastern Daylight Time)
Camden High Street
Camden Town
London, England

"They're out of the tunnel!" someone screamed. "They're out of the tunnel!"

Constable Bryan Fincham was 23 years old, and 18 months into his job on the Metropolitan Police Service. He was less than six months from the end of his probationary period, and beginning to get the hang of things, he'd reckon.

But late this afternoon they'd posted him here to the High Street of Camden Town, to help maintain calm and order. They'd evacuated the area around St. Pancras Station, and, originally, they'd said there'd be no need to evacuate from here. The train blast they were concerned about, if it came, might take down the station, but this was far enough away that there should be minimal impact.

Tell that to the people.

There'd been a steady stream of traffic moving north through the district for the past 20 or 30 minutes. It had bogged down into a bit of a jam, and moments ago people had begun to abandon their cars in the road. That couldn't be allowed.

He had grabbed the first bloke to do it, a skinny punk in a sleeveless dungaree jacket, black jeans. And boots. He and the missus had simply ditched their ancient Ford Escort MK van in the middle of the High Street. The car looked like a small ambulance. Except it was purple, with some sort of childlike representation of the planets of the solar system painted along its side. At first, Fincham assumed the old bohemian car had overheated while waiting in the traffic, but then the wanker and his girl just walked away from it.

"Hey!" He grabbed the man's elbow. "Hey now!"

It was just the first leak that gave the dam permission to burst. Within what seemed like seconds, everyone was doing it. They were all just abandoning their vehicles, getting out, and leaving. At first, they were walking quickly, with purpose. But then some of them began to run.

A fast-flowing river of people moved along the sidewalks, and between the cars. They surged past Fincham without even seeing him. To Fincham, it seemed like one of these films where the world has ended, and a horde of flesh-eating zombies are fast on the heels of the main characters.

Now everyone was running, pushing, and shoving in the narrow street. An older man fell to his knees and was stepped on.

Fincham tried to move to the man's aid, but he was swimming against the tide. A blur of people shoved past him, bounced off him, bounced off each other, a blind swarm of humanity, moving heedlessly. He pushed through them, but it was like pushing through a thicket. He'd lost sight of the man who had fallen. Was he still down?

Fincham looked to his right. No. The man was back up. He was limping to the side, holding his head. His face was a wreck, a mask of blood. He leaned against a storefront, away from the crowds, and slowly sank to the ground.

"What is it?" Fincham shouted. "What's happening?" His hands were in the air and extended as if to tell the people to:

STOP.

A young woman in tight jeans and an orange tube top stopped, but only for a second. Her eyes were wild. "The train is coming! It has atomic weapons on board. A dirty bomb! It's coming now! You have to get out of here!"

Then she was gone.

The train was coming. The explosive train. The atomic bomb train. Of course it was just a rumor. And it had set off a panic.

But was it true?

"Ah, bloody hell," Fincham said. He could stand here, ineffectually waving his arms, and wait to be blown to bits. Or he could...

Bryan Fincham, young Constable of the London Metropolitan Police Service, often known as Scotland Yard, turned and ran with the crowd.

CHAPTER THIRTY TWO

A guy down there had a gun.

But Ed wasn't staying up here. He plunged through the flaming hole in the roof of the train, his arms and legs spread, making him a huge target, like a bear.

The guy was small, small by Ed standards, maybe small anyway. Ed didn't get a chance to really see him. He was young. He reached to point his gun upwards, but Ed landed on top of him before he could aim.

The kid broke Ed's fall, but just barely. They crashed to the floor, Ed on top. The kid's head bounced off the hard flooring, his face dazed by the impact. He still had the gun in his hand.

With his left hand, Ed banged the kid's gun hand against the floor, once, twice. The gun came loose. The kid dug his free hand into Ed's face, trying to push him off.

Ed punched him. The punch came over the top and landed solidly on the fragile bones of the kid's face.

The kid had some fight in him, though. He tried to claw at Ed's face. They did a crazy, slapping, hand jive together, batting each other's hand away. Of its own accord, Ed's left hand found the kid's gun on the floor.

The kid's hand was under Ed's chin, pushing hard.

Ed looked up. There was a half-circle of people standing around, staring down at them, arms and legs braced against the seats, swaying with the motion of the train as it raced down the track.

"Is this a hijacker?" Ed asked the crowd.

People nodded. People looked confused. It was a sea of traumatized faces.

"Yes or no?"

"Yes," a man said.

"Yes!" another shouted.

A low murmur of yeses went through the group.

Good enough. Ed had the gun. He pressed the muzzle against the kid's face. The kid pushed at Ed's face, both hands free now, clawing at him.

Ed turned his face away and:

BANG!

One shot did it. The kid was dead. He was a mess, actually.

Ed didn't really look. He kneeled there for a moment, catching his breath. It had been a whale of a couple of minutes, from the bridge jump to the roof of the train, to fighting and killing this guy.

He looked up at the crowd again. The people were shaking and rolling as the train took bends in the track at high speed. For an instant, a new thought occurred to Ed. What if the train just derailed?

Better not to think about that right now.

"Where are the rest?" he said.

A man pointed behind Ed. Then another did the same. That was no good. Ed turned, half-expecting to see a hijacker standing above him, gun pointed at his head.

No. There was another group of people behind him. He got it now. He had blown a hole in the roof right in the middle of the car. People had been sitting under that spot. Not only did part of the roof come crashing down; the part that remained was on fire. People had gotten out of their seats to get away from it.

Sorry.

He looked beyond the people. Sure enough, a man had run to the door at the front end of the train car. He opened the door and passed through it.

Okay. Clean that guy up first, then go find Stone.

Ed pushed himself to his feet.

Now there was a thick knot of people between him and the door at the far end. The people were all just standing there, looking at him.

"Excuse me. Coming through."

He pushed a small man out of his way. The man barely moved. No one else moved at all. These people were in shock.

Ed had no time for this.

"Gang way!" he shouted. "Police!"

That should get them moving. But it didn't. So he simply blasted through the crowd, parting them with his body.

* * *

"I should kill you right now," the man said.

Richard Sebastian-Vilar lifted his head from the table. The drugs they had given him had worn off hours ago, but he was exhausted. He was still cuffed to the table, and unable to sit up properly. He could not stand at all.

They had left him here like this… he had no idea how long it had been. It could have been a full day. He could have been days. He knew that he had wet himself, at least twice. He could smell the stench of himself, and it was not pleasant.

The kidnapping seemed like a long time ago. He was dehydrated, and very hungry. He had a splitting headache, which could have been from dehydration, or maybe it was a hangover from the drugs.

He had given up. He had given up the hope of seeing his wife and daughter again. He had given up hope of resuming his life. He imagined the hijackers would just kill him at some point. Why even let him live?

He had noticed that the train was moving. Then he noticed that it was getting faster and faster. He glanced out the window at his table. They were outside now. He spotted shapes zipping by in the darkness of the evening. Trees, poles, buildings. There were lights along the railway, and lights in the distance as well. Everything was moving so fast that he couldn't focus on any of it.

What was the reason behind what they were doing? Vilar had no idea. No one had bothered to explain anything to him. There was no big soliloquy from a terrorist, explaining how the crimes of the West had brought us to this pass. They had more or less ignored him. They didn't care what happened to him, and neither did he. Not really. Not anymore. He'd heard an explosion a moment ago, and thought he was dead then.

He roused himself to look at the man speaking. It was a young guy, dark-skinned, dark eyes, clean shaven, in a blue dress shirt open at the collar.

The man pressed the muzzle of a gun to Vilar's forehead. Vilar felt nothing about that. He could die in the next second. It would almost seem like a welcome relief.

"I'm a Supreme Court justice," he said. "Of the United States."

The young guy shook his head. "You're nothing. You work for the oppressors. You're an abortionist and a whoremonger."

Vilar shook his head. This was where he came in. The last clear memories he had, in a tunnel high in the Pyrenees Mountains, some other terrorist was accusing him of more or less the same things.

"So shoot me. Okay? Just shoot me."

And he realized then which way he was going to vote. Perhaps he had known it all along. If he lived through this, he was going to strike down the travel ban in the conservative states. The travel ban was driven by fear. The travel ban meant that people like this, this young terrorist, would win. People of good will, who were 99% of all people, in the United States, in North Africa, everywhere, would lose.

You couldn't be afraid of people like this. You simply had to defeat them, whatever that took. They did what they did to drive a wedge through people, to separate them. The job of good government, indeed the job of the human race, was to bring people together.

The gun was still pressed to Vilar's head. But he didn't care. For the first time, he understood that he was at war. He was not above the fray, even though he had long fooled himself into thinking he was. If he ever got the opportunity, and if he had the means available, he would kill the man standing in front of him.

Suddenly, the young guy turned his head and looked to his left, back down the way he had come. The gesture was something from deep in human memory - similar to those of prey animals in the wild. Red alert. He'd heard the sound of a predator.

Dinosaur coming.

Darth Vader coming.

Death coming.

The young guy shook his head, seemed to forget about Vilar, and ran further up through the train car. At the front, he hit the button, the door opened, and he passed into the next car.

Vilar took a deep breath. He was tired.

He let his head sink back down to the tabletop.

* * *

Ed came bursting into the Business Class lounge.

The lights in here were dim. The windows along the tables were big. The design of the lounge brought the outside world in. The train was whipping. The shadows and lights of the countryside zoomed by. There were no passengers in here. At least, there didn't appear to be.

Ed crept through, one slow step at a time. The speed of the train, and its side-to-side movements, made it difficult to walk. His quarry could be hiding anywhere in here, waiting for him.

Ed tossed the dead hijacker's gun aside, into the darkness under a table. He unstrapped the MP5 from his chest, and checked it. Full auto.

205

He knew the magazine was loaded. He had two more of those. It was time to end these mothers.

His eyes were alive. His head was on a swivel.

Someone was up ahead, and to his left. A man. Thin. His head was on the table in front of him, facing away from Ed.

This didn't look right. The guy looked like bait. A trap.

Ed put the gun on him from behind.

"You! Are you alive?"

The man turned his head to the side but didn't lift it.

"American?" he said.

"Yes. You?"

Now the man pushed his head up from the table. "My name is Richard Sebastian-Vilar. I am a Supreme Court judge. I was kidnapped in Spain... I don't know when. I don't know where I am."

Oh man.

Ed quickly stepped to the thin man. There was no time to offer him much in terms of support or medical care, and he couldn't allow himself to let his own guard down. He was on a hunting expedition that could easily go the other way.

But he crouched down near the guy for a second.

"Sir, I'm very glad to see you're still alive. My name is Special Agent Edward Newsam. I work for the FBI Special Response Team. You're on the high-speed train from Paris to London. I'm here to rescue you. But I have to clear these hijackers out first. There isn't a lot of time."

He looked closely. The man was crying now. His body was trembling.

"I'm chained to this table."

Ed glanced under the table. The man wasn't lying. Those were real steel manacles under there. It was going to take time and effort to cut those things.

"Are you hurt?"

"I don't think so."

Ed nodded. "Okay. Then this is the best place for you at this moment. You're as safe as you're going to be right here, exactly as you are."

Ed wasn't sure if he was lying or not. He just didn't have the time to come up with an alternative.

"Did you see a man come through here?"

Vilar nodded. "Yes. Just a minute ago. He held a gun to my head. He went into the next car, up ahead."

Ed stood. "I'll be back for you, sir. I promise. Just hang in there."

He turned to leave but stopped.

"I have your watch, by the way."

He held his wrist out to the judge. In the gloom, with the crazy shadows zipping by, the Breitling almost seemed to glow. The blue color was beautiful.

The judge inspected it, but then put his head back on the table.

"Keep it."

Ed nodded. It was a nice watch. If he lived through this...

"I'll be back for you."

He went to the next car. There was no one in here, either. It was a much smaller car than the previous ones - more of a compartment than an actual car. Immediately he saw why. This was the front car of the train. The big steel door to the cockpit was here. This was some kind of lounge for the drivers.

A corpse was on the floor, a guy in a train driver uniform. There was no one else here. Ed toed the body just to make sure. He pushed it with his boot. It was dead weight. He surveyed the scene for a moment. There were only two doors in here - the one to the cockpit, and one to the side that was probably a restroom.

Ed barely glanced at the cockpit door. Since September 11th, they'd made these doors almost impossible to beat. It was going to be hard to do anything about that thing. Meanwhile, someone was in there, driving this train - someone with access to a detonator that could blow this whole train apart.

Ed looked at the restroom door. Would the driver open the cockpit to anyone at this point? Probably not. Operationally, it made sense that once the hijacking driver was in place, that he was locked in for the duration.

That meant...

Ed crept closer to the restroom door. He approached it from the side. He did not stand in front of it. The light on above it was red. OCCUPIED. His body swayed with the jerks and movements of the train. He reached out and jiggled the handle.

"Hey, is anybody..."

BANG! BANG! BANG!

Sudden holes appeared in the door where the guy shot through it. The door was thin metal and fiberglass, easy to punch holes through. The hijacker was decent. Give him some credit. He moved his shots around, firing blind, trying to improve his chances of a body mass hit.

BANG! BANG!

Ed took an angle on the door, planted his legs, and just tore it up with the MP5.

DUH-DUH-DUH-DUH-DUH-DUH.

The door shredded. There was nowhere to hide in there. He gave it another burst.

DUH-DUH-DUH-DUH-DUH-DUH.

Things shattered on the other side - glass, maybe ceramic. Hard to say. A body fell to the floor. Ed reached up with a big leg, and kicked the door in. He had to push it and shove it. The door was broken in the middle.

He looked behind it. A young guy, shot full of holes, was on the floor.

Okay, one more down.

That was two. Ed had no idea how many there were. He needed to find Stone. If Stone was alive in here somewhere, Ed had the sense that Stone would know what they were dealing with. After all, he'd been briefed. Ed hadn't.

Ed looked at the gleaming door to the cockpit. His poppers probably weren't going to put a dent in that thing. Even more, setting off explosions inside the train…

No good. He didn't know where the detonators were. He didn't know where or how the C4 was wired. The door itself could somehow be part of the daisy chain. In fact, that would make a lot of sense.

He nodded, turned, and hit the button to open the door to the next car, and went back the way he came. Back to the fight. Back to find Stone.

If the driver hadn't blown up the train yet, then…

A flashback came to him. When he was falling through the sky, the windshield of the train appeared to be shattered. *What did that mean?*

There was no time to think about it.

* * *

Here we go.

A hijacker stood and turned to look back. There was something happening behind them - probably something to do with the explosions from before. Luke saw it unfolding, jumped up and aimed through the shattered window.

BANG!

Shot the guy in the back of the head. A spray of blood, and the guy went back down. This was the chance. Maybe this was the chance.

Luke hit the button to his own door. It slid open and he rolled out into the foyer.

He was vulnerable here, terribly vulnerable. The dead guy on the floor was the last man who had been alive inside here.

The train was rocking and rolling, swaying side to side.

Luke jumped up and slid along the wall to the door. From his angle, he couldn't see anyone on the other side. He took a breath. This was for all the marbles.

One… two…

He spun, stepped into the door, his gun out, ready to fire. The passenger car extended out in front of him, people seated on either side of the aisle. The people seemed to lean away from the aisle, trying to protect themselves from whatever happened next. The guy Luke had just shot was here on the floor. The other hijackers were…

There was one, at the far end of the car.

The window down there shattered, like this one had. Gunshots came. The man was shooting through that door at something. He fell back, firing his gun up through the broken window.

Someone was down there, fighting hijackers, coming the other way. Alain?

It had to be. Luke hit the button and the door opened in front of him. If Alain was coming this way, and Luke had cleaned out the hijackers at the back of the train, that must mean that one guy was the last one left.

He and Alain had put the squeeze on them. The pincer! It worked.

They could finish this right here.

But the train was still moving. The pilot was still in there, running this rolling bomb into the station at high speed. If they hadn't cut power by now, it was too late.

Call in the EMP strike.

It was the last resort. Luke walked up through the train, gun out, moving fast. He pulled out the small radio transmitter, hit TALK with his thumb. His gut told him it was the right thing. This train had been tearing it up for too long. They were going to reach the station soon.

Not good. Not at these speeds.

He was going to kill this hijacker. Just walk up behind him and…

"Launch the EMP!" he shouted into the radio. "Train out of control! Repeat! Launch the EMP!"

Someone near him gasped.

"Look!"

Luke turned to his left. A man stood in a passenger seat. He was a middle-aged man, maybe 45. For an instant, Luke could see every detail about him. He was good looking, with salt and pepper hair, dark skin, and piercing, calm eyes. His five o'clock shadow said he'd been up a long time. He wore a dress shirt and a gray vest, like a businessman at a casual affair might do.

There was a gun in his right hand, pointed at Luke's head.

Luke jerked to the side.

BANG!

Missed me. How?

Luke brought his own gun around, but the man dove out into the aisle. They wrestled, on their feet, both men with a gun in their right hand, both men pushing the other's gun aside with their left.

Luke tried to brace his legs, but the train swayed, and he fell, the man coming down on the top of him. Luke's gun flew out of his hand. There was no way to look for it. The other guy still had his. Luke's hand was on top of it.

He punched the guy in the face, a hammer blow.

Again.

The guy's weak hand was his free hand. He couldn't get his gun away from Luke.

Luke punched him again.

The man made a sound, of rage, of agony, impossible to say which. "Aaaaanh!"

The man's hand was on Luke's face, pressing his head against the floor. Luke's own hand slithered down to the knife he had taped to his calf. It was taped securely, too securely. He pulled at it, trying to rip it away from the skin.

The man gave up the gun. He threw it aside. Now his right hand was free. He pushed Luke's jaw up with his left hand, exposing Luke's throat.

He punched Luke in the throat.

Luke felt the wind hiss out of him. That was a real punch. It just missed crushing his windpipe. Another punch like that, and he was done.

There was no way. Not after everything. Some guy wasn't going to punch him to death on a runaway train.

The guy reared up.

Luke pulled the knife free. His left hand was on the guy's face, trying to push him backwards. The man bore all his weight down on top of Luke.

One more punch to the throat. Luke couldn't get his jaw down to protect himself.

He plunged the knife into the man's back.

The man straightened up for a second. His eyes widened. He grunted.

He felt that.

Then he hardened again. He punched Luke again, but his fist hit Luke's face.

Luke pulled the knife out and stabbed him again.

Above him, somewhere closer now, more gunshots rang out.

BANG! BANG! BANG!

Everywhere around them, people were screaming. It was a chorus of shrieks. Luke pushed his man off. BANG! A gunshot went off near his head. His ears rang. Who was shooting? He stabbed the guy again.

The train whipped along, not slowing down at all. The speed was incredible. Shadows zoomed by the windows.

They must be very close to the station now.

CHAPTER THIRTY THREE

7:15 pm British Summer Time (2:15 pm Eastern Daylight Time)
The Skies above West London
London, England

"Rogue Six, Rogue Six, do you read me?"

The old British Aerospace Hawk 200 flew on a northbound heading across the early night sky, at the edge of the far western London suburbs. Inside the cone of the fighter jet, the sky was wide open. Far to the west, the last light of day was fading.

Captain James "Biggs" Bigsley glanced at his radar. It was quiet out here tonight. There wasn't another aircraft anywhere in the sky. Of course, that was because of the presence of Rogue Six. Rogue Six went up, and of necessity everyone else had better come down.

The plane didn't look like much in this day and age, and it wouldn't survive more than a few minutes against an American F/A-18 or the new Eurofighters the RAF had on order. But surviving a dogfight wasn't its purpose.

Biggs was fitted with a helmet, a flight suit, and on top of that a parachute harness and a survival vest. The cockpit itself was equipped with a manual ejection system the pilot could control - in case the electronics aboard the plane failed.

Hopefully, he wouldn't need any of that stuff tonight. But you never knew. The weapons loaded on here were experimental, and if the directed energy went in the wrong direction, Biggs could find himself without a working aircraft, and out in the elements.

"Loud and clear, Northholt. Awaiting your orders."

"All systems go, Rogue Six. Release the Hound."

Biggs heard the order, but he wanted to make it 100% certain.

"Repeat, Dover. I had a moment of interference there. Please repeat."

"Rogue Six, release the Hound."

"Roger that," Biggs said.

He broke his northbound heading and banked to the right, headed east over the city. He dropped altitude, coming in low and slowing to just over 300 miles per hour. The City of London zipped by below him. Just ahead, seconds from now, were the colorful lights of Wembley Stadium, shining upwards into the night. In the distance, he could see the white lights on London Bridge.

This was all laid out ahead of time. The Hound was shorthand for the Sakharaov cruise missile, which could fly a pre-programmed route. Once engaged, it would release a high-energy directed microwave pulse at everything below its flight path, sizzling electronics and electrical systems, disabling some, completely destroying others. Every vehicle sitting in traffic was guaranteed to be sitting a long time.

The pulse would not kill anyone.

Unless, of course, they were wearing a heart pacemaker, or happened to be on life support at a hospital.

Biggs shook his head. Trade-offs were someone else's department. If they wanted to deploy the weapon, he had to assume they had studied the ramifications.

Tonight's route for the weapon was to follow the Eurostar rail line from St. Pancras Station to the tunnel entrance at Folkestone, and then ditch into the English Channel. The path of destruction would be perhaps two hundred meters wide, though electrical systems outside the edges of that would be vulnerable as well.

Biggs shook the thoughts away. He needed to focus. He roared over Wembley, altitude low and getting lower. The place was empty tonight. Whatever had been scheduled was probably canceled.

Everyone in the city was trying to evacuate. He could see it below him. Thousands of cars, lorries, and buses inching, crawling, not moving at all. Streams of people running.

Here came St. Pancras Station, its clock tower shining.

"Preparing to launch," he said.

This is bound to scare the pants off a few of these buggers.

He fired the missile. He caught a glimpse of it racing out ahead of the plane, its fins deploying. Then he steered into a steep, near vertical climb, and banked hard to his right. He leveled out and headed back the way he came.

"The Hound is released," he said. "The Hound is away."

He accelerated again, pushing the plane towards its max speed. Within seconds, he topped out just below Mach 1, racing west, out toward the furthest lights of the city.

He didn't want to be anywhere near that missile when the pulse was released.

CHAPTER THIRTY FOUR

"Wow," Mark Swann said. "Are you seeing this?"

He was sitting at his "desk" in what amounted to his "office" on the second floor of the SRT headquarters. His desk was a series of thick plywood boards, mounted along a wall like a long serving table, with several coats of white paint slapped on them.

A crowd of SRT people stood around and behind him. Swann was mindful that Don Morris was in that crowd. He and Don didn't always see eye to eye, and Don seemed more than a little irritated with him lately.

The SRT was a leaky ship, but there wasn't much Swann could do about it. There might be an in-house leaker, or an all-powerful agency like the CIA or NSA could simply be pulling and decrypting Special Response Team communications. Swann was trying to put a stop to it, but he was one man. And a mere mortal at that.

"Yeah," Don said. "I see it. What is it?"

There were several video monitors on top of the boards, and a line of servers tucked underneath them. There were various other pieces of equipment on plywood shelves above his head. There were several small fans, and two portable cooling units, one on a shelf, and a larger one on wheels on the floor. Wires snaked everywhere all over the floor. Empty energy drink cans marched like soldiers along both the plywood desk and the shelves.

The monitor directly in front of him was showing real-time aerial satellite footage of London. The place was lit up like the circus was coming to town. He had been monitoring the approach of the train, as it whipped along like a guided missile toward St. Pancras Station. He had also been monitoring the vast traffic jam as the people of London attempted a desperate exodus away from the city center.

But in the past several seconds, something had exploded near the English Channel coast. A bomb had gone off, something... It was followed by sudden darkness up and down the coastal area near Folkestone and Dover.

"It looks like…"

Swann worked to zoom the footage in near the site of the explosion. There was only so much he could do. He switched to ground based cameras on the other video screens. He scrolled through a bunch of them. Several were dead. A few were still on and were pointed at an area of darkness just outside where they were operating.

"Something blew up on the coast, and it took out the power to a wide swath of territory out there. And I mean all the power. All the lights are out. Municipal cameras are out. Surveillance cameras are out. Motorway lights are out. Entire buildings and communities have gone dark."

"What would do it?" Don said.

Swann shrugged. "I don't know. Theoretically, an electromagnetic pulse could do it, but no one really admits to having them, and I was under the impression that it would take out a larger area. Could be a… I don't want to say it."

"Just say it," Don said.

Swann shrugged. "Don't quote me on this, but a small tactical nuke would probably set off an electromagnetic pulse."

"Oh my God," Trudy Wellington said.

"Obviously, it could be something else. I just don't know what."

"Has anybody heard from Ed Newsam?" Don said. "He's close to that action, and I want to know what's going on."

Swann turned around and faced Don. That was another issue. Ed had jumped off a bridge about 10 or 15 minutes ago. They hadn't heard from him since. Swann glanced at Trudy. Her eyes were wide behind her red glasses. She made a gentle head shake.

"I haven't heard from him," Swann said.

He had a hunch that Ed might be closer to the action than Don realized.

CHAPTER THIRTY FIVE

7:21 pm British Summer Time (2:21 pm Eastern Daylight Time)
Nearing St. Pancras Railway Station
London, England

Everywhere, people were screaming.

Luke fought on. He stabbed and stabbed, his right arm moving like a piston. His left arm pinned the guy's neck to the floor. Luke grunted with the force of his own movements. Beneath him, the air went out of his man like a punctured tire.

Luke looked down at him. The man's eyes were white, blank, and dead.

"Good," Luke gasped.

His heart pounded in his chest. He rolled over and lay on his back for a moment, next to the body of his enemy. The bodies had piled up in here all day.

It was a mess.

All around Luke, there was a mad cacophony of noise - screams, shouts, wails of the passengers. And beneath all that, the sound of the train itself. The train was still moving as fast as ever.

The lights were still on. That was a problem.

He'd lost his radio transmitter in the fight. He felt around on the floor under the dead guy, found it, and pulled it out. He hit the TALK button.

"Stone calling! Where's that EMP, please?"

The man's voice came on, perhaps a touch less calm than before.

"There was an error. The pulse failed in the initial launch. Reports suggest the missile self-destructed near the coastline. Repeat, EMP has failed. Please stop the train by whatever means available."

Whatever means available?

What means were those?

The voice went on. "Speed and distance indicate approximately three minutes to arrival at Pancras train station. Barriers have been erected to cushion the impact, but it won't be enough if you arrive at full speed. Not nearly enough."

"Yeah," Luke said. "Understand."

He slipped the transmitter into his pocket and pushed himself to his feet. He looked out a window. An urban landscape flew by in the near distance, moving so fast that everything was a blur.

Luke needed to find his gun. It was on the floor here somewhere.

Suddenly, a shadow loomed behind him. He turned. A giant form stood there, blocking the aisle. For a second, Luke's fevered mind couldn't place the form, couldn't make it coalesce into something familiar. It was too strange. It was too unexpected.

"Stone," the monster said.

Luke stared at it another second. Time was wasting.

"Ed? What are you doing?"

It occurred to Luke that the guy coming the other way in the pincer move wasn't Alain, and never had been. It was Ed. How was that even possible?

"*How* are you doing?" Luke said. "You hurt?"

"Only my feelings."

Luke looked at Ed again. He really saw him this time. Big Ed Newsam, muscles stacked on top of muscles, fists like concrete. His eyes almost seemed to shine in the darkness, scanning the train for more hijackers to kill.

"I thought you were a Frenchman."

Now Ed smiled. "I only know one line in French, and I ain't gonna say it to you."

Luke nearly laughed. "Try me."

Ed shrugged. *"Voulez vous ce cushe avec moi, ce soi?"*

Now Luke did laugh. With his jaw, he gestured back the way Ed had come. His jaw, his neck and throat were sore. That last guy had let him have it pretty good.

"Any of them left?" he said.

"I haven't seen any. If I did…"

Luke nodded. "I get it."

They stared at each other for one more second.

"We have to stop the train," Luke said. "We gotta get inside the cockpit. We probably have less than three minutes."

Ed nodded. "I have an idea."

* * *

"You ready?" Ed said.

Luke nodded. "Ready as I'm ever going to be."

217

They were standing under a ragged hole in the ceiling of a train car. Ed had blown that hole on his way in. The plan, to the extent there was one, was that Ed was going to boost Luke up through the hole, and Luke was going to make his way two cars up to the cockpit of the train. Ed couldn't be completely sure, but he thought that the windshield of the cockpit was shattered.

If that turned out to be true, Luke would crawl through the open windshield, subdue the driver, and stop the train.

Ed wasn't coming. There was no obvious way to get his huge bulk up and through that hole, and no time to think about it. All around them, train passengers sat frozen, watching them with giant eyes. In some cases, the passengers sat with their eyes squeezed tight. The passengers were no help.

Ed was bent over, in a squat, his hands laced together. Luke put his boot into the stirrup that Ed's big hands made. He put his own hands on Ed's broad back.

"All in one go," Ed said.

Luke nodded. "Got it. On my go."

Now Ed nodded. "Just say the word."

"Go."

Luke put his weight into Ed's laced hands. At the same moment, Ed launched his body upward. Luke straightened his leg and took the ride up. Ed heaved him into the air. Luke grabbed the ragged hole in the roof and pushed himself through it.

For a second, he hung there, hands pressed against the hot metal, his upper body above the train, the wind screaming in his face, threatening to shove him back into the hole. The train was flying along. Something was coming - some sort of horizontal metal bar, green lights descending from it.

It would take his head off.

Ed pushed his feet from below and Luke slid up and onto his stomach, his body flat to the roof of the train. The bar went by in a blur, just above his head.

"Ahh."

That was bad.

He pressed his cheek and his palms to the roof. The train was in some kind of concrete slot canyon, below street level. It wasn't a tunnel - more like a cement gash carved into the ground. Shadows of buildings zipped by, half-seen. The sky was open above his head.

Tiny sharp pieces of grit seemed to patter against the top of his head. Another metal bar zipped by just above him, less than a meter from the top of the train. The green lights cast an eerie glow, for a split second, and then were gone.

If he was standing, a bar like that would slice him in half. He slithered like a snake, keeping his head down. The forces were impossible. The train lurched from side to side, trying to shake him off.

He grabbed a metal handle and pulled himself along it. He was going too slow. They were minutes from the station.

He poked his head up. The wind roared in his face. He squinted into it.

The next green lights were far away. He pushed himself up into the wind and lurched forward in a crouch, his clothes rippling. He took a step, then another.

Another.

The lights were coming.

He hit the deck, an instant before they zoomed overhead.

Too slow. Too slow.

Go!

He popped his head up again. More green lights in the distance. How many more chances did he have?

"Gaaaaaa!!!'

He scrabbled forward like a crab, hands and feet, knees not even touching the train, moving fast now. That was the ticket.

He flattened out and slid forward just as the lights came. The familiar green glow was here, washed over him, then was gone. Instantly, he was up and crawling again. He skittered like something out of a nightmare.

He came to the gap between train cars. He lunged across it like a four-legged creature would lunge, banged his knees on the lip of the next car, took the pain without a sound, and slid forward again.

Green lights zipped over him.

He was up and moving a split second later. He had the rhythm.

Go! Go! Go!

There was no time. He moved up the train, wind screaming around him. He lost track. Up, crawl, dive, slide. Wait a beat.

Up, crawl, dive, slide.

He leapt another gap. Was this the front car of the train? It must be.

A black chasm loomed ahead. A tunnel. This must be it. The train was entering the tunnel that brought it to the station.

Time's up.

The tunnel swallowed him, sheer darkness. Pure movement. Side to side, straight ahead. The sound in here was impossible to believe.

PURE SOUND.   Screeching, screaming echoes, all around him. Humans were not designed to be exposed to this. Not to this speed, not to this NOISE.

He wanted to cover his ears, but there was no time.

If he covered his ears, he would die. They would all die.

He crawled forward, blind now.   There was so much shrieking sound, he might as well be deaf as well.   It was impossible to make sense of it.

He scrabbled across a vent, then reached an incline.   He slid forward and down, no way to stop himself now.

That windshield better be shattered.

It was. He fell through it and into the cockpit. He landed on top of the instruments. The lights were on in here. There was a man in the pilot's seat. There was blood. He was shot, his head slumped to the side.

Luke crawled across him, fell to the floor, then pulled himself to his feet.

Another man was here, dead on the floor. Both men wore uniforms of the train company. Where was the terrorist? There was no time to make sense of it.

It was slightly quieter here in the cockpit. He could hear his radio transmitter now. A voice was screaming.

"Stone! Do you read? Stone! Do you read? Seconds to impact!"

No time to answer.

He looked through the shattered windshield. The headlights of the train illuminated the way ahead.   There was something out there, something bright yellow. The terminus. It must be the terminus. That was trouble.

The fat man in the pilot seat was strapped in place.

In an instant, Luke's knife was in his hand. He hacked away the guy's binds, freed the body, and shoved it to the floor.

"Move it."

He sat in the pilot seat.

That yellow *something* loomed there, straight ahead. The train was slowing now, but not quickly enough.

The body.

The body had been strapped there to keep the train going. Okay, clever. What else? There was something heavy on the floor, like a brick. Hopefully, it wasn't some kind of toe-popper mine. It didn't matter. He had to do something.

Luke pushed it with his foot.

The radio transmitter: "STONE!"

A small pedal popped up as the brick slid off of it. The train slowed more. Still not enough. He could see the power delivery reducing on the dashboard readout.

That yellow something was RIGHT THERE.

His hands moved around the controls his eyes wild.

Bright red letters: BRAKE.

He pushed the lever forward. Hard. Instantly, the momentum changed. He was nearly flung forward as the train braked. He shoved it harder.

Put your weight on it!

He pushed.

The yellow thing. It was a tank of some kind. A barrel. A barrier? The man had said there would be barriers.

Impact. Impact coming. He braced one hand against the dashboard. He pushed the brake as far as it would go.

"Stop!" he shouted.

Yellow filled his field of vision.

WHUMPFFF.

The train hit hard, the yellow barrier exploding into a giant spray of water. It splashed into the cockpit, soaking him like a 10-foot wave.

There was another yellow barrel behind the first. The train hit that one, too.

WHUMPFFF.

More water sprayed.

The train was slower now, much slower. It hit the third barrel and broke it apart, the water sluicing all over the front of the train, but not spraying inside the cockpit.

The train hit a fourth barrel, pushed into it...

...and stopped.

The yellow barrel was huge. As tall as the train, and as wide. For a long second, it seemed to debate as to what it wanted to do. Then it popped and collapsed, water falling out in a lovely cascade in front of the train and onto the platform.

Luke sat back in the pilot's seat. He took a deep breath. It had been a while since he had breathed at all.

"Stone?" a tinny voice said.

He took the radio transmitter out of his pocket.

"Agent Luke Stone," he said. His voice was like a gasp.

"United States FBI Special Response Team. Accompanied by Agent Edward Newsam of the Special Response Team. We're here. St.

Pancras Station. Train is stopped. All or nearly all hijackers are dead. Request immediate emergency medical assistance for train passengers, and immediate security lockdown of the train and platform. Repeat, request immediate assistance."

Somewhere, wherever this transmitter went, a group of people were cheering.

"Good job, Stone," the voice said.

Stone shook his head and smiled. "Thanks."

* * *

Luke stood on the train platform. He had climbed out the windshield. He was holding a small device he'd found in the cockpit, what he believed to be the only functional detonator on the train.

Ed Newsam walked up the platform toward him. A moment ago, Ed had simply wrenched open one of the passenger doors. From here, Luke could hear the howling and moaning of the passengers. None of them had come out of the train yet.

"Some of these people, man," Ed said. "They're never gonna be the same after this."

Luke smiled. "Me, neither."

Ed looked him over. "I notice you're all wet. Soaked, really. What's that about?"

Luke laughed and shook his head. "Let's not talk about it."

Three stories above their heads, a curved dome of skylights opened to the dark night.

The station itself was entirely deserted. Not a single person was anywhere.

"Nice place," Ed said.

"Beautiful," Luke said. He had been to this train station before. He could picture it, an ornate old piece of artwork from a previous century, with this modernized section that fit the rest perfectly. They didn't make places like this anymore.

Then he thought of the dead, wounded, and terrified people on the train, and the nice moment passed.

At the far end of the platform, lights appeared. A flashlight. Another one. Then another one. Then several more. They swept back and forth. They moved quickly, coming this way. They weren't really flashlights. They were lights on the scopes of rifles, carried by either SWAT-type cops, SAS special operators, or both.

Luke put the transmitter to his lips.

222

"Luke Stone again. Agent Newsam and I are on the platform outside the train. Please don't kill us."

Ed gestured at the radio. "Can I see that?" he said.

Luke shrugged. "Sure." He handed it over.

Ed looked it over, figuring out how to work it. Then he clicked TALK.

"Be advised that US Supreme Court judge Richard Vilar is alive and aboard the train. He is in the business class lounge near the front of the train, and in need of assistance."

Ed handed the radio back to Luke. Ahead of them, the lights were everywhere, a forest of them converging.

"You found him," Luke said.

Ed nodded and smiled. He showed Luke the Breitling watch on his wrist, shining a faint metallic blue. It was pretty, no doubt.

"Yeah. I found him. He gave me the watch."

CHAPTER THIRTY SIX

September 27
2:05 pm Eastern Daylight Time
The Oval Office
The White House
Washington, DC

"I think that seals it," Clement Dixon said.

He glanced around the office. Three tall windows, with drapes pulled back, looked out on the Rose Garden. It was a bright, sunny day outside. Indian Summer, they used to call it. In the corner, the Resolute Desk - a long-ago gift from the British people - was there in its customary spot. Standing at the double doors were two tall Secret Service agents, backs straight, staring ahead, seemingly at nothing.

Here, near the center of the office, a comfortable sitting area with high-backed chairs was situated on top of a lush carpet adorned with the Seal of the President. At the moment, he was visiting with Vice President Thomas Hayes and Senator Susan Hopkins of California. They were all sipping black tea.

"In what way, Mr. President?" Susan Hopkins said.

Dixon smiled at them both. Hopkins was beautiful, of course, as beautiful as they all said, much more beautiful in person than on the TV. She wore a no-nonsense gray business suit, sensible shoes, and her hair tied in a bun. She could have worn a potato sack, and it wouldn't have mattered. That didn't sway Dixon one way or the other.

Thomas Hayes looked like Clement Dixon had just run him off the road. Dixon had heard that Hayes had his reservations about Susan Hopkins, but he could voice those at a later time. Or he could keep them to himself. The three of them were making history here. And Clement Dixon was an avid student of history.

A low black coffee table completed the look and helped tie the area together. No one ever put their coffee or teacups on there. Generally speaking, Dixon would place books on the table, depending on what he was reading or thinking about, or what subtle message he wanted to send. Today there was a fat hardcover book on there, a biography of Susan B. Anthony. He smiled. Maybe the message wasn't that subtle.

He would miss this place. He really would. Hosting people in the Oval Office was one of the great perks of this job. He silently reminded himself that he would be here, practically every day, for another 16 months. And he also reminded himself that it was for the best. He wasn't the man he'd been a year ago.

It was time to get out of the way. But he had one more thing to do before then, and this meeting was it. The whole thing had happened faster than he expected, and that was just fine. What was even finer was he had been brought inside the decision-making circle, and then he had hijacked the whole thing.

"You both understand what I'm saying here. Don't make me say it out loud. You're the perfect couple, the perfect complement to each other, and you'll be just about unstoppable. Susan, my people have done the research. It turns out you've got some of the highest positive ratings of any politician in America, even higher than mine in some cases. And unlike mine, your negatives barely exist."

"I think a lot of people don't know me very well," she said.

"They're going to know you a lot better very soon. You've got my blessing. This is the dynamic duo, and I'm honored to be sitting here with you both."

Dixon had taken a bunch of meetings in the past couple of day. The kicker was one he had with David Halstram, of all people. Halstram had been a junior staffer around the West Wing at one point, really just another young face in a young crowd. To Dixon, these days, they were practically all the same. Only one staffer here had ever jumped out at him, and he didn't like to think about that.

Then Thomas, to his credit, had spotted David's energy and intelligence. He had picked him out of the choir and elevated him to soloist. David Halstram had very quickly become Thomas's body man and nearly constant companion. The kid had a lot to offer.

As far as David Halstram was concerned, Susan Hopkins was the "it" girl. To say that he admired her was to say that the Grand Canyon was pleasant to look at. She was the woman of destiny. In Halstram's mind, the path was clear to Susan becoming the first woman President of the United States.

If Thomas Hayes cakewalked into the presidency, and Halstram was nearly sure he would, then Susan was next in line. After eight years as Hayes's understudy, she still wouldn't be quite 50 years old.

In the course of that meeting with David Halstram, the scales fell from Dixon's eyes. The moment was that profound. He felt like Saul on the road to Damascus. He had been blind, but now he could see.

This was what Dixon wanted. His life's work had been as a liberal firebrand. If the legacy of his Presidency was a seamless handoff to Thomas Hayes, which in turn would put Susan Hopkins in position to become the first woman President, that's what he wanted. That had been the promise of the women's movement these past hundred years, and it had never been realized. The time to put that in place was now, and Susan Hopkins was the woman.

Hayes was clearly reluctant, but what choice did he have? In this one instance, Dixon was going to ride over his concerns. It was for Thomas's own good, the good of his presidential ticket, and the good of America, that Susan was the running mate.

Once again, they had come out smelling like a rose. American agents, secret agents who the world would never know, had saved hundreds of lives on board that train. They had saved the train, the Channel Tunnel, and the London train station. Americans were heroes again. And the Dixon administration owned it.

The Supreme Court had just struck down the travel ban against North Africans as unconstitutional. Another victory. The deciding vote had been the man who was kidnapped by North Africans, Richard Sebastian-Vilar. Clement Dixon would almost like to send him a gift, but it would seem untoward. He did plan to have the entire Supreme Court here for a lunch, and he would share his feelings with Vilar then.

Dixon was in a celebratory mood. Hayes and Hopkins were both in a celebratory mood, as well. This tea gathering was meant to be a celebration.

The Dixon presidency was now a juggernaut. As of this morning, Dixon's approval ratings were the highest they'd ever been, he was going out on top, and if need be, he was going to flex his muscle to ram Susan Hopkins down Thomas Hayes's throat.

Thomas wanted Dixon's full support, didn't he? Of course he did. He wanted Clement Dixon's enthusiastic presence on the campaign trail, right?

Sure. Who wouldn't want the presence of the most popular president in the last 20 years on the podium with him? In that case, Susan Hopkins was Thomas's running mate. It was all unstated. He couldn't come right out and say the words, but it was there.

He picked up the phone on the small table at his elbow. The phone had one button on it. He pressed it, and two seconds later a female voice answered.

"Yes, Mr. President?"

"Mary, have them send up a bottle of champagne, will you please? Something nice. We have a lot to celebrate, don't we?"

"Yes, sir. We do."

Dixon grinned at Susan Hopkins and Thomas Hayes. They both watched him, both smiling now. Maybe Susan's smile was a little more genuine than Thomas's. But maybe not. Maybe Thomas knew it was the right decision and was pleased someone had taken it out of his hands.

"I think we're going to close up shop early today," Dixon said. "And have ourselves a drink."

CHAPTER THIRTY SEVEN

8:45 pm Eastern Daylight Time
The Tidal Basin
Near the Jefferson Memorial
Washington, DC

"I made you a promise some months ago," Bill Ryan said.

Don Morris nodded. "I know that."

"When Miles Richmond died, I told you that you didn't need to worry about having a patron in this town. You didn't need to worry about who was watching your back. Because I was the one."

They walked together on a path not far from the National Mall. It was night. Late September, still warm, people jogging past in shorts and t-shirts. Both men wore slacks, dress shirts, and light windbreaker jackets. Don's was dark blue with the letter SRT in white on his left breast.

Across the water from them, the circular dome of the Jefferson Memorial was lit up in green, almost like neon. It made a beautiful effect.

"I kept that promise."

"I know that," Don said.

He refrained from reminding Bill that Don had stuck his neck out and had put the Special Response Team on the chopping block, to help Miles Richmond get his granddaughter back. And he had done all of that as a favor to none other than Bill Ryan, Minority Leader of the House of Representatives. In a sense, Bill had owed him some protection.

But in truth, he had paid it off in spades. Bill had been in Washington a long time. He was a DC operator, and a master string puller. Don's budget requests hadn't been questioned in months. Investigations into the behavior of a few of his field agents had quietly been dropped. The FBI proper was no longer making full frontal assaults on his autonomy. They were working behind the scenes, to be sure. They were listening, and they were watching. But...

"When you wanted your men in on that train hijacking, I put them there," Bill said now. "Hayes had you riding the bench."

"I hope I don't need to thank you for that," Don said. "Those men are the best we have. I don't mean we in terms of the Special Response Team, or the FBI; I mean America. I'll put them up against any elite operators, from any country, anywhere in the world, at any time. They saved that train and all those passengers on board, and they saved a Supreme Court judge."

Bill nodded. It was a sore spot with him, Don knew. The judge had come home from being kidnapped and nearly blown up by terrorists, and days later had voted to strike down the travel ban from North African Muslim countries. Behind closed doors, Bill Ryan was probably one of the architects of that ban.

"It was good for America," Don said. "It was good for our standing in the world. We saved more than 400 people. We helped our allies. And we showed some people who is still in charge."

"I know that," Bill said.

"But thank you, anyway," Don said.

"You should get more credit than you do. You and your men. Clement Dixon and Thomas Hayes are acting like they were the ones on that train. I don't even mind it so much coming from Dixon. But Hayes?"

"We live in the dark," Don said. "The SRT is clandestine. That's by design. We can't do our work if we step into the limelight. I wouldn't want the attention anyway. I can't speak for them 100%, but I believe that holds true of my special operators as well. They're family men. They do what they do because it's right. They save lives."

They walked on in silence for a moment. The Jefferson Memorial was much closer now. Some kids were fooling around inside of it, sliding around on its marble floor. Don smiled. They kept those floors well-polished, and kids liked to slide around on it in their socks. Don sometimes got the urge himself.

"We've been friends a long time," Bill said.

"Yes."

Were they even friends? Don supposed they were. They had been freshman knobs together at the Citadel back in the dinosaur era. They'd been good friends then. Best friends, you might even have called them. They had drifted apart after that, as Don had gone into the real military after the Citadel, and Bill had gone to law school, then crawled into the snake pit of politics.

Now that he was here in DC, Don had found out that you didn't survive without protectors. They would eat you alive. They would strip the bones from your flesh. All those years away, Don had assumed that back home, they were all on the same team. America. It wasn't true. It was trench warfare here.

It seemed to outsiders like there were two teams fighting against each other, but even that wasn't true. It was a battle royale, a free for all. Some were fighting for ideals, some were lining their own pockets and the pockets of their rich friends, some were just power hungry. Some were a combination of all three. It was confusing, a constant crossfire, and you could easily get your butt shot off. Like it or not, Bill was Don's protector now.

It was good. Don needed someone, and Bill Ryan was as well-connected as they come in this town. When the House flipped back the other way, which it would inevitably do at some point, Bill was first in line to become Speaker. No one was even a close second. That would make him one of the most powerful men in Washington, and by extension, the world.

Even so, Bill sighed now as if the weight on him was too heavy to bear.

"We have to decide who we're going to be in the years ahead. We have to decide what America is going to be. The writing's on the wall. Thomas Hayes is going to be the next President of the United States. It doesn't look like there's anything we can do to stop it."

Don shrugged. Clement Dixon had invited him to lunch at Camp David in a couple of weeks, just the two of them. Of course he would go. Of course he would try renew or extend his relationship with Dixon. But Bill claimed to have inside information that Dixon was going to step down. And when Don had been in Dixon's presence recently, it certainly seemed the case that he was pulling back.

"It's possible I can have a relationship with Hayes," Don said. "Maybe the SRT can weather a transition from Dixon to Hayes."

Bill looked at him closely.

"Do you really believe that, after everything that's happened?"

Don didn't even have to think about. He shook his head.

"No. Hayes and I…"

He trailed off and let the thought hang there.

"Don, look. I respect your relationship with Clement Dixon. I even respect Dixon himself. I've never agreed with him on anything. But he's a good man. He's smart. He's tough. He's a credit to his side of the aisle. But he's from an earlier time. Don't try to establish a relationship with Thomas Hayes. The man is bad for the country. Let me ask you a question. Do you think Thomas Hayes is half the man Clement Dixon is?"

"No. I don't."

"Do you think Hayes, if he takes the captain's seat, is going to steer this ship with a firm hand?"

"No."

"He's going to campaign with Susan Hopkins as his running mate. That's what I'm hearing, and I have reason to believe it's true. Okay, suppose the super model becomes Vice President. She can't really do much harm from there. But that puts her pretty little head one bullet away, one breath away, from the presidency. Do you think Susan Hopkins could safely run a popcorn stand at a movie theater, never mind the United States of America?"

"I don't know," Don said. He hadn't given Susan Hopkins much thought before now. He'd seen her on TV a few times. She was a Senator from California. Good-looking. Young for a woman in her position. She tended to blather on about things she didn't seem to know much about, but they all did that. Bill Ryan himself did it.

Bill shook his head. "Personally, I doubt it."

They walked on for another moment. It was a lovely night, and it was nice to walk here. It was even nice to listen to Bill spout and pontificate. Maybe something would come of it one day. But Don had other things on his mind as well. There was Trudy Wellington. He needed to do something about that situation.

And Margaret was waiting for him. He needed to get home to her. He'd been coming home early in recent days, instead of burning the candle at both ends. It was good thing.

Bill stopped walking and turned to Don.

"Something has to be done, my friend. History doesn't look kindly on the ones who sit on their hands. Events get out of their control."

Don looked his friend in the eyes. "What would you like to do, Bill?"

Bill raised his hands in the air, as if supplicating the heavens. "I don't know yet. But when I do it, I know that I want you to be there with me."

CHAPTER THIRTY EIGHT

September 29
11:30 pm Irish Daylight Time (6: 30 pm Eastern Daylight Time)
Inish Mor, Aran Islands
Ireland

"It's incredible," Becca said. "I don't think I've ever seen the sky like this."

Luke didn't answer. He had seen it before, of course. Many times. But he could see a thousand more times and it still wouldn't be enough. Ed had certainly seen it, too. And Cassandra? She had grown up as a military brat. Her dad had been stationed in the Philippines at some point. She had probably seen it.

There was no light pollution here. The astounding sweep of the Milky Way Galaxy filled the dark night sky, a billion stars shining white against a black backdrop. It was how the cavemen had probably experienced it 50,000 years ago. The night was so clear, and the sky was so visible, that every few minutes another shooting star appeared.

As they watched, one made a sudden, large horizontal scrape against the sky.

"Oooh," Cassandra said. "That was a good one."

"Chariot of fire," Ed said.

"Chariots of the gods," Luke said.

"That's right."

"You can see why people used to think things like that. They didn't know what was up there. It might as well be gods riding across the sky."

They were sitting on top of the ruins of an old fortress that was thought to be more than a thousand years old. The story went that it had first come to ruin in a coastal Viking attack. Then people rebuilt it. Then it was attacked and wrecked again. And so on, the way people had always done, and would probably always do.

They'd had dinner and drinks in a pub in the tiny port town on the island, then driven their old beater of a rental car out here. They had hiked across open fields in the dark, climbing over stone walls hundreds of years old, to reach this place.

Luke carried Gunner in a fancy sack across his chest. Big Ed was carrying Jade in the same way. Both of the kids were fast asleep. Gunner was a comforting weight, pulling on Luke's chest and back.

Once in a while, he would give a kick in his sleep, or he would stretch, but mostly he hung limp and snoozed. He was alive, no doubt about that. The girls had been nervous about it, but Luke and Ed insisted. If you wanted to see the world, you slung the babies on your body somewhere, and you went.

Luke's eyes had become accustomed to the dark, but it was a night with no moon, and he could barely see the faces of the others. From the ramparts of the wrecked castle, he could see far across the islands, a light here and there shining from houses dotting the landscape. Their car was out there somewhere, parked along a narrow road on the other side of all these fields.

He was a little bit buzzed from the drinks. Becca was sitting with him, her head leaning on his shoulder. Don had given Luke and Ed two more weeks off. This time, the weeks were entirely off - they didn't have to pretend to be on loan to some international agency, or on a fact-finding tour about European intelligence techniques.

The girls had flown in from Austria. London was pretty well locked down, so Luke and Ed had met them at the Manchester airport. Then they had traveled around a bit and found themselves here.

The night was cool, but not cold. The smell of a peat fire was wafting from somewhere, possibly all the way across the island. It was a good moment.

They had done it again, he supposed. A terrible crisis had taken place. Terrorists had been bent on destruction. They had killed a bunch of innocent people, disrupted the lives of millions of others, and for what?

Then Luke and Ed had gone in and put a stop to it.

But they couldn't do that forever. One of these times, it wasn't going to work. The terrorists weren't going to stop, the kidnappers weren't going to stop, the other countries weren't going to stop. It was going to go on and on.

Luke looked at Ed. He was sitting on another wall, about ten feet across a large gap. It wasn't clear how far down the gap went. And Ed was basically a large silhouette, a big dark blotch against the night.

Ed had his wife and child with him. Ed was huge, and he was strong, and fast, but he was not immortal. One of these times...

233

Luke was not immortal, either. He knew that. For some reason, he played a little misdirection game with himself, where he thought about Ed. Ed getting shot. Ed getting blown up. Ed dying in front of Luke during a firefight. But it could happen the other way around.

The ancient people thought gods rode chariots across the sky. Ed and Luke were not gods. They were going to die, one way or another. They could die as old men, with grandchildren, or they could die as young men, a few weeks from now.

The terrorists were going to keep coming.

The wars were going to keep coming.

There were always going to be kidnappings and hijackings, and there were always going to be heavily armed men ready and willing to die RIGHT NOW.

Becca had made it clear she didn't want Luke doing this job anymore. She wanted Luke to do something else. Not to put too fine a point on it, she came from a wealthy family. Luke didn't have to work, at least, not right away. He could take time off until he found a job doing something else, years of time if he needed it.

He could get a job training recruits at Quantico.

He could get a job as a detective for a local police force.

He could get no job at all.

He'd had a recurring fantasy the past few nights. He pictured himself going back to Tangier and visiting with Eza Berrada's mother. She would invite him in, and he would sit with her in her apartment and drink sweet Moroccan mint tea.

Luke was the last person to talk to Eza. "Tell my mother," the kid had said, but he hadn't finished the thought.

Luke thought he might know what to tell her. Eza wasn't a bad kid. He had gotten caught up with the wrong people, that was all. Governments, spy agencies, terrorist organizations. They had recognized his abilities, and they had decided to use them for their own purposes. They had forced him into difficult circumstances and made him do things he would never think to do on his own. Then, after they had gotten everything they could from him, squeezed him dry, they had discarded him.

Luke reflected that he knew a little bit about things like this. He could share with her how it happened to her son. He could tell her how in Eza's dying moments, despite the pain he was in and the fear he must have felt, he had given Luke information that probably saved the lives of hundreds, and maybe thousands of people.

That would be nice. Except it wasn't going to happen. Berrada's mother would never let Luke into her home and serve him tea. Luke didn't speak more than a few words of Moroccan Arabic. Luke worked for the United States government, and technically speaking, Eza was a terrorist. If Luke and his partner Ed had never become involved in Eza's life, the kid might still be alive.

Never mind. So much for fantasies.

"It's beautiful night," Becca said now. She sounded sleepy. She sounded like it was almost time to find their way back to the car, and head to the guest house and sleep. Across the way, Ed and Cassandra had lapsed into silence. They were probably ready.

Luke welcomed that idea. He'd been sleeping like a rock these past few nights. Sleep agreed with him.

"I love it here," Becca said.

Luke nodded. "So do I." He gazed across the dark fields, framed by the staggering night sky.

"And I don't want to go back," he almost said, but didn't.

ROGUE FORCE
(A Troy Stark Thriller—Book #1)

"Thriller writing at its best. Thriller enthusiasts who relish the precise execution of an international thriller, but who seek the psychological depth and believability of a protagonist who simultaneously fields professional and personal life challenges, will find this a gripping story that's hard to put down."
--Midwest Book Review, Diane Donovan (regarding Any Means Necessary)

"One of the best thrillers I have read this year. The plot is intelligent and will keep you hooked from the beginning. The author did a superb job creating a set of characters who are fully developed and very much enjoyable. I can hardly wait for the sequel."
--Books and Movie Reviews, Roberto Mattos (re Any Means Necessary)

From #1 bestselling and USA Today bestselling author Jack Mars, author of the critically-acclaimed *Luke Stone* and *Agent Zero* series (with over 5,000 five-star reviews), comes an explosive new, action-packed thriller series that takes readers on a wild-ride across Europe, America, and the world.

When elite Navy Seal Troy Stark is forced into retirement for his dubious respect for authority, he dreads the quiet life awaiting him with his brothers and buddies in Yonkers, New York. But the quiet doesn't last long: the NYPD needs Troy's military expertise to help find and stop a major terrorist threat to New York City. To pre-empt the attack, they need him to fly to Europe and stop it at its source—using any means necessary.

Troy finds himself partnered with an Interpol agent who is as different from him as can be, and their instant dislike is mutual. But they have an attack to stop, and only a few days to do it, and together they'll need each other as they criss-cross Europe in a high-octane cat-and-mouse chase to shut these terrorists down.

But what starts off as a straightforward mission (and an opportunity to clear his name) soon catapults Troy headfirst into a global conspiracy. These criminals are more sophisticated than they appear, and even with Troy's unparalleled military skills, he and his team find themselves constantly one stop behind. With the fate of New York City on the line, the stakes couldn't be higher.

Where will they strike? And when? And can Troy stop it before it's too late?

An unputdownable action thriller with heart-pounding suspense and unforeseen twists, ROGUE FORCE is the debut novel in an exhilarating new series by a #1 bestselling author that will have you fall in love with a brand new action hero—and turn pages late into the night.

Books #2 and #3 in the series—ROGUE COMMAND and ROGUE TARGET—are now also available.

Jack Mars

Jack Mars is the USA Today bestselling author of the LUKE STONE thriller series, which includes seven books. He is also the author of the new FORGING OF LUKE STONE prequel series, comprising six books; of the AGENT ZERO spy thriller series, comprising twelve books; and of the TROY STARK thriller series, comprising three books (and counting).

Jack loves to hear from you, so please feel free to visit www.Jackmarsauthor.com to join the email list, receive a free book, receive free giveaways, connect on Facebook and Twitter, and stay in touch!

BOOKS BY JACK MARS

LUKE STONE THRILLER SERIES
ANY MEANS NECESSARY (Book #1)
OATH OF OFFICE (Book #2)
SITUATION ROOM (Book #3)
OPPOSE ANY FOE (Book #4)
PRESIDENT ELECT (Book #5)
OUR SACRED HONOR (Book #6)
HOUSE DIVIDED (Book #7)

FORGING OF LUKE STONE PREQUEL SERIES
PRIMARY TARGET (Book #1)
PRIMARY COMMAND (Book #2)
PRIMARY THREAT (Book #3)
PRIMARY GLORY (Book #4)
PRIMARY VALOR (Book #5)
PRIMARY DUTY (Book #6)

AN AGENT ZERO SPY THRILLER SERIES
AGENT ZERO (Book #1)
TARGET ZERO (Book #2)
HUNTING ZERO (Book #3)
TRAPPING ZERO (Book #4)
FILE ZERO (Book #5)
RECALL ZERO (Book #6)
ASSASSIN ZERO (Book #7)
DECOY ZERO (Book #8)
CHASING ZERO (Book #9)
VENGEANCE ZERO (Book #10)
ZERO ZERO (Book #11)
ABSOLUTE ZERO (Book #12)

Printed in Great Britain
by Amazon

27589084R00136